Dark Horse

C Fleming

That bloke off the telly

Ivan checked his watch for the third time since he'd arrived, even though the hands of his Rolex had only moved on two minutes since his last glance. She wasn't even late yet, but standing around waiting made him feel self-conscious. La Roulade was a typically pretentious French brasserie off the Strand, better class than a chain of upmarket pizza restaurants, but the bill wouldn't be as eye watering as taking her to a Michelin starred establishment out in the Berkshire countryside.

On reflection, it was a good balance for a first date, but he regretted saying that he'd meet her in such a public place. The pavement was a crush of Londoners leaving work mingling with tourists looking for somewhere to eat post shopping and pre theatre. Whilst the foreign tourists didn't give him a second glance, many Brits did a momentary double take as they realized they were passing "that bloke off the telly."

Ivan was used to the reaction and secretly didn't mind it. Recognition equaled adoration in his mind and everyone likes to be liked, right? But standing outside a restaurant like this he may as well have had "waiting for a date" written on his forehead in flashing neon.

"Ivan?"

And there she was. In a split second he looked her up and down and completed the evaluation. Wow. Decent tits, slim waist, dainty features, pretty eyes, shining bright and blue. Gorgeous blonde hair tumbling around her shoulders like a fluffy scarf and a knockout smile. Aimed at him. Oh yes, his sister had been right about this one. This one was good.

"Abigail, hello." With relief that she had turned up, he shook her hand formally, and without further ado held open the door to La Roulade and motioned for her to enter. The interior was a haven of calm from the hustle of the busy London street outside and Ivan felt himself relax.

"I don't make a habit of blind dates," he explained as they sat in a corner booth and took the menus from the penguin-suited waiter. "My sister says that I keep choosing the wrong sorts of girls – you know, ones with pretty faces but nothing going on between their ears. She kept singing your praises and so I thought 'why not'." He paused and peered at her over his menu. "I must say that it's quite nice that you're not going out with me just because I'm that bloke off the telly."

"Oh?" Abigail replied, her eyebrows raised quizzically. "Ann didn't tell me anything about what you do."

She hadn't recognized him. This should be a good thing, no prejudgment, no thoughts on his presentation style, no stalking his tweets on social media beforehand to see what his opinions were. But a part of him was offended. This was a big deal. He was a big deal. Not everyone gets the opportunity to dine with what the Daily Mail once referred to as a "national treasure".

"I present the sport for the BBC on a Saturday afternoon. You know, 'Saturday kick off'?"

She looked blank. "Sorry, I don't really follow sport. I've heard of Gazza, and I know that Raul Delgado is seriously hot, but that's about it," she added. "Although now I think about it, your name does sound familiar."

There was silence as they both studied the menu for a while. In blind date terms, both felt this was an acceptable silence rather than an awkward silence. But not for too long.

"Are you having a starter?" he asked. "I rather fancy trying the foie gras."

She pondered the list in front of her, some things were new and mysterious, other dishes sounded safer.

"I think I'll have the minestrone soup and beef bourginon," she replied, folding up her menu and placing it decisively on the table in front of her.

Ivan was thankful that she was having a starter. So many girls didn't want one, making excuses about not wanting to fill themselves up before the main course. He suspected they secretly wanted a starter but didn't want to look greedy. Bonus points for Abigail.

"So you work in marketing?" Ivan resorted to a standard opening question. His long list of sporting subjects from Chelsea's chances in the FA cup battle to The Wise Professor's stunning winning performance in the Cheltenham Gold Cup were presumably nonstarters for a girl that had no interest in sport.

"Not really," she replied, sipping at the full bodied Shiraz that Ivan had ordered. "I've been doing temping jobs for the last couple of years and the work at PMG was a 9 month's cover for maternity leave. It started off as mainly a clerical role, but they are so short staffed in marketing that they got me involved in a lot of campaigns. Strictly speaking, they were tasks that were beyond the scope of my job description, but I didn't mind. It was all good experience."

Ivan questioned the past tense and Abigail went on to explain that the nine months were up and she was about to start a new placement at Bartlett Incorporated on Monday. In Abigail's mind, this was a good thing as it meant she wouldn't have to see Ann again and face questions about how the blind date with her brother went.

She politely asked him what it was like working in television, and how he got into it in the first place. They were questions that people asked over and over again and he found it quite tedious to roll out the same answers, but at least she was making an effort to converse. Some of his dates just sat there like lemons waiting for him to do all the hard work. This girl had brightness about her.

She earned extra brownie points for managing a crème brulee for pudding too, and also for offering to go halves when the bill came, but without being too insistent. Would she be a girl who would sleep with him on the first date? There was only one way to find out.

"So," he hovered on the step outside the restaurant. "My flat's just over the river, ten minutes away. Would you like to come back for coffee?"

"It's been a lovely meal," she began in a tone that Ivan could already tell was leading to a 'but'. "But I have to be getting back."

"I'd love to see you again," he insisted, hoping it wasn't sounding too much like begging. "Can I have your number and I'll give you a ring?"

Abigail typed the eleven digits of her mobile number into his phone and pecked him on the cheek.

"Cheerio Ivan."

She made her way off towards the Strand, at a comfortable pace in her cracking high heels. Ivan stood, mesmerized, watching her go.

April fool

Torrential rain hammered persistently on the canvas roof of Abigail's tent, matching the pounding of her heartbeat. Self-pity, desperation and confusion pulsed around her body. Within the cramped interior of her new tent lay her sole possessions; one Fendi handbag containing a phone that must remain switched off, a purse containing bank cards that were useless, a couple of tampons, her sketch book that was slightly damp on the corner and a packet of polo mints. In the side pocket she gratefully found a packet of tissues and wiped the worst of the wetness from her face, raindrops that had dribbled from her once neat fringe, down the sides of her nose where they mingled with her hot, salty tears.

She blew her nose hard into a second tissue and took a deep breath. What a difference a day makes, she thought to herself, examining the streaks of mud that were now drying onto the kitten heel of her Faith shoes. She'd only cleaned the shoes a week ago in preparation for starting the new job at Bartlett Incorporated.

She almost laughed thinking back to the night before starting the job, opening her wardrobe and laying out different outfit options on her bed. She discounted the sassy Karen Millen suit with the halterneck lace top in case it was considered a little too revealing, then went to the other extreme and paired up a pretty floral Boden skirt with a 50s retro blouse. At 23 years old, Abigail was one of the few people that could carry off such an old fashioned look with ease, her baby blue eyes oozing innocence and bewilderment at the world around her. Often she wore an Alice band in her shiny long blond hair, adding to the cute submissive image even further.

"Nope," she muttered, placing it back on hangers and fishing out a plain black pencil skirt, a cream camisole and black cardigan with three quarter length sleeves. "Go for plain." She would have to spend the first couple of days taking mental notes of the other women around her in the office until she decided what look would blend in.

"They're not paying you to take part in a fashion contest," her Dad had grumbled as she did a twirl in front the hall mirror for the benefit of her Mum. "They just need you to get the job done." Which was a pity, because as Abigail folded the cardigan up into a ball to serve as a pillow for the night, she realized that she couldn't even get that part right. Just one week into the role and she'd made the biggest mistake of her short life.

It had started on the very first day at Bartlett Inc. April fool's day. The company was one of those faceless corporations set within a shiny façade. The temptation had been too strong, what with the password box there on the screen, the cursor winking away at her, testing her resolve, teasing, try me, go on, you know you want to.

Abigail caved in by 10am.

P-a-s-s-w-o-r-d, she typed into the box with her dainty manicured fingers.

Access denied.

P-a-s-s-w-o-r-d-1
Access denied.

She had no idea what the computer program was that she was trying to access, and didn't care. It wasn't even that she wanted to get into the software; the enjoyment was just trying to defeat the smug little cursor.

She certainly needed some form of entertainment to break up the monotony of the days.

P-a-s-s-w-o-r-d-0-1
Access denied.

B-a-r-t-l-e-t-t
Access denied.

B-a-r-t-l-e-t-t-0
Access denied.

She had only found out on Friday that her placement would be at Bartletts. As her last day at PMG, she was facing a period of nothingness until the agency rang breathless with excitement that there was a new opening on Monday. Abigail was needed in a hurry to cover a gaping hole in the administrative staffing, plugging the vacant space of the key person that ensures the caffeine flows for the directors, the stationery cupboard remains topped up with paper clips and the phone doesn't ring incessantly. Nearly all placements start this way for Abigail. But none had so far ended the way this one was about to.

Abigail learned that she was covering for a girl called Ellie Hardwick, PA to the head of investments, and she'd been on sick leave for several days. As usual, there was no one with the time to give Abigail a proper induction, nor explain properly what was expected of her, or introduce her to key people. Through her first morning, numerous people came crashing through the door with the word "Ellie –" about to spill from their lips before they did a double take and stopped with a surprised "oh" hanging in the air. Usually followed by "You're not Ellie" or "Is Ellie not back then?"

B-a-r-t-l-e-t-t-1
Access denied

B-a-r-t-l-e-t-t-0-1
Access denied

Abigail wondered who would have chosen the password. That was the key. If she knew who set the password, then the choices were narrowed down significantly; you just had to start finding out personal information about the password setter. Pet's names, kid's names, that sort of thing.

Before Abigail could ponder further, the phone rang on the desk, pulling her attention away from the screen for a second. In the ten minute briefing that morning she had picked up on the strict procedure over ensuring the calls are screened. Gillian Bright, some assistant something or other, had also managed to point out the toilets, the kettle and the phone before leaving her to it.

"The calls that come through to this phone will be for Neil Johnson. He's the head of investments, and he's very busy and paid too much to deal with trivial matters, so whoever's calling, just take a message, write it on that pad there and whenever he's not in the office, go and pop it on his desk, right in the centre so that he'll see it. He can then decide whether he needs to call them back. If the door's open, he's out, if the door's shut, he's in and you mustn't disturb him, no matter how urgent the caller says it is."

That seemed easy enough. Abigail cleared her throat and answered the phone using her polite and efficient phone voice.

"Good morning, Bartlett Investments, Mr Johnson's office."

There was a slight hesitation on the other end before a timid voice spoke up. "Oh hi, it's Ellie, I wondered if Mr Johnson was there."

Now it was Abigail's turn to hesitate. Clearly she is Ellie's temporary replacement, and Ellie will know that, but should she acknowledge it? Should she ask if Ellie's feeling better? Abigail decided to play dumb.

"No, I'm afraid he's out at the moment, I can take a message and leave it for his return?"

"Oh." Ellie sounded disappointed. "Just tell him I called and he can get me on my mobile. He's got the number," she added, preempting Abigail's next question.

"OK, consider it done. Nice to speak with you Ellie."

The note was written out in Abigail's best handwriting and she made her way into the adjoining office for the first time. Rather plush, she noted. Predictably there was an executive black leather swivel chair, and a vast expanse of mahogany desk, which was considerably tidy for a busy man. Matching cabinets, his own coffee maker, which Abigail would bet he didn't know how to use. Ah, pictures of the kids on the desk; one toothy grinned school photo of a girl around the age of seven. Blonde pigtails, clumsy spectacles. Another photo, this one larger with what was probably the wife holding a bundle of baby in a blue jumpsuit that said 'Party in my crib, bring a bottle' on it. Cute.

Placing the note on the middle of the desk as instructed, Abigail returned to her domain and sat back down at her notably smaller, cramped desk. On the computer screen the cursor continued to wink at her. OK, a few more tries.

E-l-l-i-e... no too short.
E-l-l-i-e-0-0-1
Access denied.

E-l-l-i-e-h-a-r-d-w-i-c-k
Access denied.

E-l-l-i-e-h-a-r-d-w-i-c-k-0-1
Access denied.

Never mind. The clock on the wall ticked away and Abigail wondered what time she could go for lunch. The phone seemed to be quiet, there was nobody to make coffee for, and no one was bothering her. Time to get on with some sketches then. She pulled out a dog-eared sketchpad from her designer Fendi handbag – a 21st birthday present from her parents that she cherished and saved for special occasions. Like the first week of a new temping job. One day she hoped she'd be able to afford to buy her own handbags – Fendi or otherwise – maybe from the profits of her latest clothing ranges.

The sketchbook contained page after page of concepts for Abigail's fantasy fashion designs, just ideas that had so far not extended beyond the page, but one day Abigail dreamed of seeing her creations on the catwalks of Milan and worn on the cover of Vogue. Or maybe just on a dummy in the window of Top Shop would be good enough. Perhaps one of the popular contestants on those singing talent shows would choose an Abigail Daycock design, and suddenly all the teenagers across Britain would want to get their hands on one for themselves.

For the rest of the morning, Abigail worked contentedly on some new designs, fairly undisturbed apart from the occasional call to Mr Johnson's phone, and a couple of people coming in to panic that the toner had run out on the photocopier, or they hadn't had confirmation of their flight to Zurich in the morning. Her tummy gave its first growl of protest around 12.30, when to Abigail's relief, Gillian stuck her head around the door frame.

"I can look after the phone for half an hour if you want to pop out for lunch."

Abigail didn't need asking twice and escaped the office onto the busy London Street, tugging her Hobbs coat tighter around her against the biting April wind.

She checked her phone. A-ha! Message from Nadine. Nadine and Abigail had met five years ago whilst studying at the London College of Fashion. Despite their shared interest in textiles and fabrics, the two girls had completely different approaches, with Abigail preoccupied by labels, the High Street, and celebrity fashion. Nadine by contrast could be found scouring car boot sales and charity shops for unusual fabrics that she could turn into something unique with the aid of a sewing machine and a swish of ribbon or a peacock feather. If Abigail wore anything from Nadine's wardrobe it would clearly look ridiculous, but Nadine's Arabian skin, mysterious features and confidence meant that she could carry it off beautifully.

"Hi Ab," said the text message. "Am free tomorrow for lunch if you are. Am skint though so will need to be cheap or your treat. Hope you can make it, xxx." Abigail smiled. That was typical Nadine; always penniless but it never bothered her.

It would be nice to see Nadine again. It had been a few weeks since they'd last met for a catch up over a bottle of wine. From the corner of the street, Abigail's nifty fingers composed a text back to Nadine stating a time and place to meet. She looked forward to hearing whatever scrape Nadine had got herself into recently because one thing was sure; Nadine's life was a far sight more adventurous than Abigail's.

Well, for now.

Tuesday morning

Nadine woke at eleven o'clock. Momentarily she wondered where she was, as the threadbare sofa she was laying on didn't look familiar, but as she slowly opened her eyes and glanced around at her surroundings, the events of the previous evening and her location started to come back to her. This was Dougie's place. She'd been at a noisy gig in Camden with Dougie, Craig and Fish, which then turned into a lock-in until goodness knows what time. The details of how she got from the pub to Dougie's flat were a bit hazy, but she felt as though she'd only been asleep for a couple of hours.

Empty bottles of Hobgoblin littered the bare wooden floor, suggesting that the drinking had continued once they got back to the flat. Or they could have been there for days, knowing Dougie. Untidiness was definitely a trait the siblings had in common. Laying amongst the glass bottles and an overturned ashtray was a lump in a sleeping bag.

Nadine sat herself upright on the sofa and tried to flatten down the checked shirt that had become rucked up from a restless sleep, as the lump on the floor stirred with a sleepy groan. A head of dreadlocks appeared from the top of the sleeping bag.

"What time is it?" mumbled Fish, spotting Nadine.

She consulted her watch. "Just gone eleven. God, I need a fag." Fish felt around the floor and pulled a packet of tobacco from underneath his sleeping bag and tossed it over to the sofa. Expertly Nadine caught it with one hand. "Roll me one too. Want a coffee?"

"Love one, but I'm meeting Abigail in a bit. Have to walk over to the City so better get cracking in a mo." Nadine expertly rolled two cigarettes and watched Fish fondly as he fought his way out of the sleeping bag and stood up, shamelessly wearing nothing but a skimpy pair of faded black briefs. He looked around the untidy room and finally located a pair of barely blue jeans slung over a beanbag in the corner, and a crumpled t-shirt tossed over the doorframe. In seconds he was transformed back into the cool musician that he'd been twelve hours ago.

He took the roll up from her with a casual wink. Nadine's brother Dougie had formed a band called "Blue Steak" four years ago with his mates Fish and Craig. Nadine was their number one supporter. Not a groupie, she'd argue vehemently, and she'd certainly never entertained thoughts of sleeping with Fish or Craig. But she adored attending their gigs, helping them shift gear around in their battered little van, keeping on top of administrative tasks – such as confirming bookings, responding to questions on their social media sites and making sure they got paid – and in return, often crashed on a floor or sofa when she couldn't afford the fare back to her cramped council flat in Tower Hamlets.

Even the name Blue Steak had come from Nadine, who was sat with the guys when they were first trying to decide on what to call the band.

"What colour underwear do you have on?" she'd asked Dougie, who peeked under his waistband and confirmed with a confused giggle that his boxer shorts were blue.

"And what was the last thing you ate?" she asked Fish. He rolled his eyes at her craziness, but replied that it had been a juicy t-bone from the Four Kings after the gig the previous night.

"Well "Blue t-bone" sounds a bit weird, but what about "Blue steak"?" Nadine offered. The three boys mumbled it around their lips a few times before nodding in slow agreement. Blue Steak stuck. A few years had passed and the band's reputation had grown from strength to strength, with a hectic schedule of gigs across London and the Home Counties. Without Nadine to schedule their lives, the three lads were a disorganized mess, and they dreaded the occasions that she took off to foreign lands, as she did sporadically.

"Right, I'd better be off," Nadine told Fish. "Say cheerio to Dougie for me… when he finally surfaces."

Grabbing her patchwork bag from the floor, Nadine tugged on her favourite duffel coat; a charity shop bargain that she'd worn continually since September last year, left the flat and galloped down the stairs. It would take a good hour to walk from Dougie's flat in St John's Wood to the coffee shop that Abigail had nominated to meet at. Not enough people walked, Nadine reflected, watching people scurry into the tube entrances. It was good for the soul to stride along, passing life above ground, breathing in the fresh air, and best of all, Nadine could smoke freely.

As she approached Little John Street, Nadine could see her friend hovering on the corner outside the coffee shop. Dressed for her office job, Abigail always looked so groomed, so demure and pretty. With her gorgeously blonde silk hair scraped back into a neat ponytail, her trim legs enhanced by three-inch heels, and a figure hugging belted coat, which Nadine could guess was designer and very expensive. Fleetingly, Nadine felt like a tramp in comparison, but couldn't care less what other people thought.

"I've only got half an hour," Abigail explained apologetically as she hugged Nadine in greeting on the street. "But it gives us time for a quick latte and sandwich in here."

The coffee shop was serenely quiet, with soft jazz music

playing at a level that the customers could talk above or relax to. Abigail winced as she paid for the lunches, and was thankful that the agency would pay her tomorrow.

"You'll never guess what," said Nadine, breathless with excitement before Abigail had even taken her coat off. These were the opening words that Abigail loved to hear.

"You're pregnant? You're sharing a flat with Noel Gallagher? You've created a hat that the Duchess of Kent wants to buy from you? I've no idea!" With Nadine, any of those things could be likely. The last time she'd asked Abigail to 'guess what' it was because she'd received a hefty inheritance from a now deceased college professor that she'd once slept with. She'd spent the money on a 3-month trip wandering through South East Asia.

"No, I wouldn't like to share with Noel Gallagher! He strikes me as being someone who's really messy!" The pot calling the kettle black, thought Abigail. She took her coat off and settled into the comfy chair opposite Nadine. "I had an email from VSO yesterday, the voluntary services thing I did before. There's an opportunity to go to Cambodia to work in the Ministry of Education this summer."

Abigail felt her heart sink a little, but kept a smile on her face. She had few friends as it was, and losing this one for months at a time was tough.

"The Cambodian government are on a mission to get all the kids signed up and enrolled in school, rather than being pulled away to help Mum and Dad gather the crops in. I think I'm going to apply, I've got nothing else lined up."

Abigail silently scolded herself mentally for being selfish, and tried to put on an enthusiastic face. "Cool. Is that where you were before?"

"No, different continent, dummy! I was in Cameroon before, that's Africa. Cambodia's over by Vietnam. I need to get the application in this week, as they are interviewing next month with a view to sending people out there in June. You should apply with me, forget all this temping nonsense … it's great experience."

Abigail pulled a face. Getting bored at Bartlett Investments wasn't exactly an experience to die for, but working for free in a hot dusty place full of temples and elephants wasn't her thing either. The thought of surviving a summer without gossip magazines, window-shopping in Carnaby Street or a daily latte (with or without blueberry muffin) was inconceivable.

Nadine could read Abigail like a book. "Well, it's not going to make me rich," she conceded, "but it makes me feel useful. And it's a laugh; I met some great people last time, most that I'm still in touch with."

There it was again, the slight pang of jealousy. Nadine's Facebook profile was packed full of photos of exploits with people around different corners of the globe, strange names appeared on her wall exchanging jokes amongst themselves that referred to events they had shared. Experiences and memories that happened without Abigail.

"So, anyway, tell me about your mystery blind date with that woman's brother," Nadine probed, raising an inquisitive studded eyebrow.

"Well... it turns out he's some famous TV presenter that I've never heard of," Abigail replied with a smile at the memory of the French brasserie. "Ann – that's his sister – completely failed to mention that he fronts the BBC's sport coverage on a Saturday."

"Wow, that's amazing. Was he hot?"

"Nah, a bit old actually. He must be pushing forty and acting like some playboy, lapping up the attention that a lot of people in the restaurant were giving him. We had a very...well, civil date but we didn't have enough in common to interest each other."

"Oh." Nadine seemed disappointed for her friend. "Are you seeing him again?"

"He asked for my number so I made one up," Abigail sniggered. "I never have to see him or Ann again so no-one's the wiser. Honest mistake!"

"Ah yes, you're latest temping venture," Nadine remembered. "Any decent looking, rich, single blokes there?"

"I only started there yesterday but I don't get to see many people actually," Abigail struggled to think of anyone male who had passed the time of day with her. Even Mr Johnson swept in and out his office with barely two words to say to her. "I spend most of the day alone in an office, sketching out a few designs to pass the time and trying to crack the password on the computer. No luck so far, but it's only early days."

"Children's names. You know – the password. If the person that set the password has kids, they're bound to use the kid's names. Otherwise, they may use the name of their husband, boyfriend, or secret lover. Or their pets." Nadine was not telling Abigail anything she didn't already know. "Or it may be something completely random - like Walrus or Peppercorn – or something."

Abigail obviously had no idea whether Ellie had kids or pets, or how she'd find out that information. And certainly no idea how to discover a secret lover! But time is one thing she did have, and she could always work her way through every name she could think of.

"What happens when you crack the password? Will it open a

big vault and get you access to huge slabs of gold bullion?"

"I have absolutely no idea, but I hope so! I could use a few slabs of gold bullion as there's a new range of women's Tissot watches that are just to die for," admitted Abigail. She sighed. "But it's unlikely. Probably nothing much happens except a program will open that I don't understand and I'll just shut it down again. But it's about winning. The cursor sits there flashing at me in the password box all day long like a stupid tease." She glanced at her watch and reached for her coat. "Well, I'd better get back; you need to start your application to VSO and I must beat the little bastard password!"

Ellie's secret

By Thursday Abigail had worked her way through all the boys and girls names beginning with A-F that she could think of. With no luck. She'd had the opportunity to ask Gillian, as casually as she could, to tell her a bit more about Ellie, but that proved fruitless. No children, no husband. A hunt around the in desk drawers also left Abigail with no clues as to her life, her personality, her psyche. Although she did find a significant stash of trashy gossip magazines that could help pass the time.

Ellie called in once again, asking to speak with Mr Johnson. Abigail's mind raced about how she could get more information from her – but what can you say to a virtual stranger? Besides, Ellie sounded uptight and anxious enough.

"Well, I passed on your message last time," Abigail explained patiently after Ellie had barked that he had yet to call her back. "And he's not here at the moment so the best I can do is to leave him another message to say that you called. Again."

There was a long awkward paused as Ellie let out a long sigh. "I can see if Gillian's around," Abigail offered, "if you'd like to speak with her."

"No," she snapped back. "It's not a matter for Gillian. Just tell him I called and I want him to call me back." And before Abigail could even say goodbye the phone was slammed down the other end.

"Blimey," said a voice from the doorway. "I could hear that from here. Stroppy madam." A young lad stepped in and introduced himself as John from "equity securities". In a split second Abigail looked him up and down. Hmmm. Clean hair, thin torso, warm eyes, but a baby face. A bit younger than her, he seemed to have an air of 'keen office junior' about him. He was wearing a suit, but not with ease. No, this one was not in Nadine's "decent looking, single and rich" category.

Abigail had looked forward to mingling with the men in this workplace. She felt that "Investment banking" had an air of sophistication and she'd been hopeful of getting a chance of meeting some rich traders that would invite her for lunch or dinner in an intimate setting, ordering a bottle of Chateuxneuf-du-pape and fresh lobster, regaling her with tales of stocks and shares. It was only day four in the placement, granted, but so far, the men were few and far between. Those she'd passed in corridors or in the lift seemed to be the wrong side of forty, or wearing something that made her shudder and reach for a phone to dial the fashion police. Bow ties, red stripey socks, braces. She sighed inwardly and turned her attention to John.

He set a stack of paperwork down on the edge of the desk for Mr. Johnson to sign. "I mean, what does she expect you to do other than take a message?"

"She should be taking it easy if she's off sick," agreed Abigail, to which John gave a little chuckle.

"Off sick, my arse. Between you and me," he lowered his voice and bent forward over the desk, "she's off *love* sick."

Abigail's heart began to race a bit quicker. Gossip. At last, after 4 days in this dull quiet office, something exciting was finally happening. She raised her eyebrows, encouraging John to spill more beans.

"Oh? Nobody's really told me much about Ellie or why she's off."

John pushed the office door closed and lowered his voice, leaning close into Abigail as he spoke. "Word in the office is that Ellie and Mr Johnson were putting in more overtime than necessary, if you know what I mean. Late meetings – an unnecessary amount of secret rendezvous at restaurants and hotels, even in Paris. She's single but he's married with kids. The dozy idiot didn't make much effort to hide the affair though. Everyone soon knew about it, what with Ellie acting like a love struck teenager. Anyway it seems that Gillian found out and is threatening to tell his wife if they don't call it off. Boom. Ellie goes 'off sick'," he waggled his fingers in the air to show his disapproval, "and now it's all a bit stalemate."

"What do you think will happen?"

"Who knows? Technically they can't sack Ellie; she's playing by the rules and getting sick notes for stress. She's the type that'll have them for unfair dismissal straight away if they try to force her out. Tribunals et cetera et cetera. Mr Johnson's not going to leave his wife, I can't see that Ellie would want to come back and just pretend that their affair never happened. I'd get settled in if I were you, you could be here a while."

He smiled and made to go for the door. "It was nice talking to you Abigail. Oh," he paused at the door. "You didn't hear any of that from me though."

"Hear what?" Abigail smiled back. As soon as his footsteps had faded down the corridor, Abigail turned to the computer.

M-R-J-O-H-N-S-O-N
Access denied.

No, she wouldn't call him Mr Johnson would she?

N-E-I-L-J-O-H-N-S-O-N
Access denied.

N-E-I-L-J-O-H-N-S-O-N-1
Access denied

N-E-I-L-J-O-H-N-S-O-N-0-1
Access denied.

She gave a sigh of exasperation, and a deep breath. Shuddering at the sentiment, she started her new line of thought.

S-E-X-Y-N-E-I-L
Access denied

S-E-X-Y-N-E-I-L-1
Access denied

N-E-I-L-I-S-S-E-X-Y
Access denied.

A twinge of doubt was starting to set in. Maybe it wasn't Ellie that had set the password in the first place. Maybe it was automated or a corporate wide password. But, she rationalized, if that were the case, she'd never guess the password and it will have beaten her. She may as well continue down this road. Even though images of Mr. Johnson wearing just his socks and boxer shorts kept popping in her head. Not nice.

I-L-O-V-E-N-E-I-L

There was a split second pause that hadn't existed on previous attempts and suddenly Abigail felt a weird plunging sensation in her stomach as the computer made a gurgling sound from deep within its hard drive and the screen started to set a program in motion.

Oh my God, oh my God, Abigail muttered to herself, half in fear and half in excitement. She'd never truly believed deep down that she would ever get beyond the "access denied" stage. A wave of gobbledygook computer code flashed over the screen and one clunk later, the screen was suddenly ablaze with figures. It was the sort of image that Abigail had seen on TV pictures of stock trading floors, codes and red and green figures, plus and minus figures, flashing and changing. This must be FTSE index, she decided. It looked like it could be a live feed of all the stock market trading in the City. None of the blur on the screen made any sense, but Abigail had the guilty feeling that she shouldn't be looking at it. If she was caught then it was obvious she'd got in via a password protected means. Computer hacking! It must be instant dismissal from this job, she figured.

A click of the door down the corridor suddenly signalled that Mr. Johnson was coming back to his office, returning from a lengthy lunch. Over the four days she had learnt to recognise the sound of his footsteps in the corridor outside, and she also knew she had about ten seconds between the sound of the door clicking shut and his arrival in the doorway. Unless by some miracle an employee would intercept him and delay him, but Abigail didn't rate her chances.

Oh my God, she muttered for the second time as a rising panic welled up inside her. She just needed to turn the screen off. But where was the sodding monitor switch? Frantically, Abigail felt around the edge of the screen, but to no avail. There didn't seem to be a separate switch like there was on older monitors.

OK, calm down, she soothed herself, the escape key normally works... she bashed fruitlessly at the escape key but the screen continued to blink an array of green and red figures and codes at her.

Oh God, she wailed under her breath, as the footsteps were within ten metres or so of the office. Turn the whole thing off? She hunted on the box that appeared to contain the brains of the machine but to no avail. What was wrong with these modern stupid computers that seemed to hide the buttons? Five years ago there would have been a really obvious big round "off" switch.

Plug. Last resort. She looked along the selection of plugs along the back of the desk and couldn't easily tell which one belonged to the computer. In desperation, she yanked at the one closest to the window. Nope, the computer still displayed the figures. Although there seemed to be an awful lot more red figures now. And more, and now even more.

As Mr Johnson appeared in the office doorway every single figure on the screen had now turned red and there was a flashing red bar along the bottom of the screen, screaming danger at her. She yanked at the second plug, but the coffee machine simply whined briefly and clicked off.

"What the..."

Abigail's insides did a final belly flip as Neil Johnson spotted the screen and started to stride over the office towards where she sat helplessly at the desk.

"I..I.." Abigail had no idea what to say and had the sudden instinct to bolt. She could feel her face blazing crimson. She was in *so* much trouble. Everything suddenly started to happen at once, doors started to open and close down the corridor, someone called out for Mr. Johnson by name, and what was normally a calm sedate atmosphere descended in a matter of moments to panic and pandemonium.

No sooner had Mr. Johnson scanned his eyes over the screen, then he was gone, hurrying out the office and towards the sounds of the workers yelling for his assistance.

Abigail pulled at the third and final plug and the screen died in front of her eyes, but it was too late now anyway. She'd somehow messed up the entire bank's trading, maybe even en route to bringing down the entire FTSE 100 index just from a bit of accidental hacking and bashing at the escape key. She may have wiped millions out the economy. People's livelihoods may go down the drain.

She'd seen pictures on the TV news over the years; workers carrying cardboard boxes packed with the contents of their desks out onto the streets after the banks simply collapsed in a matter of hours. She'd even seen the film about the chap that brought down Barings Bank. She was the next Nick Leeson!

She couldn't stay in the office a moment longer; she'd have to answer questions. Why did she hack in? How did she get hold of the password? Questions she had no answers to.

Grabbing her coat and bag with trembling fingers, she bolted out the office, and galloped down the corridor and down the back stairs rather than taking the lift. She slipped out the emergency exit at the bottom of the stairs, grateful that the door wasn't alarmed to draw further attention to her. There must be CCTV everywhere, she reckoned. Her face would be on the news.

Never in her 23 years had she been more panicked. Where could she bolt? Dashing out into the busy Strand, she merged in with the throng of tourists momentarily and practically fell in the nearest coffee shop, ordered a latte without making eye contact with the barista and went to the far depths of the seating into a dark corner where no-one would spot her and hopefully not bother her.

She took several deep breaths to calm her panic and tried to think logically. She couldn't go home, that's the first place the police would look for her. But she couldn't just disappear without letting her parents know she was OK; it would worry them sick if she simply vanished.

She pulled out her phone and scrolled though the numbers. Nadine of course. She needed Nadine. She was just about to press the call button when she remembered seeing on films how the good people always track the bad people by using their mobile phone signals. She'd have to switch the mobile off for starters and use a public call box, or an internet café. This was going to have to take some careful thinking and plotting.

By the time her latte was cool enough to drink, Abigail felt like she had some sort of plan. It was fortunate that her wages had been deposited into her bank account yesterday morning, which allowed her to withdraw the maximum daily cash limit from a cashpoint close to her workplace. Rule number one - No using debit or credit cards, which are the first things the police would possibly track, it was strictly cash only from now on.

Rule number two – disguise. She hurried into a faceless high street accessories store and bought a hat and some shades. The shades would look silly on this cool April afternoon but may foil her images on the CCTV somewhat. Wrapping her long blonde hair into a makeshift bun she tucked it up inside the hat, transforming her appearance instantly. If anything she looked like a pop star trying to disguise herself from the paparazzi.

Rule number three – get to a place that non-one will think of looking. Abigail scanned the underground map on the back pages of her diary and opted for somewhere out to the East. She wondered whether the police would already be sat outside her parent's house in leafy suburban Richmond waiting for her to return, or one of her parents to return. She checked her watch and calculated that they would have to wait quite some time before her Mum arrived back home; tonight was parent's evening at the school where she taught, and Thursday nights were her Dad's darts night at the pub.

Rule number four – No mobile. She noted down some key phone numbers into her diary and reluctantly switched the mobile off. It was a wrench, but as soon as she'd done it she felt strangely liberated. No one knew who she was or where she was. They could no longer track her by the phone signal, no longer follow her transactions, nor the journeys she made. Her Oyster card remained at the bottom of her handbag, she would buy a Travelcard using cash and travel east.

There was no particular reason that she chose to get off the Central Line at Gants Hill station. She'd just jumped on an eastbound train and waited until she felt the instinct to get off. A suburban town like Ilford should have just what she needed, enough anonymity and randomness, with the amenities required.

From the tube station Abigail wandered somewhat aimlessly down the main street following her finely tuned instinct to direct her towards shops. Bingo, a phone box. The phone call home was going to be tricky; she'd have to blatantly lie to the answer machine. Perhaps the police were tracking the phone line home. She'd have to be brief too in case they tracked the call and her anonymous cover of Ilford was blown.

"Hi Mum and Dad," she began, a little too breezy. "Just to let you know I'm going away for a while. Sorry for the short notice, I've met someone at work – a man - and we've decided to be spontaneous and take off for a while on a short holiday... I don't really know where we're heading, but don't worry about me and I'll keep checking in to let you know I'm OK. So, take care, love you both."

Abigail slammed the phone down, her heart racing with guilt and anxiety. A gust of wind rammed against the side of the call box, sweeping a stray McDonalds burger carton into the glass. Everything suddenly felt ominous and threatening, even the gang of teenagers walking back from school, bashing each other in turn with their schoolbags eyed her suspiciously as they passed the call box.

A call to Nadine would calm her down. She fed more money into the machine and dialled Nadine's mobile number, which once again, led Abigail to a voicemail. She couldn't lie this time.

"Hi Nadine, it's me. You may have seen the news today, I think I might have done something to the stocks and shares as I managed to crack that login code I was telling you about. I'm worried that I've done something so awful, and am getting away for a bit... just until the fuss dies down. It's probably safer not to tell you where I am, but I'm safe. I've switched my mobile off so you can't get through to me. Oh, and I've told my parents that I've run away with a bloke from work. I know, it's absurd, isn't it? I never do anything spontaneous. Anyway, take care, I'll be in touch soon."

Hesitantly, she hung up. That was that. She paused momentarily in the phone box, a little safe haven of calm that she didn't want to leave. Outside the hustle and bustle of the world carried on around her regardless. Right, she pulled herself together, mustering up an ounce of courage that threatened to crumble at any moment. Accommodation came next.

Turning off down a side street and away from the bright lights of the High Street she found a series of small guesthouses competing for trade. They looked ideal, larger than family run places that could create suspicion, but not massive corporate chains that may have already been put on alert from the police.

She chose The Gables at random and walked up the steps into the hallway where a bored receptionist of unknown European origin looked up from the book she was reading. The décor was tired; cream woodchip wallpaper that was fraying in the corners, large wooden chunky furniture, deep red spiral patterned carpet.

"I'm looking for a single room?" It was a question more than a statement.

The receptionist tapped at her keyboard, although Abigail could see a row of keys attached to pebble shaped wooden key rings hanging from hooks above the receptionist's head. There were clearly plenty of vacancies. How many people would be looking for a room in Ilford on a Thursday night in April?

"The rooms are sixty pounds a night. How many nights are you staying?"

"Probably just one," she replied, thinking of how quickly the five hundred pounds would vanish in her purse if she stayed much longer. The receptionist grabbed a key from the hook and passed a registration card over the counter.

"Please fill in your details. Do you have a credit card?"

"I'm paying cash," she replied, thinking about rule number one. The receptionist seemed slightly startled momentarily, but shrugged. Abigail looked at the registration card. Name. Well, clearly not Abigail Daycock. She could no longer be Abigail Daycock.

She glanced up and the first thing she saw behind the reception was a calendar hanging on the wall. A-P-R-I-L she wrote in the Forename box. She was very tempted to put her surname as Showers, but couldn't risk drawing attention to herself that way. S-M-I-T-H she wrote in the space for her surname. You couldn't get more anonymous than that. Equally, she made up a fictional home address in Newcastle, and scrawled an illegible signature across the box where indicated.

The room was as she had expected from the décor of the reception. A single bed that looked as if it had been modeled on a wartime reconstruction; thick blankets and a lime green bedspread. The walls were cream and plain, but wall papered, with a couple of random pictures hung to break the monotony. On closer inspection, one was a scene from the Lake District, the other a black and white pencil drawing of a poppy. Probably picked up in the bargain bin at a charity shop, Abigail noted, with their mismatched frames and lack of connection to anything. Least of all Essex.

She sat wearily on the bed and wondered whether Nadine had picked up her phone message yet. She knew her parents wouldn't have been home to pick up their message. There was still time to scrap her half-baked plan and just return home and face the consequences. Police, prison, who knew what fate waited for her? She couldn't forget the screen full of red figures, the feeling of the panic welling up in the atmosphere as workers yelled for Mr

Johnson.

No, Plan A would have to stay in place she figured. She only had the clothes she was sat in, so she needed to go shopping. Clean pants were the bare minimum. She opened her purse and spread the cash over the bedspread. Minus the sixty pounds she'd just handed over, she was left with four hundred and forty pounds from the cashpoint, plus two pounds eighty nine in loose change. That would only allow her to stay on the run for six nights, if she stayed in guesthouses, which she clearly couldn't afford to do. That also left her no money for food. She could get more money from the cash point at a later date, but that action would risk alerting the police to her whereabouts. No, four hundred and forty pounds would have to last as long as possible. Guesthouses were too pricey, hostels would require ID, and she wasn't prepared to become homeless, nor go home. She couldn't turn up at any friend or relative's place and put them in an awkward position of harbouring a fugitive.

That left one thing, she figured. She pulled her coat back on, picked up the chunky room key, and headed back towards the High Street. She needed to go shopping before they shut.

At Wit's end

And so that's how we come to find Abigail – or April as she is now getting used to being called - sat cross legged in her tent, sobbing like a six year old on a Friday evening. Normally a Friday evening would involve a Chinese takeaway with her parents followed by a few alcopops down the local pub with Nadine, or catching a film at the Odeon with a large bag of rapidly melting maltesers. But this Friday was different and the start of a new life on the run.

From her four hundred and forty pounds budget, she'd invested in a two-person tent, a sleeping bag, a pair of leggings, a pack of underpants and a sweatshirt. Lugging the purchases into a pharmacy, she also bought a flannel, shower gel, toothbrush and toothpaste.

In her distress, she'd overlooked the need to buy any casual shoes, so was now unable to bring herself to wear the leggings and sweatshirt with the kitten heels, so had had to set off from the guest house on Friday morning still wearing her smart work clothes from the day before. At least she had clean pants on in case of an accident.

"Stupid cow," she cursed herself from her tent. "Where the bloody hell am I going to be able to buy any shoes around this godforsaken place?" Besides which, there was no way she was going back out in the rain today. It had started out dull and overcast from the moment she left the guest house in Ilford, full to brim with cooked breakfast, strong coffee and as much toast as she could stomach. Tottering back to the train station in her tight pencil skirt and heels, lugging bulging carrier bags from the Army and Navy Store and Marks and Spencer, she must have looked an odd sight. At least it was London and odd sights were commonplace and didn't attract too much attention.

There was no plan of action, except to get to the countryside where she would find a small campsite and lay low for a while. She'd never actually camped before. She'd gone to camp with her junior school class back in the mid nineties, but she couldn't recall any tents being involved then; just large wooden shacks on the edge of what seemed like a huge forest with bunk beds built into the sides of the walls, and a proper canteen serving nourishing hot meals. Not the sort of camping that involves heating baked beans in makeshift saucepans over a tiny camping stove, like she'd seen on TV.

Shit, she realized, she hadn't bought a camping stove. She was proving to be rubbish at this survival game.

At the mainline station in Ilford there was a large UK map

showing spaghetti lines sprawling north, east, south and west back into London. Abigail stared at it in awe. She could go anywhere. She followed lines with her fingers, she could go towards Dover or Brighton, back to the seaside resorts that she'd been taken to as a child with her parents and Aunty Pam. Abigail suddenly experienced a nostalgic rush of memories of candy floss and slot machines, donkey rides and sandcastles. Looking north, her eyes gazed up the lines towards Norfolk or Lincolnshire. In a day she could go all the way up to the Lake District, Oxenholme, Blackpool she read on the map. Looking west she poured over the South West, places she'd heard of but never been to; Barnstaple, Paignton, Redruth, Torquay. Or what about the Cotswolds, she wondered. She'd overheard a girl at Bartlett's talking about a romantic weekend her boyfriend had planned in a pretty thatched cottage in the Cotswolds. Where was that, she wondered, following lines across Oxfordshire and Gloucestershire. The names sounded adorable; Moreton-in-Marsh, Evesham, Ashchurch.... Were they places in the Cotswolds? There was one way to find out, she thought decisively. I'll go there.

"A single to Cheltenham Spa please," she asked at the desk. She was still aware that the police could be looking for her, and maybe they'd put stations on full alert, issuing her picture. She kept her head down and avoided eye contact, her hat covering her long blond hair again.

"That's fifty four pounds," the sullen woman mumbled from behind the glass. It's unlikely that she'd have bothered to make eye contact with Abigail if she could; this was London after all.

Having lugged her bulging carrier bags onto the train, across the London underground and onto the Cheltenham train at Paddington Station, Abigail was surprised that only three hours later the view from the window was turning into green luscious valleys, pretty streams and rivers and small towns with quirky stone facades. She could fit in here, she decided. Horsey people were rich; maybe this is where I meet my handsome millionaire husband, she thought. Maybe she should get some chic outfit that nodded to the riding community; fake jodhpurs and ankle boots with tweed jackets and floaty scarves.

With what, though? Her purse was now down to £270 and some loose change. That was unlikely to go far in Gloucestershire's boutique shops.

The train terminated at Cheltenham and Abigail stepped down and followed the flow of pedestrian traffic towards the town. One photocopied OS map from the library later, and Abigail was tottering off in a southerly direction wondering just what the hell she was doing. A camping virgin, drifting off into unknown territory to put up her tent somewhere, with just one change of clothes and less than three hundred pounds to survive on until goodness knows when.

The enormity of it hit her then, heading out of town, alone, her future spread out in front of her with a big question mark. Even the sky seemed to be conspiring with her darkening mood. The early breaks of sunshine had given way to increasing cloud, which as the afternoon wore on were turning ever more grey and hostile. She'd walked for two and a half hours when the first small drops started plopping to the ground. Her kitten heels had started to rub the heel of her foot and the handles on the carrier bags were digging into the palms of her hand.

According to the map, there should be a campsite right on the edge of the village of Sloth, and it couldn't come soon enough. The city was now miles behind her, the roads had become narrower and now on an unclassified country lane, the traffic had vaporized into thin air and all she could hear were birds chattering in the hedgerows and the distant hum of a combine harvester in the field. Or was it a bi-plane? Abigail's knowledge of the countryside was quite rudimentary.

She passed a sign on the side of the road welcoming careful drivers to the village of Sloth, and the road widened slightly and there were a few cottages and bungalows lining the sleepy street through the village. A pub, she noted, The Carpenters Arms, looking quite dejected in the grey blustery afternoon light. A chalkboard sign outside informed passers by that the pub proudly served Douwe Egberts coffee, which Abigail would have murdered for, were it not for the need to get to a campsite and get set up. She felt exhausted by the day's events and it wasn't even four o'clock yet.

The houses stopped and the road narrowed once again, leaving Abigail plodding on a small grass verge. The rain was starting in earnest now, and she shoved the paper photocopy of the map into one of the carrier bags to try and keep it dry. She had a small umbrella somewhere in the depths of her handbag, but no free hand to carry it, so the raindrops fell freely onto her un-waterproof coat and the dampness of the grass started to soak into her expensive shoes.

With great relief she spotted a hand painted sign at the side of the road, "Wits End Caravan and Camping" and a wonky arrow pointing up a long gravel track that seemed to constitute the driveway. In her work heels she wobbled up the gravel, past a modest detached house and into a large field, where there were a few caravans parked up but they were seemingly bereft of any life. Abigail spotted a brick outhouse at the edge of the field, with a makeshift wooden sign on the door. "Reception" it announced.

Hurrying over to get out the rain, Abigail, opened the door and entered the gloomy interior, surprised to find no-one there, an empty office with a computer unattended on the desk. The computer was on and humming gently to itself, and Abigail wondered with a shudder whether – if she were to take a closer look - there was a password box flashing its curser. There was a buzzer to press for attention, which Abigail did, and waited, taking in her new surroundings. The place seemed to need some attention, she decided. Everything looked very temporary and amateur. Surely it doesn't cost much to buy a proper sign for reception?

"Hiya, Sorry!" came a male voice, as a lad of around Abigail's age came bursting through the door. "Hi," he beamed, and if he was surprised to find a pretty single young lady, dripping in her work clothes and laden down with soggy carrier bags, he certainly didn't show it. "How can I help?"

"I was after a pitch for the night," she replied, hoping the terminology was correct. "I've got a small tent." Needlessly, she indicated the carrier bag containing the virgin tent.

"Sure." He squeezed past her and sat down at the desk. "Let me just take a few details." He tapped on the keyboard and brought the computer back to life. "Can I take your name?"

"April Smith." The lie seemed to slip off her tongue with surprising ease. Her heart was thudding slightly in case his next question was a request to see some ID.

"And how many nights will you be staying?"

"Probably the week. Until next Saturday." She had thought this one through on her long walk from the station to Wits End. She'd had time to think up a whole cover story for anyone that asked. It didn't seem as though this lad was bothered to hear it though.

"That's fine. It costs ten pounds a night – we ask that the tents are pitched over by the toilet block, anywhere along the hedgerow there. If you need food, the pub in the village does fairly decent grub and a wicked range of cider. There's also a small shop in Sloth for all your basics. Other than that, Cheltenham's the nearest slice of life – I believe there's a bus that comes along the lane here twice a day in each direction... unless you've got a car?" He wasn't requiring an answer Abigail decided. He could surely tell from her disheveled appearance and all her belongings that she had arrived on foot. She pulled out a few notes from her purse, trying to disguise the fact she had wads more, and handed over the payment for the week.

"Thank you." He shoved the cash in the drawer of the desk, not even bothering to count the notes nor lock the drawer shut.

Security in Sloth was a far cry from London. "Is there anything else I can help you with?"

Abigail hesitated. "I don't suppose you can help me put up the tent?"

Jumble

Abigail woke on Saturday morning with the early dawn light bursting through the canvas and a cacophony of birdsong in stereo from the hedgerows and the trees surrounding her pitched tent. She was relieved to find that she'd fallen asleep fairly easily, but then she had been exhausted from the uncertainty of the day, the train journey and the long walk from Cheltenham, the wind and rain, finished off with a damp fight with her new tent.

Thankfully Dan had been a Godsend, offering to lend a hand to get the tent up as quickly as possible in the awful weather. As they battled to pull everything from its new packaging, she'd learnt that Dan was the son of the campsite owners, home for the Easter holidays from Loughborough University. Initially, she'd tried to pretend that she knew what she was doing with the tent, but it was fairly obvious that this was the first time she'd ever struggled with flysheets, tent pegs and guy ropes.

Dan's curiosity had got the better of him and he'd asked what brought her – alone – to Sloth. With so little equipment. Abigail couldn't help blushing, and decided to try out her back-story for the first time.

"Is it that obvious that I'm a beginner at all this?" she grinned, trying to thread a long pole through the narrow sleeve. He took the pole from her, gently twisting it as he pushed it through.

"Just a bit."

"Well, I've been dared by my friend," she explained. "She bet me that I wouldn't be able to survive a week on a campsite on a limited budget and not being able to have my normal possessions – like my car, mobile and laptop and so forth. I'm a keen internet blogger, so I took the bet and decided to blog about my experiences."

Dan paused and raised an eyebrow. "It seems a bit of an inconvenience just to prove a point to your friend. And you'll probably end up ruining your shoes." He looked pointedly at her work shoes, now caked in mud.

"Well, I'm always up for a challenge," she responded. "I'm very competitive. And as for the shoes..." she looked down at her beloved pink heels from Faith and remembered buying them with some birthday money from her parents. She felt like crying. "They're only shoes. I can clean them."

"Just don't wear them inside the tent," he warned. "They'll probably pierce the ground sheet and then you won't be able to keep much dry. The ground's pretty sodden from the rain."

"Noted." Abigail stood back to admire the tent now that it was upright. The inside was a lot smaller than her bedroom at home, but at least her possessions didn't amount to much or take up much space. "Thanks a lot for your help – sorry you've gotten so wet."

"Not a problem," he responded with a grin. "It was much quicker with two people than struggling on your own. I'll leave you to it."

She'd sat inside the tent as the sun sank down over the horizon, wondering what to do with her Friday night. It was then she had started to feel sorry for herself and began to snivel. Damp, cold, miserable, alone, on the run.

However, the early Saturday sunshine and the deep sleep helped her to feel much better as the sun rose the next day. She looked at her watch, expecting to have slept in, but was disappointed to see that it was only six thirty. And she needed the loo, which meant putting on some layers of damp clothes to cross over the field to the toilet block. Damn this camping lark.

It occurred to her as she fought with her clothes in the confined space that she didn't have a towel, so a shower – and even a wash - would be out of the question today. She'd have to make a trip back into Cheltenham – although at least Dan had said there was a bus and she wouldn't have to walk back again in her soggy heels.

The toilet and shower block was freezing cold and Abigail couldn't imagine taking a shower in the place anyway. It was like something out of a concentration camp, with grey stone, mould-ridden tiles, bars on the frosted glass windows and clumps of hair in the plugholes. She suddenly appreciated her parent's lovely warm semi in Richmond even more. And people did this camping thing for fun?

For three hours, Abigail lay in her sleeping bag waiting for the rest of the world – apart from the birds who were already going about their business – to wake up. Her tummy began to growl with hunger and she realised that it was a long time since she'd actually eaten anything. Dan had mentioned that there was a small shop that sold basics, so that would be first priority, she decided.

Without a can opener, cutlery, nor any way of heating food, Abigail soon realised that breakfast options were a little limited. She wandered around the cramped shelving in the Spar, fantasizing about beans on toast, or egg and bacon, but ended up picking up a packet of crisps and a large chocolate bar. She'd have to develop a strategy, she realised, as this sort of diet was not a long-term prospect. But for now, calories were utmost importance and that was found in the junk she held in her basket.

"You must be from the campsite," the lady smiled behind the

counter. Abigail's paranoia kicked in and she wondered whether she smelt that bad already. The lady rang the crisps and chocolate into the till. "Provisions for a day walking in the Cotswolds?" she said, seemingly by way of explanation.

"Oh, no – it's sort of breakfast," she explained weakly. "I've not got.. I – er – forgot to bring my camping stove." The lady looked sympathetically for a moment, and Abigail handed over the money. "I don't suppose you'd know what time the bus to Cheltenham comes through do you?"

"Oh, not until Monday now. It doesn't run at the weekend."

Abigail's heart plummeted in despair. What the hell was she supposed to do for forty-eight hours trapped in this tiny little village with no adequate clothes, washing or cooking facilities, or entertainment? She didn't even have a book with her.

"Maybe you could get a taxi? I think there's a number of a local firm on the parish noticeboard over the road."

A taxi, of course. Abigail perked up, thanked the lady and wandered across the road to look at the noticeboard. There was a listing of Church services, a faded flyer about Mitsy – a lost black and white kitten from the Abbey Road area. A Ramblers poster about the next set of walks starting from the village well. There didn't seem to be a taxi number, but there was a bright coloured poster that looked fresh advertising a jumble sale at the Church.

"In aid of the Sloth Brownies. Clothing, books, cake stall, bric a brac, hot refreshments. St James Church Hall Saturday. 10am – 1pm. 10p entry."

Abigail had never set foot in a jumble sale in her life; that was more Nadine's scene, but she could at least buy a book to read and get a hot cup of coffee. She glanced at her watch and was pleased to see that it was approaching ten o'clock already, so she wandered down Church Lane and could hear a bubble of excitement as she approached. There was a long line of people snaking from the door of the Church Hall back to the roadside. It was mainly pensioners, chatting animatedly about the local gossip of the day, waiting for the doors to burst open.

Self-consciously she joined the end of the line and the couple in front of her turned and smiled curiously, nodding a welcome. They looked as though it had taken a lot of effort to walk here on their elderly legs and they had a trolley on wheels with them. Whether this was for support or to fill up, Abigail wouldn't like to bet.

"Hello," Abigail replied. She was desperate to break into her supersized chocolate bar, but it didn't feel right to munch away somehow. Someone was pulling open the big wooden doors of the hall, and there was a wave of excitement, as the crowd seemed to press forward. Abigail was fascinated.

"Ooh, here we go, get ready," the lady in front of her said, half to Abigail, half to her husband. Abigail presumed that for a village of this size and activity, a jumble sale was going to be a highlight. She had her 10p at the ready and dropped it into the bowl on the table at the entrance as she'd seen others do, then followed the couple into the hall. She paused and gazed around in wonderment at the scale of this. Trestle tables lined every wall of the hall and were piled high; there was clothing over half the tables, a teetering mound of shoes, piles of books, bags, and jewellery. Where did they find so many unwanted items in a tiny village this size?

To the left hand side of the hall, through a gap in the tables was yet another side hall, and Abigail could sense there was another hive of activity through there too. She hesitated, unsure where to start. The customers were launching themselves into the task at hand with gusto, pulling clothes from the piles, holding it up, placing it against them for size. Elbows were flying, a few people shoving to get a better view.

The table with books on seemed to be quietest, so Abigail decided to start there. Her eyes skimmed over the spines of Reader's Digest titles, Mills and Boon romances, some kids books, thrillers, spy novels. There was no order to the pile; a missed opportunity thought Abigail. They could be sorted into themes, and then placed alphabetically on the table. Nevertheless, she pulled out last year's Booker Prize winning read from underneath a hardback on caring for your houseplants.

"I'll take this one please," Abigail said to the lady behind the table.

"That's ten pence," the lady replied, "Although if you find two more, you can have three for twenty." Abigail remembered the lack of space in her cramped tent and politely declined the offer.

She moved along to the shoes. Instantly her eyes fell onto a Kickers sports shoe. Ideal. She grabbed it and desperately hunted for the other one. Why on earth hadn't someone tied the show laces together on the pairs? It could be anywhere. The girl behind this section of table was about Abigail's age, and started hunting through the shoes for the twin.

"What size are they?" Abigail asked, trying to find an indication inside the shoe.

"Um, I'm not sure – you'll have to try it on," she replied. "Here – here's the other one." Abigail kicked her own heels off and slipped on the trainers. Perfect.

"Twenty pence?" The girl said, more as a question than a statement. Abigail had the feeling that if she could have haggled down to ten pence and been successful. But twenty pence was a bargain, and she happily handed over the cash.

Her heels were now officially demoted. However, the trainers would look much better with a pair of jeans. She eyed up the tables piled high with clothing and guessed there was no order to this chaos either and it was a case of just diving in to see what she could find.

It only took a few minutes for Abigail to get the hang of it, grabbing anything that caught the eye, hold it up, instant decision, chuck it back on the pile, where usually another person's hand would come shooting out of nowhere and make a claim on it.

"Oh this is amazing!" Abigail grabbed a denim jacket in her size and noticed from the label that it was from a designer shop.

"That was mine," said the girl behind the table, the same girl that had sold her the shoes. "I can't quite fit into it anymore."

Abigail glanced her up and down and could see how she'd probably been about the same size once but was just carrying more padding.

"I've given up on the hope of shifting this baby weight, so I've had a bit of a clear out of my wardrobe so you'll probably find some more bits and pieces of mine around the place."

"Jeans?"

The girl nodded and silently started to help Abigail to rummage through the pile. Within minutes there was a pair of skinny jeans and some bootcut jeans that looked immaculate. A couple of hoodies, a selection of t-shirts and a denim jacket later and Abigail thought she'd better stop for fear of not being able to carry it all.

"Well, thank you for your help, I shall get lots of wear from these," Abigail told the girl, handing over the two pound coin. What a bargain, and what a thrill. Abigail wondered why she had always scoffed when Nadine raved about the gems she's uncovered at weekend jumble sales across London. She'd have to join in next time. If there was a next time.

A smell wafted into Abigail's nostrils just as she was heaving her bulging carrier bag out towards the exit. Bacon! She'd forgotten all about the refreshments part of the jumble sale. The side hall was a hive of activity, with nearly every table full of people – mainly pensioners admittedly – enjoying pots of tea, cake, buttered toast and a good catch up on village gossip. On the makeshift counter Abigail eyed the array of home baked cakes, flapjacks, buns and felt a nostalgic yearning for the days that she'd help her mother bake cornflake cake on a Saturday afternoon. A handwritten price list confirmed that the refreshments were also a bargain, with a bacon buttie and a cup of tea for £1.50.

The buttie was enormous, stuffed with bacon and oozing with butter, to which Abigail added a squirt of red sauce. She found a table in the corner from where she could observe the social etiquettes of the gathering like David Attenborough watching a pack of exotic wild animals in the jungle. Most had finished their drinks but looked as though they were settled into the chair for at least another hour. The pace of life in Sloth was obviously far removed from the hectic work breaks she took in London, grabbing quick coffees here and there. What else would people do on a Saturday in a village this small? No wonder the jumble sale was a highlight for the villagers.

After half an hour (Abigail decided that nobody else showed signs of moving, so she should enjoy her time leisurely) she saw the girl that had sold her the clothing come in and have a word with the lady in charge of the catering. There was talk of the hall getting very quiet and a discussion around logistics of where the leftover items were headed. With empty time stretching out in front of Abigail like a dark void, it suddenly became very obvious to her what she had to do.

"Would you like a hand with anything, clearing up wise?" she asked. The two ladies looked momentarily startled. "I've not got any plans, and as it's for charity, I wondered if you needed an extra pair of hands?"

The older lady's face softened. "Oh, that's really kind, er...."

"April."

"April. Perhaps in about quarter of an hour once the last people have left you could help Kate here box up all the leftover clothes and bric-a-brac and carry them down to Mrs. Angel's cottage. We're going to put it all in her spare room until the next event."

April beamed with a sense of purpose. "Great. I'll just pop my purchases in my ..." she stopped herself saying 'tent' in the nick of time. "place, then I'll come back and give you a hand Kate."

Twenty minutes later, Abigail was getting stuck in, helping Kate to pack away the leftovers, folding clothes into bin bags, and stacking bric a brac into cardboard boxes. They made small talk about each other's lives, and Abigail discovered that Kate had lived in Sloth all her life. Abigail couldn't imagine how somebody had reached their mid twenties and still be living in the confines of this tiny hamlet. The people were friendly enough, the scenery was stunning but surely that wasn't enough? If you opened the cages of the lab rats, their natural instinct would be to run away, into the unknown, rather than stay in their captivity. Kate seemed to Abigail to be a bright intelligent girl; she seemed wasted here in the confines of Sloth. She silently admonished herself for being judgmental.

Abigail cautiously stuck to her cover story about the bet that she'd made with her friend and the blog she was supposed to be writing. She admitted vaguely to living in London and was "between jobs" in the fashion industry. Kate appeared to lead an exhausting life, will a full time job as a dental nurse in Cheltenham, and a two year old toddler in nursery, and a jump jockey husband called Callum who was off working at different racecourses around the country most days.

"On top of everything, I'm having to look after Eddie and Jeremy at the moment too," she explained.

"Eddie and Jeremy?"

"My Mum's beagles; Eddie the Beagle and Jeremy Beagle." Abigail laughed. It appealed to her sense of humour and she immediately wanted to meet Kate's mum. "She's gone to Australia for a month to visit an old school friend and so she's left the dogs with me to look after. For small dogs, they've got so much energy and seem to need endless walks. Oh, and a huge appetite, they eat everything!"

For a moment, Abigail hesitated, on the brink of offering to walk the dogs. Was that too forward, when they'd only just met? She had plenty of time on her hands at the moment and could certainly use the exercise. There was nowhere to use her Blast24 gym membership card in Sloth, and if her breakfast was going to decline into mars bars and packets of crisps, rather than the fruit salads and cereal she ate at home, then she'd definitely need to do something. She let the moment pass, and continued to stack the leftover paperbacks into a cardboard box.

"So, who sees this blog that you write?" Kate asked, keen to take the attention away from her life and deflect it back to Abigail.

"I haven't actually started writing it yet," she confessed. "As part of the rules of the bet, I wasn't allowed to bring a laptop with me, so I'll need to go into Cheltenham and use the computers in the library. I'm not sure if the library's open at the weekend so it'll be my first job on Monday morning."

"You don't need to go all the way to Cheltenham," Kate replied dismissively as she deftly folded a pile of children's clothing and stuffed them into a black sack. "We've got a computer at home you can use."

"Really?" Abigail was surprised at the spontaneous generosity and wished she'd made the offer about walking the dogs. She made a mental note to repay the favour, but not just yet. She felt that would look too false. "That's really kind, are you sure?"

Kate paused from the task in hand and regarded Abigail fondly. "Of course. We're around tomorrow evening if you want to call in. Callum will have to show you the computer as it's his thing really, and he should be back by seven as he's in Huntingdon tomorrow. I don't have much time to do anything on it. Although I do sneak in the odd game of Block Blast."

Abigail thanked Kate again and smiled to herself. She'd been here in Sloth less than 24 hours and already had a friend and an invite. If she were lucky, maybe Kate would feed her too? And lend her a towel? The boxes and bags were now pretty much finished and ready to go.

Luckily Mrs. Angel lived just two doors down from the Church in a pretty ivy strewn cottage set back from the road. There were four slightly wonky stone steps to ascend before negotiating a rickety wooden gate that led to the garden path to the door. The front garden was ablaze with daffodils, overgrown buddleia bushes, rose bushes and the lawn could do with cutting as the recent rain and sunshine was making everything perk up and grow rapidly.

"Hello Mrs. Angel," Kate greeted the rotund pensioner as she answered the door. "We've brought the leftovers from the jumble sale."

"Oh yes, Kate dear, bring them on in." Kate introduced Abigail, although laden down with a cardboard box of books. Abigail had no free hand to shake hands. "How did it go this morning? I was hoping to come along but my back's been agony this morning. Don't ever get old," she advised, shuffling up the passageway in front of the girls, placing a pudgy hand on the wall to steady herself now and then.

"It was pretty busy, most of the village turned out. Catherine was still counting the proceeds when I left, but it's looking very promising."

They were instructed to take the boxes upstairs and dump them in the back bedroom, so Abigail followed Kate up the narrow staircase. The cottage smelt of baking, an aroma that – despite eating a huge bacon roll an hour earlier – made Abigail's mouth water.

The came down the staircase into the hallway and found Mrs. Angel waiting at the bottom holding out a £20 note to add to the proceeds of the jumble sale. After an obligatory protest, Mrs. Angel insisted and Kate took the note.

"She's so generous," Kate explained as they headed back down the garden path to collect the next batch of boxes and black sacks. "She's always splashing her money around, buying people things, donating to causes. She says she's got nothing else to spend it on."

"No family?"

"Not in the village. I think she has grown up grandchildren in Scotland, but they rarely seem to visit. Shame, she's a lovely old lady, but she's got plenty of friends in the village."

As they returned with the second batch, the kettle was whistling away in the kitchen towards the back of the cottage. "I hope you've got time for tea and cake when you've finished," Mrs. Angel said, more as a plea than an invite. Kate shrugged at Abigail, who shrugged back.

"I've left Aidan with Val, and the dogs will need a walk in a bit, but I can stay for a little while," Kate replied. "I think by the time we've shifted the rest of the boxes, we'll have earned a cuppa."

With the cup of strong hot steaming tea (served from a teapot with a knitted cosy to keep it warm) came a large chunk of lemon drizzle cake. Abigail bit into it and felt the moistness prickles her taste buds into action. In London she would never have dreamed of having such a diet laden with calories, fat and sugar, but not knowing when and where the next meal was coming from had changed her outlook on life. They'd made nearly a dozen trips between the church hall and Mrs. Angel's cottage, filling her spare bedrooms to the rafters with boxes and black sacks, so time was marching on towards lunchtime anyway.

Abigail glanced around the sitting room, finding it quite stereotypical of a woman of Mrs. Angel's age and era. She suspected she'd lived here most of her adult life, with chunky dressers cluttered with photographs of family portraits, a myriad of china ornaments, a plant pot with a healthy looking hyacinth providing a splash of colour and a desk calendar that still displayed dates for March.

There was no sofa; just four individual armchairs made from tapestry fabric that were quite worn, but partially covered with crocheted blankets, and a random assortment of cushions. A battered leather poufee sat randomly in the middle of the crowded room with yesterday's Daily Express folded on top. "PANIC AS BANKS" read the start of the headline, turning Abigail's stomach as she caught glimpse of it. The rest of the headline lay on the underside of the paper so she had no idea how the sentence finished but she didn't want to know.

"Terrible business with those banks," Mrs. Angel said, spotting that Abigail was looking at the paper. "That's why I never put money in them, never have. It's much safer to keep it where I know I can access it anytime I want. Don't trust the computers, can't rely on them. I know Mrs. Baker from bridge club couldn't pay for her holiday deposit. She made a special trip into Cheltenham to go to the travel agent and spent over an hour with the lady choosing a holiday – I think it was a cruise – and then the card wouldn't work. She went out to use one of those holes in the wall, but that wouldn't give her any money either. So she went into the bank and there was a big queue of angry people all trying to demand the same thing. And the manager of the bank was pulling his hair out saying there's nothing he can do, as it's a problem all over the country with the computers. Stupid things. The money's still all there it seems – well it has to be – but what's the point if no one can get at it? Were you two affected at all?"

Abigail said nothing but could feel a hot flush of shame sweep across her face and prayed it wasn't noticeable to the others.

Kate shrugged. "I haven't tried to get any money out since everything crashed, but I know Val had her debit card refused at Morrisons yesterday. That must have been embarrassing, as she had a huge weekly shop piled up on the conveyor belt and no way of paying for it. It's a real mess."

"I took a lot of cash out on Thursday ready for this trip," Abigail said, "so I don't know whether I've been affected yet." The irony. The whole trip was a result of the fiasco. Her whole life had been affected by one stupid password. If only they knew the half of it. Abigail sipped her tea to create a lull in the conversation.

"So have you just moved to the village?" Mrs. Angel asked Abigail, thankfully diverting the conversation to another track. Once again, Abigail described the backstory to Mrs. Angel, not lingering too much on the blogging part, which she presumed would be beyond Mrs. Angel's comprehension.

"Well, if you're ever in need of food, I've always got plenty here," Mrs. Angel offered generously. "Or if it gets cold and you want a warm place to sleep, you're very welcome."

"That's very kind," smiled Abigail, not believing that she would ever take her up on her offer. "I'll bear that in mind." She munched a mouthful of cake thoughtfully. "I have a bit of time on my hands, so if you need anything doing, just shout up, I'd be happy to help."

Mrs. Angel heaved herself onto her feet, sighing as she reached full height and pausing to rub her back. She glanced out of the small wooden window onto the front lawn. "Are you much of a gardener?"

Abigail had never touched a garden in her life. At her parents' suburban Richmond semi, the garden was always neat, the grass kept mown in a tidy rectangle, with the edges trimmed around the fishpond. The colourful borders were lined with an array of bushes that flowered with proud bursts of their reds, yellows, pinks and purples throughout the warmer months, and on the patio there were tubs, containers and hanging baskets full of marigolds and pansies and other assorted floral displays that nodded and smiled happily in the breeze.

But none of it was thanks to Abigail, she reflected. It just seemed to be there and happen magically. Both her Mum and Dad could be seen "pottering" around in the garden some weekends, wandering casually around with a pair of secateurs. And she recalled many trips to garden centres on a Sunday afternoon when she was too young to protest and be allowed to stay at home, strolling through displays of every living thing known to man from fruit trees to gladioli. She was bored to her core, but her parents reveled in it, stopping to point at plants, inspect leaves, read the little "care for your plant" cards that stuck up from the soil. Abigail only went on the hope she'd be allowed a buttery flapjack with her milkshake in the cafe at the end of the trip.

"Gardening?" she asked, stepping up to look out of the window with Mrs. Angel. How hard could it be? "I'd be happy to give it a go." Her subconscious sniggered at the thought but she dismissed her reservations. As long as Mrs. Angel had a lawn mower and something to cut those rampaging plants with, she felt confident that she could tackle it. It couldn't be any harder than making a pair of trousers, could it?

She agreed to come around on Monday morning, pleased with how her mental diary was now filling up. When she'd woken in the tent that morning, she had a long stretch of emptiness ahead, and here she was after five energetic hours of helping with a jumble sale, with a Sunday evening appointment to use Kate's computer to write the fictional blog, and a date on Monday with Mrs. Angel's garden. Beyond that though, a lifetime on the run seemed an onerous prospect. She wondered how long she could stay in Sloth before the police closed in on her. Someone would spot her picture online or in the news, put two and two together and blow her cover. Maybe Kate or Mrs. Angel already knew her identity and were trying to stall her until the police could arrive. Abigail's stomach took another plunge of fear.

Little did she know that she was also to be occupied that evening too. On returning to Wit's End campsite, she met Dan walking the opposite direction down the driveway.

"Settled in OK?" he asked. "You've got a change of clothes I see," he nodded towards the jeans that she'd bought that morning for 20p. Kate's old jeans of course, although Abigail wasn't about to admit that though.

"Yes, I don't think I'll be needing the short skirt and heels any time soon," she responded wistfully. A new job in the hustle and bustle of London seemed a long way off from the green fields and slow pace of Sloth. Maybe they should have been added to the leftover jumble bag, she mused.

"Oh, you've got a few other tenting neighbours," Dan continued. "It'll be busy in Sloth over the weekend as there's the folk festival taking place at the airfield up the road. It's an annual event that brings in an interesting bunch of campers."

Dan chose his words carefully. The festival was a mecca for middle class, middle aged groups and couples who yearned for their student days; smoking pot, drinking strong dry cider and mellowing out to the sound of pennywhistles and banjos. Thankfully, they'd all be packed up by Monday and be heading back to their middle management desk jobs. "Oh, it does mean that the pub will be pretty busy tonight though if you're planning on eating there, so probably best to book a table in advance."

"A table for one," Abigail scoffed before she had time to stop herself. There was an embarrassed pause for a second before Dan's face lit up. "Why don't you come to the house? Mum and Dad are going out and I was planning on making a vat of chilli and having a few mates round, a beer or two. You'd be very welcome."

Abigail hesitated. This sounded like a chat up line. Or a sympathy vote.

"Come on," he persisted. "It's silly you being all alone with nowhere to eat for miles around, and I'm going to have so much chilli con carne I won't know what to do with it all."

"All right," she agreed. "But I'm not coming empty handed, what shall I bring?"

"That's more like it! Just bring whatever you fancy drinking and a big appetite."

Appetite wasn't top of the list following Mrs. Angel's huge slab of lemon drizzle cake, but Abigail knew she'd be ready for something else later. Quietly satisfied that she had yet another appointment lined up, she went back to her tent, which as Dan had pointed out, was now accompanied on each side by new arrivals.

The sun had managed to dry out the ground enough to allow the neighbouring residents to spread blankets outside their tents while they lay, smoking roll up cigarettes and reading books. Abigail smiled and nodded at them and felt aggrieved that she didn't have a blanket to use, so sat inside her canvas reading the book that she'd bought that morning at the jumble sale.

By six o'clock, her tummy rumbled. She wandered over to the shower and toilet block to put some make up on, noticing that all the festival goers had now packed up their blankets and had vanished, presumably to the pub or to the festival itself. It was so dark and dank in the toilet block. The window sills were bare, with the cold wind whistling in through the cracks. The stone floor was damp, one of the fluorescent light strips flickered and people had scribbled graffiti on some of the toilet doors.

Not quite the Ritz, but it was all she could afford, she told herself, trying to see through the dim light whether the eye shadow was the right shade. And at least it meant a free meal tonight. Grabbing the two bottles of wine from the tent that she'd popped out to the shop to buy a little earlier, she made her way down to the house, where Dan opened the door and greeted her like a long lost friend. He was wearing a "Kiss the chef" apron over black jeans and a Nirvana t-shirt.

"Come in'" he invited and she stepped into the hallway that smelt immediately of warm chilli con carne. She could hear a guitar being strummed in a distant room, and he led her down the hallway and into a bright, airy lounge where a small group sat gathered on the large sagging sofas.

"Everybody, this is April," Dan announced, and there was a general friendly chorus of "hi" in reply. "This is my girlfriend Mandy," he introduced, indicating a girl a few years younger than Abigail. She looked at Mandy in awe. Her triathlon-toned body was being shown off under a tight black lycra dress, which she wore with high dernier tights and killer red heels. She had a gorgeous mass of silky brown hair that tumbled past her rib cage, which she flicked effortlessly away from her face when she smiled her greeting. She could give Princess Kate a run for her money with her flawless complexion made up with perfectly applied cosmetics. Abigail felt much underdressed in her jumble sale jeans, trainers and sweatshirt.

"...and that's Adam from Fry's Farm down the road, and that's Penny - his little sister."

Fortunately, Adam hadn't made any effort either though, she noted with relief, sitting in his ripped jeans and plain white t-shirt. He had the guitar on his lap.

His little sister Penny looked about twelve, a gangly awkward age where her teeth were in braces and she was probably just trying out bras.

Abigail worried momentarily about the odd assortment gathered around the coffee table, and what they would talk about, but as the drink kept rolling, they made it very easy to join in the conversation. They asked Abigail the usual questions about whether she had brothers or sisters, what her parents did, and Abigail was able to answer truthfully without giving away too much about her identity. In return she learnt that Mandy and Dan were at university together in Loughborough, both studying sports science. That would explain the amazing body then. They were still on a long Easter break, which Adam ridiculed them for, being a lazy drain on the coffers of the hardworking taxpayer. Adam worked on the family's dairy farm along the lane, working long days that started ridiculously early and seemed to Abigail to have very little respite, even on a Sunday. She suspected there was very little money to be earned there either.

"And what about you April?" asked Mandy, "Are you at uni?"

"Er, no, I didn't go to university," she lied. "I left college in London a few years ago and have been doing temping jobs here and there trying to decide what line of work I'd be interested in."

"Have you got any ideas of what you'd like to do?" This girl was very direct, decided Abigail, feeling under scrutiny suddenly. "I mean, what sort of things are you interested in, and what are you good at?" This felt like a job interview.

"Well," Abigail took a slight pause as four pairs of eyes were directed straight at her, waiting for her answer. "I have a pretty full range of admin and IT skills, but I don't want to end up simply in an office job, but I guess it helps that I can build websites, create forms, manipulate numbers on spreadsheets and things. I've just finished a temping role in a marketing agency and picked up quite a bit of knowledge and skill around marketing campaigns, advertising and that sort of thing. I'm good with a sewing machine and enjoy playing around making clothes and accessories. I can cook, although I don't think I'd want to do that for a living – far too hot and sweaty and I'd probably lose the enjoyment of eating. So I don't know. I guess I'm waiting for a calling."

"Well talking of food," Dan replied, thankfully diverting the attention away from Abigail "I am about to dish up the feast!"

They all took their places at the large dining table in the corner of the lounge, and Dan placed a large pot of steaming chilli con carne in the centre between them. A mound of rice followed, along with an array of accompaniments including yoghurt, lettuce and tortillas.

"Oh," exclaimed Penny, examining the contents of the ladle that she was about to spoon onto her rice. "It's meat. I've decided to become vegetarian."

"Don't be silly," Adam scolded, "Just eat up. You can become vegetarian tomorrow. I mean, the cow's dead and cooked now, so you eating Dan's yummy chilli won't make any difference to this animal, will it?"

"I suppose not," she reasoned, allowing the food to tumble off the ladle onto her plate. Abigail chuckled.

"Well that was easy," she complimented Adam. "You should work in negotiation, not dairy farming!"

"Nah," he replied. "I just know how to convince my sister of things. Besides, she loves meat; there's no way she'd ever become vegetarian. She'd end up starving in our house if she does."

"No I wouldn't," Penny retorted.

"You would! There's no way any of us would cook you a separate meal."

"Then I'd make my own."

"Yeah? Like what? What would you cook yourself?"

The challenge threw her momentarily, and she put her fork down to think more clearly. "I'd cook.... Potato. And ..um... chips. Maybe some rice."

The argument appeared to end there, and everyone chomped away in silence for a few minutes, making occasional noises to indicate that the chilli was delicious.

"So," Abigail said moments later to no-one in particular, "Tell me about the people of Sloth. Who should I look out for and who should I avoid?"

"Well, you've obviously met my good self and Adam, and we are the people that the entire village centres around," Dan playfully boasted. "You haven't met my parents yet I don't think – they're pretty laid back and cool about most things. My Mum's got this bee in her bonnet at the moment about customer feedback – she's designed a new form to see what our campers really think about the place."

"April should fill one in," offered Mandy. "And perhaps April could then give your Mum feedback on the feedback so to speak. With all your experience in marketing and office work, you'd probably have a flair for that sort of thing." Abigail sensed a snipe, but let it go. It was probably her paranoid imagination; it had been running on overtime lately. Being a police suspect on the run tends to do that to a person.

"I'd be happy to," Abigail replied. "What does your Dad think about the idea?"

"He's happier just talking to guests to get informal feedback. Plus he's never touched an Office document or spreadsheet in his life. They've been here twenty-five years and I don't think much has changed in that time. 'If it ain't broke, why fix it?'" came Dan's impression of his Dad.

"You'll probably come across Kate and Callum," said Adam, getting back to the subject of who was who in the village. "Kate's one of those people that gets herself completely involved in everything. The church, the WI, the fundraising committees, the fetes and festivals."

"You say that like it's a bad thing. I think Kate's pretty incredible," countered Mandy. "Small villages will only thrive if there's people willing to glue everybody together and I see Kate as definitely the glue. Superglue."

"I've actually come across Kate already," Abigail said. "We met at the jumble sale at the Church hall this morning."

"Ha! There you go!" Adam grinned as if his point had been proved. "But I bet Callum wasn't there, he's hardly ever around. Seems to work seven days a week all over the place. I'm amazed they've got a kid – how have they found the time to make a baby!"

"Her husband's a jockey, right?"

Mandy let out a small gasp at Abigail's lack of knowledge, "He's not just *any* old jockey; he's practically a celebrity in this village! He landed the Cheltenham Gold Cup last month and could be in with a chance of winning the Grand National next week. Some people think he could also be nominated for Sports Personality of the Year."

"Well, I've also met Mrs. Angel," Abigail went on. Mandy was making her feel quite foolish. "She seems lovely, and her cake is to die for."

"Oh she's such a sweetheart," Dan concurred. "She taught me to play piano when I was younger. I never kept it up though. Sadly."

"And she used to baby sit me when I was a nipper, and for Penny too."

Hearing her name and realizing that she had a chance of being included in the adult conversation, Penny pushed her empty plate aside and sat up.

"We played shops in her kitchen for hours," Penny reminisced. "With real money too – not these plastic coins and things, but proper paper notes and coins. Some of them were like ten pound notes."

"That sounds like Mrs. Angel – she stashes cash around the house like she was hoarding newspaper or something," Dan said. "She's never trusted the banks."

"And now she's looking like the sensible one what with all of this banking mess kicking off," said Mandy decisively, looking firmly at Abigail. A stab of paranoia hit Abigail suddenly. Did she know something? Was her cover blown? Is that why she's been a bit prickly and condescending towards Abigail all evening?

"Until she gets burgled and loses the lot," replied Dan, who started to gather up the empty plates. Mandy jumped to her feet and began to top the wine glasses up, and open fresh cans of lager for

Adam and Dan.

"There's not too many other people to note," Adam continued. "The landlord of the Carpenters Arms is Roger. He's some relation of the Ashingtons. He only took the pub over at Christmas so he's trying to turn it around after it got a bit run down."

Simultaneously, everyone drifted back over to the sofas with glasses in hand and settled back down on the comfy furniture to let the food go down.

"We think he's gay," Dan said. "He used to be in the army and he left suddenly and came back to this village to take on a crappy pub." Abigail couldn't follow the logic of how his actions must result in him being gay, but Dan handed her a sheet of A4 paper and their attention was taken away from Roger, gay or otherwise.

"Here – perhaps you can tell us what you think."

The form was the "Customer satisfaction survey", typed fairly neatly in Times New Roman font. Abigail hated Times New Roman but didn't say so as it seemed quite a picky point. It launched straight into question one.

"I think that there needs to be a couple of lines explaining the purpose of the survey," offered Abigail. "Just something like 'we are keen to find out the views of our campers, and appreciate your time in completing this short survey for us.'"

"Isn't that fairly obvious though?" sneered Mandy. "It does say 'Customer satisfaction survey' in the title."

"It's a good point April," Dan replied, overriding Mandy. "It certainly sounds a lot friendlier, even if it's obvious. Have a go at answering the questions too." He handed Abigail a pen.

Question One asked how the customer would rate the site on a scale of one to ten.

"Hmmm, that's a bit vague," Abigail said, hoping that she wasn't coming over too negative. "What does your Mum mean by "site"? That could be the grounds, the facilities, the overall experience of staying here, the friendliness of the staff? If it's an overall rating for everything, then the question should come at the end, and say that it's an overall score."

There followed an uncomfortable silence and Abigail glanced at Mandy just at the point she was rolling her eyes at Adam in mock despair.

"There's also nowhere to write comments to explain your score. If I give this a one out of ten, how will you know what's wrong with the site, and how to improve?"

If Dan regretted giving Abigail the survey he didn't show it.

"There is a comments box on the back," he pointed out and Abigail flicked the paper over to see a large box taking up most of the reverse side with the heading 'Your comments'.

Question 2 asked whether there was anything that needed changing about the site. There was a small space under the question that would allow only a few lines of text. Abigail pointed that out.

"Well, how much would you want to write?" Dan asked, a tone of frustration creeping into his voice.

Abigail thought for a few moments. "There's quite a lot I could put in there and you may find some customers fill it in unhelpfully by not explaining what they mean. For example, I may put in "toilet block". Personally I think it's cold, dank, uninviting and could use some tender loving care to make it better, but if I just write "toilet block" you aren't going to know what my gripes are with it. It may be better to make the question more solution focused, such as 'What improvements, if any, would you like to see to improve the site'? So in my toilet block example I might instead write 'Get some curtains put up in the ladies toilet block and install heating.' Do you see what I mean?"

"Do you know what I think we should do?" Dan asked rhetorically. "I think I should give you a pad of paper, 7 days and a mission to bring back a revised questionnaire for my Mum, because this one needs a lot of work." He took the questionnaire from Abigail, tore it decisively in half and handed it back to her with an A4 pad of blank paper. "Would you mind?"

"Not at all, it'll give me something to do. I hope your Mum doesn't think I'm a bossy boots though."

"Nah," Dan waved off her concerns. "Just leave her to me."

"Why doesn't April make the curtains for toilet block as well?" Mandy asked, with a thick undertone of sarcasm. "She's a whizz on a sewing machine after all?"

"You know what? That is a brilliant idea!" Dan enthused as Mandy's face fell. "Would you be up for that? I could give you some money to cover the cost of any material and you could come in here and use Mum's sewing machine. Only if you had time - and wanted to of course, I wouldn't want to impose on your break. We can give you a few extra night's stay as payment... if you wanted to stay a bit longer than a week, and can put up with the cold dank toilet block that is."

Abigail was momentarily speechless as the offers were all coming at once. Staying beyond a week hadn't been her plan, but maybe a few days extra wouldn't hurt. Before she had chance to agree, little Penny scampered over to her side and tugged at her sleeve.

"April – I've got the best idea. You can buy material for the curtains at the market tomorrow over at Weird Al's fields, and we can go together, because I'm not allowed to go on my own but it's OK if someone takes me and I can never find anyone who wants to go because Adam says the market is full of crappy bits of rubbish that no-one wants to buy." She finally took a breath and Abigail glanced at Adam to ascertain his take on the situation.

"Don't feel pressurized to take her..." he started apologetically.

"Weird Al?" Abigail questioned.

"Yeah," replied Dan thoughtfully. "Nobody really knows how he came up with that nickname. He's got a few acres down the lane and doesn't do anything with it except let it be used for a car boot sale and market every Sunday morning. It's the biggest one in the area, and there's a material stall there, Penny's right about that."

"Please," begged Penny, tugging Abigail's sleeve insistently.

"Well, as long as it's OK with your Mum - why the devil not?"

Penny cheered with excitement and clapped her hands together, and Abigail wondered how much more socializing would appear in her diary in the next 24 hours. Compared to London where everyone went about his or her own lives, this country life ironically seemed much more sociable. Yes, you were subject to gossip and scrutiny, but Abigail sensed there would always be someone to turn to in times of need. And who could be more in need at the moment than our fugitive on the run?

Weird Al's bargains

"Play me the message again," Fish demanded as he, Nadine, Craig and Dougie sat around on the packed up band equipment after a euphoric gig at the Steaming Sheep. The landlord had called last orders half an hour ago and the pub was finally coming down from its noisy high an hour ago, where Blue Steak were belting out "Mustang Sally" to a drunken crowd who bounced up and down on what little sticky dance floor there was.

"Right, listen carefully," scolded Nadine, who had already played the answerphone message to them twice already. Distractions and short attention spans had disrupted the first two plays, but she finally had all three of them listening intently. She turned the volume up a notch on her phone.

"Hi Nadine, it's me," came Abigail's voice shakily from the speaker. "You may have seen the news today, I think I might have done something to the stocks and shares as I managed to crack that login code I was telling you about. I'm worried that I've done something so awful, and am getting away for a bit... just until the fuss dies down. It's probably safer not to tell you where I am, but I'm safe. I've switched my mobile off so you can't get through to me. Oh, and I've told my parents that I've run away with a bloke from work. I know, it's absurd, isn't it? Anyway, take care, I'll be in touch soon."

"What login?" asked Dougie. As the eldest member of the band, Nadine decided he was the one to take control of the situation. Nadine explained what little she knew about the password box at Bartlett's, and how Abigail had been trying to guess the word.

"Should we be worried about her?" she asked the trio. "She sounds really scared."

"Well, there's not a lot we can do, is there?" said Craig bluntly. Nadine glared at him for his lack of sympathy. "She doesn't say where she's gone and we have no way of contacting her. She says she'll be in touch soon so I say you should wait and let her get in touch."

There was an awkward pause and Nadine was horrified to feel her eyes welling up with tears. "I'm just really scared for her as she's never really been away from home properly before. Especially not on her own like this. She could be anywhere." She broke off as a tear made its escape down her cheek.

Dougie shifted over and perched a buttock on the Marshall speaker next to her. He put an arm around her and pulled her in towards his chest.

"Don't worry babe," he soothed. "Why not stick a message on

47

her Facebook wall – she might be able to get a glimpse of that?"
Nadine nodded glumly. Anything was worth a try.

Sunday morning started bright and promising, and at Fry's Farm, Penny woke up excited as she remembered that she was able to go to Weird Al's market that morning with the newcomer to the village. The farmhouse was deserted when she scrambled down the bare wooden stairs at seven o'clock as her parents were already out and about getting the herd into milking. There was no sign of brother Adam either, who was also no doubt roped into jobs around the farm.

Penny shooed one of the many cats off the arm of the threadbare corduroy sofa in order to retrieve a bungee for her hair, and without bothering to brush her shoulder length brown tangled mess, she scraped it back off her face using her hands and manhandled it all into a misshapen pony tail.

She found her ankle boots in the porch; brown, scuffed and well worn, but the most comfy footwear Penny owned. Tugging them on, she then skipped off down the muddy driveway, deftly skirting around the puddles as she went. There hadn't been any heavy rain since the downpours of Friday, when Abigail had arrived in Sloth, but the driveway was so poorly maintained by Penny and Adam's father that the potholes had filled with grimy brown water and not had chance to drain away. Once out onto the lane, Penny turned right and made the five-minute trip to Wit's End campsite.

Once again Abigail was woken earlier than she would have chosen by the tweeting of birds in the hedgerows that lined the camping field. She'd had a disturbed sleep anyway, what with her mind buzzing from the conversations that previous evening, then just as she was on the hazy brink of falling asleep, the first of the revelers from the festival started to arrive back to the camp site, singing out of time and out of tune whilst telling each other to "shush because people are trying to sleep". Ignoring their own advice, they decided that two o'clock in the morning was a suitable time to sit outside their tent with a guitar and have an unplugged music session.

Finally she'd dozed off fully and was starting to dream about a talking mouse that was riding on a big wheel at a fairground, when she was woken with a jump as another festival go-er tripped over a guy rope and fell into the clash and bang of metal pots and pans that were stacked alongside the washing up bowl outside another camper's tent.

The light permeating through the canvas, Abigail read some

more of her jumble sale book before deciding that seven thirty was a respectable time to surface and get dressed.

"Ah you're up at last," a little voice said as Abigail unzipped the tent and drew back the door. "I've been waiting ages – the market opens at seven and you have to get there early to get the best bargains. Come on!"

Abigail had planned to at least go to the toilet block to brush her teeth, but Penny's flushed excited face convinced her that she should just let them rot for one day. Together, the unlikely duo set off down the sleepy Sloth main street, Abigail guarding the thirty pounds that Dan had given her to buy material with the previous evening, and Penny with two pounds of pocket money. She was looking for second hand books in the "Sylvia Downton mystery series" and sometimes was lucky enough to pick them up for less than a pound each.

"Have you read any?" she asked Abigail, who confessed that she wasn't familiar with Sylvia Downton.

"I've read fourteen of them," Penny said proudly. "But there are thirty eight in the whole series so I've got a lot more to read." She proceeded to describe to Abigail that Sylvia was a schoolgirl detective in a boarding school, who had an amazing talent for solving school mysteries. "In the first one, the school cat goes missing and Sylvia discovers that the cook had kidnapped it and was planning to put the cat into the casserole for the students to eat, but her evil plan was foiled by the schoolgirl."

"That sounds a bit grisly," observed Abigail, who preferred to challenge herself with booker prize winning fiction, and the odd indulgence into chick lit. "Are they all like that?"

"Some of them, yes. The last one I read was about Sylvia solving a mystery about the science teacher, Mr Crumble, who was stealing some of the potions he used in the chemistry class to make nasty smells. He had a plan to make stink bombs with them and try to get some of the naughty students he didn't like to discover the stink bombs so that they would let them off and hopefully get expelled." The girls paused and stood in the grass verge momentarily to let a car pass. "But of course, Sylvia discovered what he was doing and the headmaster ended up sacking the teacher instead."

It occurred to Abigail that Penny was quite a lonely child. She didn't seem to have a great deal of people her age in the village and so presumably buried herself into books instead. Looking at Penny's clothes, Abigail also deduced that the family probably weren't rich, or just didn't care about outward appearances. Penny could be described as scruffy, with mud-splattered leggings and a plain beige jumper that looked hand knitted by someone without an eye for detail. She wasn't wearing any accessories, her ears were unpierced, all her stubby fingers were unadorned by rings and even her hair wasn't brushed.

Abigail glanced down at herself and thought maybe she shouldn't be so quick to judge. She was still wearing Kate's jeans and the sweatshirt that she'd worn continuously since the jumble sale the day before. Her stock of clean pants would soon be getting dangerously low and she longed for a deep hot bubbly bath instead of the cold mouldy showers in the toilet block on site.

"Look, we're nearly here," chirped Penny as they rounded the corner of the lane. Abigail could instantly smell the welcoming aroma of burger vans, and realized that she hadn't eaten anything yet that morning. Up ahead she saw a buzz of activity in the field to the right, vans, stalls, cars displaying goods on tables, and a mass of people milling through the mess like disorientated ants. Cars were pulling into the field from the opposite direction, there was no-one else arriving on foot like Penny and Abigail.

"Are you hungry?" Abigail asked Penny, as the scent of burgers teased her nostrils too much. "Fancy a burger or a hot dog?"

"I haven't had breakfast," she admitted, but there was a hesitation in her voice. "I'd rather not spend my money until I know there's no Sylvia Downton books."

"Well I can treat us to breakfast. It's on me." Abigail started to head towards the burger van.

Penny looked doubtful for a moment before nodding and following. "I feel a bit bad though because I can't buy you anything in return."

"Don't be silly. I like treating people." Abigail ordered two burgers with congealed onions and salivated as she squeezed red sauce over the bun. "You know, that's one thing they could do with at Wits End is somewhere to be able to get breakfast," mused Abigail, biting hungrily into the burger. "Or just hot food and drinks in general. Maybe I'll put it on the feedback form."

"What – like a café on site?" asked Penny, nibbling her burger with dainty finesse compared to Abigail.

"Or someone to drop off hot food around the tents first thing in the morning. Like a bacon buttie delivery service. I wonder if that would work?" She glanced at Penny, who shrugged. "You see, there's probably other people like me have come unprepared for cooking food, so unless I eat junk like crisps or chocolate for breakfast, I haven't anything to eat."

"But most people that go camping aren't like you." Penny

observed. "Adam was saying last night how odd it is that you have come away all on your own and obviously have no clue about camping. Then Dan said you'd arrived in a short skirt and high heels with a brand new tent." Penny giggled. "I wish I'd been there to see it."

Abigail felt a sting of hurt. She knew Penny wasn't being nasty, but to know that the others had been discussing her was a worry. In what context were they talking about her unsuitability for camping? The paranoia started rising again, were they dissecting her arrival egged on by Mandy, suspicious and subliminally remembering the girl on the run having brought down the banking system? Or were they just taking the piss out of her? Either way, it wasn't a nice feeling. Abigail screwed up her empty burger packaging and hurled it into the bin with an uncharacteristic wave of fury. She took a deep breath and reset her feelings. Don't take it out on Penny.

"Right then," she strode forward into the swarm of people and began to trudge alongside the other car booter bargain hunters as if caught in an undertow sucking the pair along the row of sellers. It was the first time that Abigail had been to a car boot sale and her eyes darted around from the items laid out on blankets on the ground, to table tops, to hanging on clothes rails. It was obvious that some of the sellers were families that had issued an ultimatum to the kids to fill a set amount of bin bags with books and toys that were no longer played with. Heaps of soft toys, dog eared books, battered board game boxes and jigsaw puzzles mingled in with the adult's offerings of CDs, crockery, jewellery and unwanted presents.

Other sellers were evidently here week in, week out and were making their living from trading out of the car boot. Nobody clearing out their loft would own four copies of "Dirty Dancing" on DVD, Abigail reasoned, and tried to bypass these stalls.

"Oh my goodness," Abigail breathed in amazement as she passed one of the stalls displaying a lot of loft clear out clutter. "A pair of UGG boots!" She picked them up lovingly and inspected the tread on the bottom of the sole. "Barely worn." The fleecy lining was soft and luxurious to the touch, and Abigail stood stroking the boot like a cat for several seconds.

"Not really the weather for those sorts of boots at the moment," Penny said dismissively, flicking through a pile of children's fiction that had been dumped unceremoniously in a cardboard box on the ground.

"They're size five," grunted the overweight lady behind the table. Abigail glanced at her and nodded enthusiastically. Size five was perfect. In her head she mentally calculated that the RRP for a pair of the boots would have been around £120, but they were probably from last season if not the season before, so deduct around thirty pounds. Plus the light wear and tear to the tread, and small blob of grey dirt that may or may not come out on the heel. But anything around fifty pounds would be reasonable.

"How much?" she asked tentatively, thinking of her finite financial resources.

The lady shrugged. "Three quid?" she replied more as a question than a statement.

A disbelieving laugh escaped Abigail's lips. "I'm sorry, how much?"

The lady misunderstood Abigail's reaction and looked offended. "Oh OK," she conceded with another sigh. "I'll take two pounds fifty."

"Two pounds fifty," Abigail clarified, handing over the money quickly in case the seller realized her mistake. She clutched the boots to her chest and thanked the lady, before urging Penny to walk away from the stall. She still expected the lady to call out after her, realizing the mistake and yelling that she'd meant two *hundred* and fifty.

"They'll be too hot to wear this time of year," repeated Penny. "They'll look stupid." Abigail rolled her eyes.

"But they're UGG boots. They are normally really expensive to buy new, and they're in brilliant condition. I'll keep them and wear them when the weather gets colder." She couldn't stop smiling with her bargain. "They would have cost about a hundred and twenty pounds new."

"A hundred and twenty pounds for a pair of silly boots!" Penny exclaimed. "That's just ridiculous."

Abigail opened her mouth to explain about the use of the most luxurious sheepskin in the world to make UGG boots, the exacting standards of the company that goes into producing each pair, the quality control processes and the durability, comfort and style that is synonymous with the brand name. Not to mention the costs of importing twelve thousand miles across the globe. But Penny continued.

"If I had a hundred and twenty pounds to spare there is no *way* I'd spend it on a pair of boots."

"Go on then," challenged Abigail. "What *would* you do with a hundred and twenty pounds?"

Penny didn't hesitate. "I'd buy my Mum a bundle of chickens and a cockerel to replace the ones the fox got. She would then save a load of money by getting a free supply of eggs, as well as being able to breed to get some more chickens to eat or sell. It was awful when the fox got all the chickens. It just ripped a load of their heads off and left a disgusting mess in the yard. Yuck."

Abigail didn't have an answer. She felt rather humbled by this twelve year old that had no desire to spend a small fortune on herself. Her first thought was for setting up a sustainable solution that would benefit the whole family.

They'd reached the end of the first row of cars, and Abigail realized that she'd been strolling for ten minutes without even looking up. The hypnotizing effect of watching piles of stuff at ground and thigh level meant that they'd walked several hundred metres without realizing it. The pair turned the corner and began to make their way along the next row.

"Look April – camping gear!" laughed Penny pointing to a box on the ground near the wheel of a battered jag. Penny began to rummage, giving Abigail a running commentary as she went. "Foot pump for a blow up bed, tent pegs, a ground sheet, more tent pegs... oh, a camping stove!"

Abigail joined Penny's side and took the camping stove from her. It looked in good condition, although Abigail would be the first to admit she didn't have the slightest clue what she was looking at.

"How much for this?" she asked the man hovering for a sale.

"That's a cracking stove that is," he replied. "Almost new, like, we only used it a couple of times. We were going to go and do all this camping then the missus got pregnant and we never seemed to get around to it, so we decided to get rid of all the camping stuff. Never going to get around to going I shouldn't think. That's a whole canister of gas in there, and there's some pots and pans if you're interested." Abigail realized that he hadn't answered her initial question.

He bent down to have a rummage in the box, and pulled out two dainty saucepans and a frying pan. Like the stove, they seemed barely used, just as the man had said.

"You can take the lot for a fiver."

It seemed a no brainer. The ability to be able to cook hot food, heat up water for hot drinks, and not have to eat out would be a Godsend going forward. Abigail had no idea how long she would be on the run, surviving from day to day on her dwindling funds. Although five pounds was a bit out the budget, it was a long term investment.

Before she had time to accept, Penny butted in. "Oh that's such a shame. We've just bought these boots and only have two pounds fifty left." She sighed dramatically, folded her arms and looked directly at the man challengingly.

There was a momentary stand off as the twelve year old held her stare at the middle-aged man. He sighed. "Oh go on then, I'd rather not be lumbered with them at the end of the morning. I'll take two fifty."

"Great, can we keep the box to carry them in?" Penny had morphed into a bossy little madam under her newfound confidence. Between them they packed up the camping gear into the cardboard box, threw the boots on top and paid the man.

"We only came for material!" observed Penny. "We'll have to get a taxi back if we carry on like this."

The pair continued to wander up and down the rows of wares, pausing here and there to browse through piles of books in the search for Penny's 24 unread Sylvia Downton paperbacks. It was only half past eight, but already the sun was starting to penetrate, stamping its authority on the day and Abigail realized that she was likely to get very hot in her jeans.

"Hello Penny," came a cheery male voice as they wandered past a stall in front of a muddy land rover.

"Sam!" exclaimed Penny in delight.

Abigail looked him up and down and saw a pleasant lad around her age, with copper colour hair, unruly and unkempt. It was bordering on ginger to be fair, but Abigail decided to be kind and give him the benefit of the doubt. He had a slim build, kind blue eyes and a smattering of cute freckles running riot across his nose and cheeks. On first impressions, there was possible potential there.

Abigail hovered next to Penny through the pleasantries awaiting an introduction; but Sam took control when it was obvious that the twelve year old hadn't learnt the etiquette of introducing two people to each other.

"I'm Sam," he said needlessly, stretching his hand over a pile of DVDs to shake Abigail's. "I went to school with Adam, Penny's brother."

"April," she reciprocated, shaking his hand, then wondered how to explain her connection to Penny. "I'm staying at Wit's End – the campsite in Sloth - and bumped into Penny who needed company coming here this morning."

If Sam found the explanation confusing, it didn't show on his face.

"I'm having a bit of a clear out ahead of looking for a new place to live," he said, indicating the piles of CDs, books, DVDs and knick-knacks on the trestle table in front of him.

"You're moving out of your Mum and Dad's place?" asked Penny. Sam blushed, an admission of living with his parents whilst in his twenties was obviously something to be ashamed of. Abigail wanted to reassure him that she too was still living with Mum and Dad at the age of 23, but wondered whether that was giving too much information. Her policy whilst being on the run was to be frugal and vague with personal information, especially to virtual strangers. "Where are you moving to?"

"I haven't started looking properly yet, but I'd like to find a flat in Cheltenham if possible."

"It's going to take a lot of DVD sales to earn enough cash for one of those," Penny said bluntly. "Cheltenham's a very expensive place to buy a house," she added as an aside to Abigail.

Sam reached over the table and shook a charity tin. "This is all for charity," he clarified. "Brain injury trust... you know, after Buddy." The three of them fell silent, Penny chastised.

"Anyway," Sam continued, "the search has slowed down for a bit, especially now I'm out of action." He held up his right leg, which the girls could then see was covered in plaster from the knee down to the tip of his toes, which were poking out of the oval hole at the end.

"Oh no, what have you been doing?!" Penny scolded.

"Football. Four weeks ago now. I went in for a tackle with some guy from Tewkesbury and I came off worse. That'll teach me."

"How long will you have to keep the plaster on?" asked Abigail politely.

"Could be up to another four weeks or so. It's driving me mad as it's starting to get to the itchy stage."

Abigail winced. She'd never broken any bones thank goodness, but knew how much it hurt just to snag a fingernail.

"So," Sam continued, diverting the conversation away from his injuries, "have you found much to buy?" He was looking pointedly at the cardboard box that Abigail hugged to her body.

"Oh, just some camping gear to top up what I brought with me," Abigail replied dismissively. Penny gave her a loaded look and then turned her attention back to Sam.

"And your winter boots. She spent money on thick furry winter boots Sam, like she's really going to need those in this weather."

"Hey you can never have too many pairs of boots," replied Sam generously, with a supportive grin at Abigail. "Do you want to leave the box here while you carry on looking round?"

"That's a brilliant idea," Penny enthused. "We really only came for some material because April's going to make some new curtains for the toilet block at Wits End. She says she can sew really well."

Abigail had almost forgotten the purpose of the visit and

glanced at her watch in case the market was going to pack up any time soon. It was only twenty to nine; Abigail suspected the market would run for a few more hours yet.

Bundling the cardboard box onto the driver's seat of the battered land rover, the pair bid farewell to Sam and continued to roam the stalls. Gradually the car booters gave way to more and more commercial sellers, and Penny spotted the material stand.

The vendor had gone to the effort of making what looked like a semi-permanent structure out of the back of a flatbed lorry, with colour coordinated rows of material displayed across a rising angle, splaying out the wares for all to see.

"I have no idea what I'm looking for," Abigail admitted, taking in the array of colours, textures and patterns. "I guess something fresh and clean looking."

"Like this one?" Penny suggested, pointing to a cream material splashed with bold yellow daisies across the surface. Abigail went up and felt the softness of the fabric and tried to imagine it at the edges of the dank, mouldy windows of the toilet block.

"That could work," she conceded, "with some bold yellow tie backs maybe?" She started to gather up the items she needed and instructed the vendor to cut her the right lengths of cloth.

"April – look at this!" shrieked Penny. She was rummaging in the offcuts bin at the side of the stall and had found a length of black satin with cartoon red devils dancing all over it. Their spears were pointing at zigzag angles across the material and the devils were pulling faces at each other. "That would make a brilliant dress, wouldn't it?" She held it against her body in a pose and Abigail could instantly see the potential of turning the material into one of her bespoke designs.

"I could turn that into a dress for you," Abigail said modestly. "I've got some dress designs sketched out in my notebook back in my tent."

Penny's jaw dropped. "Really?" Her eyes widened as though Abigail had just offered her the world. "You'd do that for me?"

"Sure, come on, add it to my pile here."

"I'll buy the material," Penny stated adamantly. "If you're going to the trouble of making me a dress the least I could do is pay for the material." She suddenly sounded very grown up. "Besides, everything in this tub is fifty pence." The illusion was quickly shattered.

"Right, I don't think we'll be able to carry anything more." Abigail stated as she took a grip on the bundle of folded material that the salesman had failed to put in a bag for her. They began to saunter back towards Sam's land rover to collect the abandoned box.

There was a bit more of a commotion crowding around Sam's stall as they approached and initially Abigail was hopeful that Sam's items were selling well.

"Nah – that's just his sister and their dogs," said Penny knowledgably. His sister's called Charly and she's going to be the next Zara Philips."

"What, royalty?" Penny said the most bizarre things at times.

"No," Penny giggled in reply. "She's a brilliant rider – show jumping, point to point, dressage."

Charly was politely introduced to Abigail whilst two energetic border collies sniffed around her shoes and crotch. Charly looked younger than her brother but shared the same slender build and easy manner. She'd been spared the ginger, no, *copper* hair in favour of a mass of dark brown curls that bounced around her shoulder blades. She hadn't escaped the blaze of dark freckles on her flushed cheeks.

"Excuse my appearance," she breathed. "I've just been taking the dogs for a run across the fields whilst Sam does his ...er...enterprising. I thought about running home and leaving him here, but I suppose I'd better drive the invalid back home." She dropped a peck on his cheek and patted his bum playfully. Sam squirmed, embarrassed.

"We'd offer you a lift back," she explained as she reached for the cardboard box and handed it over to Abigail, "but with the dogs, Mr pegleg here and all this leftover merchandise, it would be a bit of a squeeze."

"Oh it's not a problem," Abigail said quickly. "It's not very far to walk back. And it's such a lovely day."

"I'm praying it's like this next Sunday for the party," Sam mused. Penny gave an excited squeal.

"I can wear my new dress! April's going to make me a new dress, we've just got some wicked material and April has some of her own designs that I can choose from," she gabbled breathlessly. "It'll be like a one off designer dress from the April Smith collection, and I'll be the first person to show it off. Will it be ready for next Sunday, I hope so!"

"Yes, we can have it ready for next Sunday," smiled Abigail and Penny whooped. "Party?"

"It's our annual post Grand National party at our folk's place," Sam explained. "It's become some sort of annual tradition to celebrate the end of the jumps season. Are you planning to be at Wits End until next Sunday? If so, you are more than welcome to come along."

Abigail shrugged vaguely.

"Hog roast, copious amounts of alcohol, bucking broncho, midnight shenanigans in the hot tub, everyone that's ever known my Dad coming along to suck up to him... you get the picture."

"Sounds like a fun way to spend a Sunday evening," conceded Abigail. But it was still seven days away. The longer she spent in one place, the greater the chance of being tracked down. She couldn't promise.

An hour later, Abigail and Penny sat cross legged on the grass outside the tent. Water was boiling in a saucepan on the new gas stove to make tea, and Abigail had her sketch book spread out in front of them. They were all designs for adults but Abigail had every confidence that they could be scaled down to smaller child sizes, as long as they weren't inappropriately tarty. Penny inspired her to consider working on a teenage range.

"Some of these are crazy!" giggled Penny, looking at page after page of weird and wacky ideas that had fallen from Abigail's head onto the page. "But I like this one."

She pointed out a dress that was thankfully on the less tarty end of the scale, with a fitted bodice and full pleated skirt that was longer at the sides than at the front of back. It would look OK made up with the red devil fabric that Penny had picked out that morning. In fact, if Abigail could get hold of some red ribbon, she figured that the material could be complemented by a scarlet sash across the waistband and maybe a matching trim for the bodice.

Stage one was access to a sewing machine and a tape measure to get Penny's measurements. Once they'd finished their tea, the pair headed over to the bungalow where they found Dan's Mum, Mrs. Witt, alone in the house.

Dan and Mandy had gone up to Birmingham for the day, she told them as she shuffled them into the lounge. Mandy was competing in a Midlands regional swimming gala.

"Well, there's my sewing machine," she said, needlessly pointing to a mid range machine sat on a small makeshift table under the sunny bay window that looked out over the driveway. And I've got a sewing box in the cupboard here."

As Mrs. Witts was showing the pair where to find things, Dan was concentrating on the road ahead as he pulled his Dad's Vauxhall into the middle lane of the M5 to overtake. The radio was playing an R and B tune from a few years back, and he tapped his redundant clutch foot in time to the beat, feeling the sun on his face. He was content. He relished any opportunity to be driving, and enjoyed watching the swimming competitions that Mandy entered with tenacious regularity; she was extremely good and often came home with a medal, trophy or cup as well as the flush of pride.

Mandy should have been mentally preparing for the task ahead, but she was preoccupied with other thoughts. That April girl from last night's gathering had unsettled her. There was something not quite right about her story, and she'd aired her concerns to Dan as soon as April had said her goodnights. Dan, with a typical testosterone approach to women, had laughed off Mandy's doubts.

"Why would she not even bring a proper case for her clothes," Mandy declared, turning down the car's radio and turning towards Dan.

"Hmmm?" Dan hadn't a clue what Mandy was on about now.

"That April girl. She says that her friend set her a challenge. Fair enough, but it would have been planned in advance enough for April to pack a proper case rather than arrive with carrier bags and inappropriate clothes. Who travels for several hours in short skirts and heels?"

"What does it matter?" sighed Dan, who had got bored quickly of this line of conversation last night.

"I think she's run away from something. That's the only explanation." Mandy dwelt on this thought for a second. "It would make sense. I wonder what."

"Could be anything," Dan replied testily. "An argument with her boyfriend, parents, boss..."

"She's very attractive."

There, that was the underlying cause of Mandy's unease, even if she didn't recognize it herself. "Don't you think?" Little blonde bitch waltzes into the campsite with her baby blue eyes and within 24 hours is sat eating Dan's chili con carne and telling everyone what a great marketing ace she is.

"She's not unattractive," replied Dan tactfully.

"I think she fancies you."

"Oh she does not!" There was an uneasy silence as both pondered this last possibility. Dan felt a small blush of excitement at the thought that perhaps Mandy was right and that the cute blonde did find him hot.

"Right. That's why she's given up her Sunday to go and buy material for you and make you some curtains."

Dan knew that any response was going to wind Mandy up any further, so remained silent. He pulled into the inside lane and indicated to take the slip road off to follow the dual carriageway towards Birmingham.

The curtains turned out great. Once Penny had been measured for her new dress, she left Abigail to the productivity of the Witts' front room, and skipped off back to the farm where no doubt her mother would scold her for not having left a note that morning to say what time she would be returning.

Abigail enjoyed having an entire quiet afternoon to sew. It was a luxury she rarely afforded herself these days, and Mrs. Witts was busying herself in the kitchen and barely disturbed her. The curtains didn't take much time to sew, and just involved cutting the long length of fabric into identically sized curtain pieces, lining and hemming them and creating the tabbed tops. She then set about cutting the shape of Penny's dress from the red devil fabric, pinning it into place and was about to start hand sewing ready for a fitting when the peace was disturbed by a furious Mandy crashing through the front door with an obedient Dan shadowing her.

From the sanctuary of the lounge, Abigail could hear Mandy in the kitchen ranting to Mrs. Witts about the injustice of being beaten by a tenth of a second, how it wasn't fair and her plans to lodge an appeal. Clearly the competition hadn't gone her way. Mrs. Witts didn't get much opportunity to interject, but Mandy didn't require her to. An occasional murmur of sympathy in the right places was all that was necessary.

"Oh hi," said Dan, spotting Abigail in the window. He'd got bored of Mandy's complaining, as he'd had nothing but a continual sulky tantrum since leaving Birmingham, and wandered through into the lounge. "You found some material then?"

At first his eyes fell on the red devil fabric with horror, imagining his rustic toilet block transformed into a Hallowe'en den. But Abigail indicated the pile of sunny floral curtains ready to hang.

"All done. I presume there is the same number of windows in the gent's side of the block. I'm just working on a dress for Penny to wear to the Grand National party next Sunday."

"Cool. These are great." He inspected Abigail's handiwork with genuine enthusiasm. It was a relief for him that they had turned out OK, having entrusted a stranger with spending the site's profits on transforming the décor without consulting his parents. It could have been an expensive disaster.

From the kitchen they could hear Mrs. Witts trying to offer Mandy a cup of tea, but the spurned swimmer wasn't finished yet. She had not started to describe the cheating tactics of the winning contestant who was clearly a "silly bitch" and made so many sly moves that the organisers didn't seem to spot.

"We're going over to the pub for supper tonight, will you join us as payment for the curtains?" Dan asked Abigail, ignoring the commotion that his girlfriend was creating. He flicked his head towards the kitchen in acknowledgement. "She'll have calmed down by then... I hope."

"But you gave me the money for the fabric already," protested Abigail.

"Well, to pay you for your time then. You didn't have to spend your Sunday working on these for us. I insist," he added after her hesitation.

Abigail glanced at her watch. It was already half past five and she'd agreed to go to Kate's house at seven, which she explained to Dan.

"Tomorrow night then?" he replied. She nodded in surrender. "She'll definitely be calmer then!"

O'Casey hospitality

At seven o'clock that evening, Abigail found herself on the doorstep of Kate and Callum O'Casey. It was in the newer part of the village, a small cul-de-sac of ten identical detached properties that dated back to the 1980s. The house had a tiny patch of front lawn, protected by a knee-high wall, and a path leading up to the front door that was centered between two uPVC bay windows.

Abigail rang the doorbell and heard the instant barking of the two dogs in stereo, followed by a harassed shout. The words "Come in" could just be made out, and Abigail cautiously opened the front door into the hallway. Never in her twenty-three years of living in London could she recall anyone ever shouting "come in" before. Eddie and Jeremy immediately greeted her, the two bum waggling beagles, with their tails making a dull slapping noise on the doorframe as they fought for her attention. The stairs were ahead of her, with a neat study to the left and the lounge, where Kate's voice had come from, to the right.

She pushed her way through the dogs, which continued to fuss around her, and stepped into the lounge. There were children's toys all over the floor, an ironing board set up with a basket of clothes spewing out the top, a coffee table strewn with dirty mugs, glasses and oddments of paper.

"I'm through here."

Abigail picked her way across the floor, stepping over plastic trains and rag dolls, dog chews and a copy of the Racing Post (which had clearly been trampled many times by paws and other human footsteps) and found a bright, open kitchen at the back of the house. The kitchen was also a hive of activity, with pans steaming on the stove, ingredients for something laying on the chopping board half finished. At the table sat Kate's little boy in a booster seat, bashing a plastic beaker against the table top, making a "Ba, Ba, ba" sound with every slam against the wooden surface.

"Have I come at a bad time?" asked Abigail, instantly feeling like she'd intruded on a hectic part of the day.

"No, not at all!" replied Kate brightly, seemingly unaware of the chaos around her. "Callum's not back yet, and I'm just getting little man off to bed in a minute. Grab a seat. Fancy a glass of wine?"

Abigail sat at the kitchen table next to the toddler, trying to ignore the continuing "Ba, ba, ba" tune and the beagle that was sniffing her crotch. The other beagle had turned his attention to an empty metal food bowl and was intent on pushing it around the tiled floor, trying to lick out any invisible leftovers.

"This is Aidan," she explained, grabbing the beaker away from the toddler, and deftly reaching for a bottle of wine from the fridge before Abigail had even replied. She was a multi tasking whirlwind in the kitchen, Abigail observed with admiration. "And Aidan is going to have to go to bed without saying goodnight to Daddy as he can't seem to get himself home on time again."

Abigail couldn't tell whether Kate was genuinely upset, or just having the usual sort of moan that helps us get through the day. She stirred whatever was in one of the saucepans, waltzed over to Abigail to place the glass of wine in front of her and scooped up Aidan in one swift movement.

"Right, excuse me just a moment, I'm going to put this one to bed, back in a minute."

Abigail sat quietly looking around the kitchen, which was oddly tidy compared to the bombsite of the lounge. A welcoming smell of roast chicken wafted from the depths of the oven, but Abigail was determined not to impinge on anyone else's cooking today. She sipped at the refreshingly cool white wine that Kate had poured for her, drinking in the momentary serenity.

It didn't last long, the front door crashed open and Abigail heard a male Irish voice unleash into a monologue.

"Only me, sorry I'm late, that feckin' Alfie Bartlett clobbered me just as I was about to leave to see if I could pick up an extra ride 'cos Liam Hendry that feckin' useless knob from Glasgow dropped a weight on his toe or something earlier in the afternoon and had to go to hospital to see if it was broken so.. Anyway, I'm back now and…oh!" He stopped ranting as soon as he reached the kitchen and realized that Kate wasn't there.

"Kate's upstairs putting Aidan to bed," Abigail explained, as though she'd known him all her life. "I'm April." Considering the volume and tone of his voice, Abigail had expected somebody large and imposing to walk in the kitchen door. Contrary to her expectations, Callum was not much taller than her, and probably weighed only 150lbs. Wearing a lightweight jacket and khaki shorts he looked like something from a scout camp.

His face transformed from its stressed ranting into a beaming smile. "Well Hello!" He stretched out a hand for Abigail to shake. "Kate did mention something about a friend coming over to use the computer."

He poured himself a glass of tap water at the sink and crashed down in the seat at the table next to Abigail. He took a big dramatic sigh. Abigail could see the resemblance to Aidan, the big dark eyes and shockingly black curly hair.

"Busy day?" asked Abigail politely, for want of something better to say.

"Long day, yeah. Been up to Huntingdon, which isn't a million miles away but it's a faff to get to, cross country and all. Traffic was feckin' awful as I hit the soddin' pensioner's rush hour. Sunday evening drives back from wherever it is that pensioners seem to go to."

Abigail's geographical knowledge wasn't good, and she couldn't have pointed to Huntingdon on a map, and would probably have struggled to pinpoint Cheltenham's whereabouts before Friday.

"Do you keep your horse in the village?"

Callum looked at her blankly, and for a moment she panicked and wondered whether she'd misunderstood his job. "You're a jockey, right?"

Callum grinned, then chuckled softly, then began to laugh loudly. Hearty belly laughs at her stupidity. Abigail blushed in confusion.

"I don't ride my own horse. I ride for other people," he explained when he'd managed to stop laughing. "I'm freelance so I could ride for say, Alfie Bartlett, Robin Ashington or Brian Coldax, all at the same race meeting." He chuckled again. The thought of having his own horse seemed to tickle him.

"Oh," replied Abigail apologetically, not having the faintest clue who any of the people were. "I'm not a country girl."

Kate's footsteps could be heard galloping down the stairs, and she swept back into the kitchen. Barely acknowledging Callum's presence, she took the wine from the fridge and topped her abandoned glass up, before adding more to Abigail's.

"I hope you're hungry," she said, directing the question at Abigail. "I think I've done far too much." She took a diary from the dresser and brought it over to the table, where she sank into the chair opposite Abigail and Callum with a similar sigh to Callum's a few minutes earlier. "Right. Next week. Where are you tomorrow?"

Callum reached into the inside pocket of his jacket and pulled out a smartphone, which he fiddled with momentarily.

"Kempton. Tuesday Exeter. Looking to stay over, as I'm at Fontwell Wednesday and Teddy Graves is travelling over so can give me a lift."

"Oh crap, you're not here Wednesday? I have that doctor's appointment after work and so I can't collect Aidan from nursery. I told you that last week. You were going to keep Wednesday clear."

"I was? Sorry babe, can't rearrange this one."

Kate took a deep breath and gulped at her wine. "Then I suppose you'll head straight to Aintree," she growled.

"Correct," he replied, almost proudly.

"You're bloody useless," Kate grumbled, then ruffled his hair to suggest that she wasn't entirely cross with him. "And you stink – didn't you shower before you left?"

"Didn't get chance as I picked up an extra ride from Bartlett, and you wanted me home by seven and..."

"Go and bath, you smelly idiot, and April and I will have a nice meal, and talk about you behind your back. And say goodnight to your son while you're up there, but don't get him excited."

Callum rose from his seat, stretched and loped out of the kitchen. Abigail glanced at her watch and wondered whether she'd ever get time to write this blog tonight.

"Anything I can do to help on Wednesday?" Abigail offered, watching Kate dish up the roast with a small element of guilt. Kate hadn't given her chance to refuse the meal. "I could pick up Aidan from nursery if it helps?"

"It's OK, I can just tell the nursery that I'll be late to collect him. I was just trying to make Callum feel bad. It didn't work though, did it? Water off a duck's sodding back."

She was carving a third portion of chicken onto a small plate with salad for Callum, whilst Abigail and herself would be indulging in roast potatoes, parsnips, stuffing and thick gravy. Abigail realized that she had in fact eaten nothing since her bacon buttie at Weird Al's fields that morning.

"You could come and walk Eddie and Jeremy in the morning though," she replied as an afterthought. Abigail nodded enthusiastically. "I'll show you where we keep the spare key in a bit, just let yourself in and make yourself at home."

Upstairs, they could hear Callum singing Wonderwall very loudly and badly as he ran the bath water. Abigail wondered whether he was always like this, or showing off for her benefit. Kate brought the plates over to the table and went back to the fridge to rescue the remaining wine.

"Now then, tell me what you've been up to since yesterday."

It was hard to believe that it was only the day before that they'd met each other at the jumble sale in the village hall. Abigail started to tell her about the evening at Dan's, where she'd also met with Adam, Mandy and Penny.

"What did you make of Mandy?" Kate asked, with a knowing smile. "Was she a bit, er, biting at times?"

Abigail nodded slowly, remembering the put downs and the odd snide comments that had worried Abigail into thinking Mandy knew something about her secret.

"Oooh, I bet Mandy is so jealous of you!" Kate observed. "She gets funny with anyone that might be a threat to her relationship with Dan. Can't blame the poor girl really, rumour has it that her younger sister ran off with her fiancé a week before the wedding. She used to be a bit bitchy to me, but now I've put a few more tyres round my middle and married Daniel O'Donnell up there," she indicated the ceiling through which Callum could be heard singing the 'green, green grass of home', "she seems more civil."

"How *did* you meet Callum?" Abigail asked with interest. Although Kate had lived in Sloth all her life, she didn't seem to be integrated into the horsey set, and the combination of her easy going nature and Callum's brash Irish ways seemed to be at odds.

Kate put her knife and fork down momentarily and smiled. "He came into the dental practice out of hours after a fall at Cheltenham. He'd knocked three teeth out and needed some reconstructive work. Not a pretty sight actually, but I stupidly offered to drive him home." She paused a chuckled at the memory. "Seems the morphine made him a bit frisky and we ended up making an Aidan on our first meeting."

"Oh shit," gasped Abigail in horror, clamping her hand over her mouth.

"My mother was horrified as you can imagine. She still thinks she's twenty-five in her head, and couldn't bear being a grandmother at forty-five. I can't believe that I was actually that stupid."

"Did you think about having an..." she couldn't bring herself to say the word 'abortion', not with Aidan in the house, it seemed wrong. Kate got her drift.

"No, I started by telling Callum and then there was no option of that. Catholic family, I was straight up the aisle within a month and had to pretend he was a honeymoon baby. Luckily no-one in Sloth or Cork seemed that bothered enough to do the maths. I don't regret him though, he's great." She lowered her voice. "Callum wants to get him a brother or sister but I really haven't got the energy."

Abigail found that difficult to believe as she watched Kate gather up the empty plates, whisk them into the sink and pile dog food into the metal bowls for Jeremy and Eddie. Abigail continued to tell Kate about making Penny a dress and finding some bargains at the market that morning. It had been a busy couple of days, not to mention meeting Sam and Charly and getting invited to their Grand National party next Sunday.

"Oh course, that's next Sunday. I must ask Val whether she can babysit for us," mused Kate. "We can share a taxi up there if you like. No doubt Callum will have far too much to drink. It's the one day of the year he lets himself indulge and makes an even bigger fool of himself than usual."

"Charly seemed very nice," Abigail recalled. "Penny describes her as the next Zara Phillips."

"She's a talented rider by all accounts. Got her sights set on Badminton next month." Abigail had no idea how a game of badminton fitted into the equestrian world, and remained silent. "And Sam's a sweetheart. He was in my class at school and hung around a lot with the girls. I wonder if he's gay though."

Abigail hadn't got that impression, but had only a few minutes of polite conversation with him to base her judgment on. She glanced anxiously at her watch. Whilst it was nice sharing Kate's home and having the casual girly gossip that was the backbone of her friendship with Nadine, she was also eager to get on with her blog. You could argue that there was no reason for Abigail to keep up the ruse, and not bother going through with writing a blog, but once she'd got it into her head that she was there to document her time away from home, she felt it would be therapeutic to go through with it.

She'd also got Mrs. Witt's questionnaire in her bag to work on, and was hoping to see whether she could message Nadine via Facebook without logging in.

By eight o'clock, the dogs were fed, Callum was clean and had finished up his chicken salad and Kate was pulling on her trainers to take Eddie and Jeremy for a short walk down the lane.

Callum led Abigail into his study where a large screened Apple Mac took pride of place on the neat desk. He explained that Kate wasn't allowed near the study for fear of spilling drink on his keyboard, as she was a 'dozy mare most of the time.'

He sat her down in the main swivel chair and pulled up a small beanbag from the corner so that he sat dangerously close to her as he fired up the computer and ran briefly through the icons that she may need. Abigail had worked extensively on Macs at the placement at PMG, and knew everything he was telling her, but let him explain away.

He smelt great, clean from his bath and the smell of shampoo drifting from his damp black curls. For a second, Abigail briefly understood how Kate could have got herself in so deep on their first meeting. She made a mental note to ask Kate to borrow a towel before leaving that night.

"This is pretty by the way," he said changing the subject suddenly. He was referring to a small fabric bracelet that hung loosely on Abigail's dainty wrist. It was woven from rainbow coloured threads with the word "AB" sewn in bold black; a present that Nadine had brought her back from her last overseas trip.

Callum ran a finger slowly over the bracelet and looked into Abigail's eyes. "Ab?"

"It's short for Abril, the Spanish word for April," she gabbled, relieved that she'd managed to pull the lie from the depths of her brain. "A Spanish friend made it for me."

His fingers were still resting seductively on her wrist.

"Anyway," she pulled her hand free. "I'll be fine from here. I'll shout if I get stuck."

"Right you are," he replied briskly, standing up from his beanbag and placing it back into the corner, the tensions of the moment dissipating like a burst bubble as quickly as they occurred. He left the study and Abigail tried to clear her brain for the task ahead, swiftly setting up a webmail email address and then an account with a blogging website.

One girl and her tent – Part One
April Smith
Sunday 7th April

My name is April Smith and I have been working in a series of comfortable office jobs. My friend has challenged me to leave this safe world behind and see if I can survive for a week with no phone, no Internet, a limited amount of cash and no bank cards.

April re-read the start of her blog and sighed. That sounded boring. She highlighted the text and struck the delete key and thought for a moment. Her placement in the marketing company had surely taught her about gripping the reader with the opening lines. Make the reader want to carry on. She poised her fingers over the keyboard and began to type again.

There is a picture in the boardroom of my office that carries a quote from Mark Twain that says, "Courage is resistance to fear, the mastery of fear – not absence of fear." When I boarded the train at London Paddington with only the clothes I was wearing, a limited amount of cash, a tent and a return ticket to Cheltenham, I must admit I felt an absence of courage and nothing short of pure fear.

My mission was given to me by my friend, who accused me of leading a sheltered and privileged life, and she challenged me to survive without my middle class support network of luxuries that most of us take for granted. My family, my smartphone, my warm bed, my wages and my sense of daily structure and routine have all been taken away from me.

Abigail felt tears well up and stopped typing for a second.

This *was* therapeutic, she decided. She needed to take stock and tell the anonymous world how she was feeling, even if it contained just a few omissions of the real truth.

I arrived in Cheltenham with no real plan except to find a campsite. With no smartphone to reference a place to stay, I went to the library to look up the large-scale maps of the area. This was my first revelation, as I haven't stepped in a library for many years. They are such a valuable resource for the community, free to use and I fear that if people carry on buying their books from the bumper deals that supermarkets are able to tempt people with, they will be in danger of dying out. I think back to my bookshelves at home, crammed with books that I bought, read once and hang on to, even though I'll never read them again. The first change I will make is never to buy a new book again, and to seek out books at the local library.

So, armed with a photocopy of the map, I made my way on foot to a small hamlet around seven miles from Cheltenham and accepted some help putting up my brand new tent. I admit I am a virgin camper, and in my preparations I overlooked a lot of basic essentials. Like something to cook on. Not even the use of my smartphone – if I were allowed to use it – would help me out there.

Boredom was one of my fears but I have found the courage to be able to keep busy. Thanks for the friendliness of the people in the hamlet, I have been able to volunteer at the jumble sale, been entertained at a dinner party, been taken to the local market and car boot sale and managed to indulge in my passion for sewing. And I've only been here 48 hours.

Let's see what else I learn and what other fears I will have the courage to master in the next 48 hours.

Abigail stopped typing. She could have written more but didn't want to outstay her welcome, sitting unsociably away by herself in the study of her new friends. It was already gone nine o'clock. She clicked the upload button and her masterpiece was live. Easy as that.

She longed to open Facebook and check up on all that was happening back in her world. News, silly posts, photos, messages. A snapshot on the buzzing life of Abigail Daycock. Although she had the web browser open, she couldn't risk logging in. But maybe next time, she pondered, she could find a way around her anonymity.

She shut down the browser and padded across the hallway to the lounge door where she saw Kate and Callum relaxing on the two seater settee with the two beagles sprawled over their laps. The TV was on; a Sunday night hospital drama that Abigail often indulged in watching at home.

"All done?" asked Kate, shifting along the sofa, upsetting both beagles in the process, who leapt to the floor and trotted a lap of the lounge for no reason. She patted the small amount of space on the seat between her and Callum. "Come and join us, top up of wine?"

Abigail squashed into the middle of the sofa, acutely aware that her leg had no choice than to touch Callum's bare skin, and accepted the glass that Kate had already poured in anticipation of her arrival. You couldn't get a better example of hospitality than this.

Monday

Nadine woke on Monday morning with the sun promising yet another glorious day ahead as it pushed its way assertively through the curtains in her flat. In contrast, she felt apprehensive. The disturbing nagging feeling ate away at her as she pulled her phone from the bedside cabinet and hit the Facebook icon to see whether there had been any response to the message she'd sent Abigail yesterday. There were a few notifications; to play the latest highly addictive jewel game, Fish had written a comment in an event listing for the weekend's gig and Nadine was tagged in a photo from an Easter party a few weeks back where she was dressed as the Easter Bunny drinking goodness knows what from a goldfish bowl. Nothing from Abigail.

Nadine would have been relieved to see Abigail right that minute, lighting the gas on her new stove ready to fry some bacon for a monster breakfast of bacon butties washed down by a large caramel latte and poppy seed muffin. She'd got chatting last night to the young couple in the tent pitched next to hers, who had described how they were going to drive to Cheltenham before breakfast to get some take away coffees. In Abigail's new world of bartering, she offered to make them a couple of bacon butties in return for bringing her back a coffee and muffin. It was piggy, she knew, but she'd need the energy to tackle Mrs. Angel's unruly garden.

The campsite was very bare that morning. The tenting couple pitched next to Abigail had just been passing through on their way home from Cornwall to Carlisle, and had decided to break the journey for one night. There were a few motorhomes parked on the hard standing, mainly containing retired couples that seemed to spend most of their waking hours sat inside reading or doing crosswords or jigsaw puzzles. Abigail wondered why they chose to pay to do that sat in a field and not do it for free at home. In the pitch nearest the house was a large caravan containing a family with three young noisy children and an Alsatian dog that barked every time a car went down the lane. Fortunately very little traffic ventured through the village, but it still made Abigail jump when the dog suddenly broke out into a series of vicious barks until the noise of the car had faded away.

It was the calmest Abigail had seen Sloth. The schools were all back now from the Easter break, leaving just the university students including Mandy and Dan to drift back when they could be bothered. Technically the colleges were all back, but for the likes of Charly, getting in the final hours of preparation for Badminton horse trials were far more precious than studying for her forthcoming A' level exams in business studies and maths.

There was nobody in the village shop earlier when Abigail went to get the bacon, so she glimpsed sight of the headlines on the row of newspapers on the counter top. Speculation about a royal pregnancy, an apology from a Cabinet minister about an inappropriate remark over benefits claimants and the Daily Mail leading on an item about pensioners being worse off under a new tax proposal. Nothing about the banking system then, she noted with relief. No grainy images of Abigail gleaned from CCTV cameras as she made her escape into the Cotswolds. That was probably Friday and Saturday's headlines.

Fuelled by her breakfast and the first latte she'd consumed since leaving London, Abigail made her way to Mrs. Angel's cottage and the tangled mess of garden that greeted her.

"I haven't been able to get out and do anything with it since the end of last summer," Mrs. Angel apologized, leading Abigail very slowly up the rear garden path towards a small black shed at the back. The shed was unlocked, something else that Abigail noted was a world away from the spate of thefts from sheds in London, forcing everyone to install the strongest padlocks they could get their hands on. Inside, the air was musty and a shaft of sunlight fell through the middle of the shed, illuminating a rainbow of dust particles. It evoked a memory in Abigail that she couldn't quite put her finger on. Childhood, attics, warm summers.

Mrs. Angel pointed out the flymo mower, the extension lead, and an array of garden implements from hoes, rakes, shears, trowels, and pruning knives. Abigail had very little idea what to do with most of them, but was confident she could make it up as she went along.

She began with the grass. Taking the flymo, she plugged it in with the extension lead that Mrs. Angel had left dangling out of the kitchen window, and methodically made her way up and down the lawn. It wasn't quite the Wimbledon stripes she was hoping for but certainly prepared the canvas in a satisfying way. Tucking the flymo back into the shed, she began with the strimmer; luckily something she'd seen her Dad use around the edges of the lawn back in the distant world of Richmond. This wasn't so hard after all!

With a rake, she tidied up the clippings and weeds that she'd pulled up by hand and almost filled one of the many green sacks that Mrs. Angel had put to one side.

"Cup of coffee!" called Mrs. Angel at the precise moment Abigail was beginning to feel parched. With a brief wave from the end of the garden, Mrs. Angel left the steaming mug on top of the recycling box and retreated back into the kitchen. Abigail took the opportunity to take a break for a moment and stood sipping the coffee, surveying her work so far. It wasn't a great deal to show for two hours work, and her back was starting to ache from bending and moving in ways that her muscles were unused to, but it was rewarding. Although, like cleaning – where once you remove the dirt from one area, the other areas start to show up their filth – the tidier one piece of the garden became, it showed up the scruffiness and overgrown nature of the rest of it.

Onwards and upwards, Abigail repeated the mowing, strimming and weeding on the smaller front lawn before retreating back to the rear lawn and starting to prune back the overgrown bushes.

By two o'clock she was utterly exhausted but largely finished, although she eyed up the patio stones and decided they looked filthy. A winter of muck and damp had left a surface full of mouldy graffiti, which would probably come up really well with a stiff scrubbing brush and some warm water with bleach. She'd watched her Mum perform miracles on the flagstones at home each spring, sprucing up the patio and cleaning the garden path. She was wavering between just getting the job done and vowing to come back, when Mrs. Angel appeared once more at the back door.

"Oh what a smashing job! Thank you so much!"

"I think I'm just about done," replied Abigail, wiping a sweaty brow and pulling a stray blade of grass from her fringe, "although I can just clean up these patio slabs if you've a stiff scrubbing brush and..."

"Well don't worry yourself about those now," Mrs. Angel interrupted dismissively. "Lunch is ready."

Abigail's tummy growled on cue and she realized that despite the breakfast feast that morning, she was ravenous. She hadn't expected lunch for a second, but she should have realized that Mrs. Angel wasn't going to let a mealtime slip by without offering up reward.

On the wooden table in the kitchen Mrs. Angel had laid out two places with steaming bowls of beef stew and hunks of crusty bread in a serving bowl in the middle. Abigail tucked in with gusto.

"I like to have a proper meal in the middle of the day and then just something lighter in the evening, maybe a sandwich," Mrs. Angel explained. "I always have done, probably from the war years when we were labouring during the day and needed to take more in."

Abigail listened, fascinated, as Mrs. Angel described how she volunteered to be a land girl at the age of sixteen, which was how she came to be living in Gloucestershire today. She'd grown up in

Liverpool, but moved south to help with the war effort, and stayed in the area ever since. She was always musical and when the war ended, trained to be a music teacher, and taught in schools in Cheltenham and Gloucester until she retired in the 80s.

Abigail asked about family and Mrs. Angel looked wistful.

"I have a daughter Carol, who's in Edinburgh now." There was no pride in the description, which Abigail found unusual. She suddenly seemed sad. "She was living locally and teaching drama in the Cheltenham girl's school. All settled, married to a lovely chap called Mark and bringing up Isabella – my grand daughter. Isabella's a lovely little thing. I say "little" but she'll be twenty this year. You remind me of her. Anyway, for reasons that I never fathomed, the marriage broke down, and then she met Graham. He's a doctor – no, a *surgeon.*" Mrs. Angel half smiled and pulled a face to suggest that she'd been corrected on this too many times in the past. "I never cared much for Graham, he seemed to care only about himself and his career. He got a promotion and transferred to Edinburgh. I hoped that might mean the end of the relationship but no, she moved up with him, taking Isabella with them. Now Isabella's working up there and they haven't got the time to come all the way back down here and see me."

"That's really sad," Abigail observed, wishing there was something she could do. "When did you last see them?"

"Christmas... two years ago," she added before Abigail had chance to state that that was only a few months ago. "They invited me up to Edinburgh for Christmas the year before last, but how on earth they thought I'd get up there God only knows. I don't drive, the train takes forever and a day and it's too complicated to fly. At my age."

Abigail realized how lonely Mrs. Angel's life must be. Despite the camaraderie of the village life, there didn't seem to be anyone in particular looking out for Mrs. Angel. She wondered how she got her shopping done and made a mental note to offer before she left.

Another amazing cake followed the stew, this time coffee cake with buttery icing and almonds decorating the top.

"Oooh, "where in the world" is about to start," Mrs Angel said, checking her watch. She became animated suddenly. "Do you normally watch that?"

"I don't usually get to see daytime TV, I'm at work."

"Oh, you've got to come and see this, I think you'll like it. The jackpot's up to about ten thousand pounds."

Relieved not to be scrubbing the patio stones, Abigail sank gratefully into the largest chair and made herself comfortable, as Mrs. Angel put the correct channel on and explained the rules of the quiz show as it went along. Within minutes she was gripped.

The panda car arrives

Dan couldn't really grumble about being asked to hang the new curtains in the toilet blocks; he'd encouraged Abigail to make them after all. With a resigned sigh, he took the pile of material down to the grey dismal structure along with a pair of stepladders and his Dad's toolbox to start work on brightening up the place. The trouble with improving one tiny aspect, he reflected as the curtains instantly brightened up the dank surroundings, was that it showed up all the other numerous flaws of the toilet block.

There was ingrained dirt along the windowsills. Maybe they needed to be sanded down and repainted in fresh white emulsion. The grouting on the tiling above the sinks had turned a tired shade of grey with patches of green mildew that the everyday cleaning wouldn't touch. It was possible that a good scrubbing with bleach would help to make that shine white again, but there was graffiti on the insides of the toilet doors that would take something far more industrial to remove. "Maxi was 'ere, August 2009" read one unimaginative scribble in marker pen. "David is lush" claimed another. Dan wondered idly whether he should ask April if she was in the market for a special deep cleaning job while she was here. It was certainly over and above the remit of their regular cleaner, Betty, who wiped down the surfaces, half-heartedly mopped the floor now and then and poured bleach down the toilets.

He'd managed to get the curtains up in both the male and female blocks, as well as fit the tiebacks, when Mandy came to find him. It was getting near to six o'clock and they had promised to take April to the pub as reward for making the curtains.

"What it needs now is a vase of real daffodils on the window sill," she observed in a voice that tried to mock April. Dan didn't pick up on her tone, and nodded.

"Good idea – that can be your task for tomorrow." He glanced at Mandy, who had changed out of the jeans and t-shirt she'd been wearing when he last saw her at lunchtime and was now sporting what she referred to as her "nice tit top"; a clingy cotton smock top that plunged at the neckline where her push up bra did the rest of the job. Her tanned legs were now bare and she wore fairly skimpy denim shorts and flip-flops. The outfit suggested she'd just thrown together a few items to cool her down in the heat, but Dan knew her better than that. Her bum looked knockout in the shorts, and along with the nice tit top, she was sending a clear message to April that she had plenty to offer Dan.

With psychic timing, Abigail was just leaving her tent as Dan and Mandy walked out of the toilet block nearby and she concurred that she was ready to head to the pub. She took one look at Mandy and instantly felt underdressed. She'd been so sweaty after undertaking the gardening at Mrs. Angel's place that she'd had a quick shower and could only find some jeans and a plain t-shirt to wear that were clean. She'd have to think about getting some washing done soon; her stash of clean pants was down to just a few pairs and she didn't fancy trying to wash them in the shower block on site.

"I'll just put these tools and bits away, but you girls go on ahead and get the drinks in."

Awkwardly, the two girls headed off across the site and down the driveway together, Mandy enquiring politely about April's day. Abigail described the gardening and the nice time she'd had chatting to Mrs. Angel and describing how they had been watching the telly together that afternoon.

"You'll be making yourself indispensible at this rate," replied Mandy mysteriously. "Then you'll never be allowed to leave. Sentenced to an eternity in Sloth. God, can you imagine?"

Abigail didn't really see what was so wrong with spending an eternity in Sloth, although she was only basing that on less than four day's residency so far. They entered the darkness of the pub porch through the squeaky wooden front door. It was low beamed and quiet, with no music, just the hum of a fruit machine flashing its neon lights to itself in the corner.

"Drinks are definitely on me," insisted Abigail, needlessly, as Mandy had made no move to get her purse out. Mandy shrugged and said she'd have vodka and coke and Dan would have a pint of anything that tasted of lager. Initially there was no one serving, but within minutes they heard a shuffling and hopping sound and Sam's smiling face appeared from the door at the back of the bar.

"Hiya!" he greeted, immediately recognizing Abigail from the car boot sale the day before. "It's a small world here in Sloth!"

"You work here?" Abigail asked, cursing herself for the stupidity of the question. Of course he worked here, that's why he was behind the bar.

"Well, I help out now and then," he replied. "It's my Uncle Roger's pub so he's taken pity on me with my inability to do other work at the moment," He indicated his plastered leg, "and given me a few shifts, washing up, pulling pints, that sort of thing. Charly works here too sometimes, and I'm covering a few of her shifts as she's bailing out to get more showjumping practice in." He seemed to realize he was waffling and stopped talking abruptly, looking from Mandy to Abigail expectantly. Like an enthusiastic puppy, he paused to see how he could please them.

"What can I get you?"

"A pint of lager, a vodka and coke and... a white wine please."

"You'd better ask her for ID," said Mandy lightly. "I think that's her secret; she's working undercover for trading standards trying to get landlords prosecuted for serving underage drinkers."

Abigail's heart lurched. Mandy had obviously not bought her back-story and was suspicious of her purpose for being in Sloth.

"You're not serious?" replied Abigail with a forced laugh, although she could feel a hot flush gushing over her cheeks.

"Oh I don't know," replied Sam, leaning over the bar to inspect her more closely. "There's not a single wrinkle on that pretty young face of yours, and I am supposed to ask for ID on anyone who appears to be under 21. And you certainly could pass for someone who is under 21..."

Sam had stopped pouring the lager, and was waiting expectantly, while Mandy lingered in expectation. Abigail realized that she was going to have to play along. Protestation could rouse even more suspicion.

"I'm not sure what ID I've brought with me," mumbled Abigail, opening the card side of her purse and pretending to browse through the selection.

"There's your driving license!" Mandy said, indicating the pink top of the card. Damn.

Carefully Abigail removed the card and slid her thumb subtly over her name. She presented it to Sam, with the date of birth clearly on display and showing she was definitely over 21.

"Thank you Madam," grinned Sam, and continued to pour the lager.

"I bet you've got one of those embarrassing photos, haven't you?" teased Mandy as Abigail made to put the card back in its slit. "Come on, let's have a look."

Quick as lightening, she snatched the card playfully out of Abigail's hand and danced away from the bar before Abigail could react. She went and sat at the table by the bay window at the front of the bar and studied the card, grinning like a Cheshire cat at her prank. Trying to calm her panic, Abigail paid Sam and carried the drinks over to the table.

"Your real name's Abigail then?" said Mandy, handing the card back to Abigail.

"Yeah," said Abigail casually, her mind reeling. "My little brother couldn't say Abigail when he was little and it came out sounding like April, so that kind of stuck." She was glad Mandy didn't realize she'd given Dan a false surname as well. The similarities between the names April and Abigail were thankfully close enough to blag, as she had done when Callum questioned the "Ab" bracelet.

"You said on Saturday that you don't have any brothers and sisters," replied Mandy. Shit, that girl had a sharp memory.

"Er, nephew, I meant, not brother." Abigail realized her mistake as soon as it tumbled out of her lips and Mandy was going to pick up on it. With a quizzical raise of the eyebrow, she said the inevitable. "How do you have a nephew if you don't have brothers and sisters?"

"Oh, well, you know what I mean," snapped Abigail, taking a gulp of her wine, flustered and embarrassed. There was an awkward pause as Mandy mirrored her action with her glass of vodka and coke.

"No, not really, but chill." She smiled. Not a genuine friendly smile, but more a mocking smile, sympathy for the squirming wreck sat opposite her. "If you're embarrassed about the name Abigail and wanted to change it, I can't say I blame you. I would have done the same."

Abigail was too relieved to be let off the hook than be angry at Mandy's insult. Thankfully, as if on cue, Dan came bursting through the door, complete with his cheery smile. He acknowledged Sam who was wiping down the bar, and came to sit down on the velvet bench next to Mandy.

Abigail was relieved when Dan arrived, the atmosphere changed instantly. There was suddenly easy conversation between the three of them and together they chose a handful of tracks on the jukebox that Sam managed to break into so that they wouldn't have to pay. They munched their way through typical pub grub – ham, egg and chips for Abigail, an aubergine bake for Mandy and beef madras for Dan, and enjoyed another round of drinks without the ID debacle of an hour earlier. Few other people arrived. An elderly gentleman that Sam recognized came to nurse a pint of bitter on a bar stool, and a quiet couple came in and sat in the corner with a bottle of wine.

At seven o'clock, Sam swung over to their table on his crutches announcing that he'd knocked off now, and could he join them? Squaring the triangle, he sat next to Abigail and rested his plastered leg on the stool next to him.

"So what's new?" he asked to nobody in particular, to which Mandy pitched in with the description of her unfair defeat at the swimming gala yesterday. Dan caught Abigail's gaze and raised his eyebrows in mock exasperation. Abigail smiled back, understanding.

Suddenly her attention was drawn out of the window where

two policemen had just pulled up in a panda car. Her heart began thumping quicker as she watched them get out of the car and look up and down the quiet lane. She took a deep breath, telling herself not to panic; they may not be looking for her. To her horror she saw them cross the lane and head towards the wooden doors of The Carpenter's Arms.

"Excuse me a second," she muttered quickly to her companions and shot out of her seat, walking purposefully towards the back of the bar where she prayed the ladies toilets were located. The lady behind the bar pointed through a side room, and Abigail couldn't walk any quicker without breaking into a run as she pushed her way into the ladies. It had probably looked to the group as though she was being ill, she reckoned, but didn't care against the bigger picture of being caught by the police. It was cold in the toilets, two cubicles with the tiniest window at head height within the stall that was obviously against the outside wall. Even Abigail's petite frame couldn't have squeezed through the gap to the outside world, so she'd have to wait and hope the police didn't find what they were looking for. Only Mandy knew her name was Abigail, so her future was in the hands of a jealous cow that made no secret she didn't think much of Abigail. She waited a few minutes, looking at her reflection in the mirror. She couldn't hear anything beyond the door of the toilets except for the faint beat of a Shakira song; one of Mandy's jukebox choices.

She waited for what felt like half an hour but in reality was only ten minutes, before cautiously leaving the shelter of the ladies and back into the dim light of the side bar. Her heart jolted as she saw the policemen sat at a small round table close to the pool table, sipping at glasses of orange juice and chatting casually to each other. Abigail avoided looking at them, but as she passed through into the front bar, she got the sense that they weren't watching her. No suspicion, no talking into their radios.

Trying to get her heart to calm back down to a normal rate, she forced an apologetic smile as she sat back down.

"Are you all right?" asked Sam, concern all over his baby face.

"Yeah, sorry about that, just felt a bit dizzy, but it's passed."

"Are you sure, you look a bit pale?" Sam placed a caring hand on the back of her shoulders and rubbed gently. She winced as he hit a sore spot; the muscle being one of many victims to several nights sleeping on the ground and a morning of bending and squatting in Mrs. Angel's garden.

"I'm a bit stiff," she explained, as Sam removed his hand as quickly as if he'd been scolded. "I've not got enough padding for this sleeping on the ground lark."

"I have just the solution," declared Dan, rising from his seat. "Dan's magic hands. We've just been studying sports massage on the course. Let me give you a massage."

He stood behind Abigail and took her hair in his hand to smooth it over her shoulder, exposing her neck to him.

"You tell me where," he instructed, placing his hands firmly on the muscles leading up between her shoulder blades, and beginning a slow steady circular pressure. Abigail made a moaning noise to affirm that was exactly the spot. He continued, increasing the pressure gradually.

"Can you handle it a bit harder?" He asked, to which Sam spluttered childishly into his lager and Mandy sat stony faced.

"I can take it a bit harder," Abigail replied, partly to play along with the innuendo and partly to increase Mandy's obvious displeasure. Dan seemed completely unaware that his girlfriend was far from impressed with his behaviour.

"Right, that's enough," Mandy snapped after five minutes. She rose to her feet. "I am going to whip your ass at the pool table," she stated competitively to Dan, taking his hand from Abigail's shoulder and dragging him off towards the back bar, where the pool table lay empty, and where the policemen continued to sit. Abigail almost felt relaxed again.

She bought another round of drinks for herself and Sam, and took Mandy's vacated seat so that she was sitting opposite Sam, which made for easier conversation.

"So how's the sewing coming along?" he asked Abigail, remembering their brief conversation at the car boot sale the day before.

"Good," she nodded. "The curtains are finished and already in their pride of place in the toilet block. Penny's dress is nearly there – I'll take it down to her for a fitting soon and then I need to go into Cheltenham to get some ribbon for the finishing touches. You don't happen to know what time the bus goes along this lane into Cheltenham do you?" she asked as an afterthought.

"Bus? I didn't realize there was one." She may have well asked what time the space ship went judging by his reaction.

"I haven't got a car with me," she explained, somewhat apologetically. "So I'm reliant on feet or bus. Never mind."

"You could take a taxi," he suggested. "I am taking taxis everywhere at the moment with my leg like this; another thing that's driving me crazy. I'm so used to being independent and driving myself everywhere, now I have to rely on taxis."

"Or Charly," Abigail replied, remembering her driving him home from the car boot sale.

"Yeah, my Mum drives me around too, when she hasn't been drinking. But I can give you a number for a taxi firm." Abigail didn't relish the thought of what a taxi would cost both ways into Cheltenham, especially as she was only going for a small piece of ribbon and to wash her underwear at a launderette. But she smiled gratefully.

"So is your sewing thing a full time profession?" he asked, and Abigail launched into her vague backstory about temping and writing the blog. "I like working, but I can't ever see myself earning serious money," she admitted. "That's why I need to meet a man with a bulging bank balance to help me live a life of luxury."

"You're in the right place," he replied thoughtfully. "These villages are crowded with trainers, owners, and jockeys."

"Well I wouldn't be interested in a marrying a jockey, if Callum's anything to go by. I spent yesterday evening with him and Kate and his schedule doesn't seem to fit around a relationship and family life at all. Poor Kate, having to put up with that sort of lifestyle."

There was a pause as they sipped their drinks. Sam had no response to Abigail's reaction to Callum's lifestyle.

"So is the pub work a full time profession for you?" she reflected back at him. He smirked quietly to himself.

"No, I just help out a bit here. I mainly work for my Dad, doing jobs around the stables. He owns a racing yard." Abigail sensed he was being purposefully vague, but wasn't that exactly what she'd just done to him?

"What do you like doing for fun?" she asked, realizing that the conversation was heading exactly the same direction as it had with Ivan Costello a few weeks earlier. She really needed to learn some questions that weren't so predictable.

"Football, obviously," he replied, unconsciously waggling his broken right leg. "Going out with the lads, playing golf, paintballing, clay shooting, ski-ing... do you ski?"

"I've never tried," replied Abigail, realising that she'd never done a single thing on Sam's list. She really should take more exercise and get some more varied interests.

"But riding is my first love," continued Sam. "I enjoy anything on horseback, jumping, point to point, hunting.." It took all of Abigail's courage not to screw up her face in disapproval. "Can you ride?"

"I've never tried," sighed Abigail.

"I'm shocked. How do you get to be in your twenties and never been on a horse? I was in the saddle before I could walk."

"I've lived in London all my life," Abigail replied in protest. "I'm not sure if that's an excuse, but if you're not born into a horsey family then you don't ever come into contact with any. Although we had a family trip down to the New Forest once and I stroked one of those wild ponies that graze on the sides of the road. Scared stiff of it I was." Sam regarded her with an expression of pity and she was feeling like the most boring twenty three year old on the planet.

"I like riding a bike," she offered.

This was a bit of an exaggeration too, since Abigail hadn't taken her bike out of the garden shed for at least five years, and only ever went on Sunday bike rides to please her dad. She just remembered returning after ten miles with a sore bum and aching limbs.

"Well there's your transport problems solved then," he countered. "My Mum's got a bike you're welcome to borrow if you can't find the bus times. It's only about 7 miles down the hill to the City. And if you wanted to come and pick up the bike tomorrow, you can have your first ride on a horse."

Abigail hesitated. Seven miles down the hill meant seven miles coming back uphill, and she'd not ridden a bike for years. This was not the easy task he made it sound. And as for getting on a horse…

"Sounds great," she heard herself saying. Mastering courage was the task she'd preached about in her blog, and what would be more courageous than this?

"Are you free tomorrow?" he asked. "I'd better get you on a horse before you back out." Abigail nodded in agreement and Sam drew a rough map on the back of a beermat of how to find his house, which was in Upper Maisey, 2 miles away.

As Abigail tucked the beermat into her bag, there was a triumphant cheer from Mandy as she sashayed her way into the front bar. "Beat the pants off him," she boasted. "Who's up for a game of doubles? Girls versus boys?"

The Ashington Yard

Abigail looked properly at the beermat the following morning before setting off and smiled at the detail Sam had gone to when preparing the map for her. As well as marking on all the roads in Sloth, he'd pointed out certain landmarks, such as Callum's place, annotated with observations such as "lazy fecker". He'd drawn cartoon cows and horses, a tractor with Adam on it, and Mrs. Angel's garden with stripes on the lawn following Abigail's handiwork.

It was actually very straightforward to find his parents' place, and the extravagant artwork hadn't been necessary. She headed on the quiet lane opposite the pub for a mile through Lower Maisey, crossed at the crossroads and looked out for the red barn on the corner of the field (drawn on the map of course). Opposite the red barn was a pair of brick columns guarding either side of a graveled driveway. A plaque on one of the columns declared this to be "Ashington Yard". She was in the right place.

Turning into the driveway she gasped at the sight. The driveway led to a block paving area that would easily house ten cars; already parked there was the land rover that she'd seen at the car boot sale on Sunday, a sensible looking Volvo, a Volkswagen Beetle and a sporty Porsche boxster. Beyond the paved area she spotted the house. Mansion would be a better description. The estate agents had described it as "a Mediterranean style residence in a good position set within two acres of mature landscaped garden, offering a high degree of seclusion and privacy." Since the Ashington family had bought the place in the late 1980s they had extended the stabling to the rear of the property, and created an indoor and outdoor school for the horses. To the left hand side of the house, they had installed a heated outdoor swimming pool screened by a low wall and surrounded it with a covered patio area containing a built in bar-b-que that would cater for hundreds. The infamous jacuzzi nestled against the side of the house at the side of the pool area.

This was the kind of place Abigail had dreamed of living in when her Plan A came to fruition and she'd married her rich banker or international footballer. This family reeked of money, and Abigail was breathless with excitement to take a look inside at their lifestyle. She found the front door by following a crazy paved path off the driveway to a grand glass door nestled next to the double garage. She pressed the doorbell and heard a loud rendition of "oranges and lemons" play away inside the hallway to announce her arrival. It was 9.30; she hoped she wasn't too early. Sam hadn't mentioned a time, but she had woken early as she did most mornings with the sun penetrating her canvas and the birds tweeting their hearts out. Although she took her time getting up, showering, choosing an outfit from her diminishing supply of clean clothes and making a bacon buttie, she found that the time moved very slowly and she had to read for an hour before feeling it was late enough to set out to visit Sam.

She sensed movement inside the house and the door opened to Sam's smiling face. Abigail apologized in case she was too early, but there seemed to be plenty of activity already buzzing inside, so she didn't feel as though she'd judged it wrong. Sam lead her through an amazing light and airy hallway through to a kitchen that was bigger than her parent's entire ground floor back in Richmond. There was a large granite island in the middle of the kitchen with bar stools circling it, upon which Sam's Dad was sitting nursing a cup of coffee with a copy of the Racing Post spread out before him.

"Dad, this is April," Sam introduced. "April – my Dad, Robin."

"Hello April." Robin looked up and smiled and scrunched his nose up in a carbon copy of Sam, although that was where the genetic similarity ended. Robin was greying at the temples, with no signs of the reddish hair colouring that Sam inherited, nor the freckles adorning the cheeks. He was of a stocky build; certainly not fat, but middle age had crept up on him and placed a cushion of padding around his torso.

"Hello Mr Ashington," Abigail replied politely, to which he insisted she call him Robin.

"And this is my Mum," Sam had moved on his crutches over to the window where a tall thin lady stood gazing absent mindedly out over the valley below. She turned slowly and blinked, as though waking from a dream. "Mum – this is April, she's the one that would like to borrow your bike," he reminded her, as though explaining to a child.

"Oh, hello April."

Abigail looked her up and down and ached to give her some fashion advice. Her long straight brown hair was in desperate need of a brushing, and was probably too long for her age anyway. She'd applied make up for make up's sake, rather than using cosmetics to enhance her appearance, and the pinky eye shadow clashed with her baggy orange top, with a horrific crimson lipstick that didn't quite reach the edges of her lips. It looked as though she'd put on blusher with a paintbrush. She was wearing a black mini skirt with bare legs, her knobbly knees on full display, dressing like a teenage girl a third of her age.

"Would you like a drink?" asked Sam, bringing Abigail's

attention back to him. "Tea, coffee, juice?"

"Or wine?" prompted Sam's Mum.

"Oh, I think it's a little early for wine," started Abigail before noticing that Sam's Mum had a glass of red wine in her hand. "For me," she added hurriedly. "But coffee would be great – milk and two sugars."

Abigail took her place at the breakfast bar opposite Robin, who politely stopped reading and folded his paper up, removed his glasses and slid them into his breast pocket.

"Sam tells me you're living at Wit's End down in Sloth," Robin said, which Abigail translated as "What on earth are you doing sleeping in a tent on your own in the middle of nowhere?" She launched into her back-story once again. Every time she gave the explanation, she embellished it a little further with a few more added details, so it wasn't just about surviving without technology and comforts, now it was about overcoming fears and mastering courage. Robin listened attentively and nodded encouragingly in the right places. Why did Abigail feel like she was having a job interview? Looking into Robin's warm attentive eyes, she desperately wanted to impress him.

"And are you single?" Robin blurted out unexpectedly.

"Dad!" shrieked Sam in embarrassment, pausing from the coffee making to make an exasperated face at Robin. Abigail blushed slightly and Robin shrugged in protest. He couldn't see what was wrong with the question.

The kitchen however, went silent waiting for Abigail's answer.

"Yes, I'm single," declared Abigail. "The last date I went on was a bit awkward. It was a blind date with a chap who presents sports shows on TV and I didn't recognize him. I had no idea who he was."

"Not that Ivan Costello was it?" asked Charly, sweeping into the kitchen and catching the tail end of the conversation. "He's gorgeous." Charly swooped over to the fridge and helped herself to a carton of orange juice.

"Yes, that's right," relied Abigail, remembering suddenly. The awkward conversation, the age gap. "It was Ivan. Everyone in the restaurant kept looking over at him and he was loving every minute you could tell."

"I can imagine that," said Sam, placing the mug of coffee in front of Abigail. "He came here before the Cheltenham Gold Cup to pre record a feature about the yard, and talk to Dad about our hopefuls for the festival. He struck me as being a bit arrogant."

"Are you seeing him again?" asked Charly, wide-eyed and enthusiastic.

"No." Abigail hesitated. "He asked me for my number and I'm ashamed to say that I gave him a false one."

"I wish you'd given him my number instead!" laughed Charly. "I'd go out with him in an instant."

"You're too young for boyfriends," scolded Mrs. Ashington, which Abigail thought was fairly harsh considering Charly was old enough to drive. "And haven't you got to be at college today?"

"No Mum, I've got study periods all morning," she replied, exasperated. She was wearing jodphurs and a jacket and had clearly been out riding so far that morning. She gave a sly wink at Abigail as though confirming that she really *should* be studying.

"And I've asked her to help me out too," added Sam, sticking up for his sister.

"We're taking April out for her first ride on Grace."

Mrs. Ashington appeared to tut, and drained her glass of wine. Abigail wondered whether it was her first glass of the day.

"Right, I'd better be off," Robin declared, standing from the stool and pulling a smart suit jacket over his shirt. "Exeter beckons."

"Giving the Black Banana a run?" asked Sam. Abigail smiled to herself, wondering whether Nadine had sat down with the horse's owner and asked them what colour their underpants were and what they had last eaten. If it was a good enough way to name a band, it could work perfectly well for racehorses.

"Yes, bring him back down to two miles and see whether he can do something to please his owners. Cheerio all." He pecked his wife on the cheek and waved as he made his way out of the kitchen towards the hallway. Abigail liked him immensely and had only been in his company for five minutes.

She drained her coffee and sat dreading the moment she'd have to get up on that damned horse.

"Shall I give you a tour?" asked Sam, noticing that she'd finished. Excellent. A mechanism to delay riding that horse and a chance to have a nosy around this palatial Ashington home.

She followed Sam on his crutches through the kitchen's second doorway; one that didn't lead to the main hallway, and found herself in another wide corridor. Sam continued to the far end and motioned out of the glass panel in the door.

"Pool and hot tub outside there, then we've got a shower area here," he opened the first door inside the hallway to show off a room that looked like the changing room of some posh sports club. There was a wooden bench with coat hooks for changing, with a large frosted glass area screening an enormous shower. A hairdryer was installed on the wall along with a mirror that stretched across the entire width of the area. "It gets a lot of use when we have pool parties and someone wants to come and dry off."

Abigail nodded politely. It was twice the size of their poky family bathroom back in Richmond.

"Next door is the study stroke library. It's actually doubling up as my bedroom too at the moment, as I can't manage the stairs." He banged the plaster on his right leg with his crutch, then winced, as he'd evidently hit it harder than he meant to.

Peering through the door that he held open, Abigail's mouth fell open. The room was easily twice the size of their lounge at home, and that was considered roomy. The wall on the far side was lined with shelves, packed with books of various shapes and sizes. There was a desk within an alcove to the left, toppling with documents, letters, paperwork and an old laptop. A camp bed was set up to the right, unmade sheets and blankets leaving the area looking a mess. Stray clothes were strewn across the floor surrounding it. Typical boy, sighed Abigail to herself.

"I love this room," enthused Sam, swinging himself inside on his crutches. "It seems Mum and Dad have kept every book, newspaper, and magazine they've ever bought and just hoarded it in here. I've got no idea why. They rarely come and get anything to read."

Abigail followed Sam over to the bookcase and started browsing through the titles. There were a great deal of books relating to horses, racing, autobiographies of jockeys and trainers. Another section held gardening books, cookery books and Abigail guessed that Mrs. Ashington had stashed that selection there. Then there were a bundle of fiction books, romance novels, crime books and thrillers.

"Oh, Sylvia Downton books!" exclaimed Abigail, spotting a long set of matching covers. "Penny was hunting for these at the car boot sale on Sunday."

"Charly used to drink those up. I think the whole set is pretty much there. I'm sure she won't mind if Penny takes the ones she needs. I'll mention it to her on Sunday."

Instead of leading Abigail back into the kitchen, the hallway veered round to the left of the kitchen and on the left hand side opened out into a lounge that Abigail could have stayed in for weeks on end and never been bored. There was a vast expanse of squashy sofa set around in a horseshoe shape facing a massive plasma TV on the wall. To the other end of the lounge, a pool table stood in front of a large natural fireplace. There was even a bar tucked into the corner, complete with a row of spirits on optics and pumps for the beer.

The room was flooded with sunlight, the southerly wall being completely glass, leading straight into a roomy conservatory stuffed full of beanbags and wicker furniture. The doors to the conservatory gave access to the large lawn and views over the stables below and the greenery and the woods beyond that.

"Wow, this is amazing. It's a far cry from the views you get from my house," Abigail reflected, remembering the concrete and traffic to the front and back of their property. To the end of the lawn, they watched as Charly was back on her horse, practicing sharp turns in the showjumping ring.

"She's incorrigible," laughed Sam. "She's got A' levels coming up in a few weeks and we just can't peel her off Oscar. Come on, I'll show you the yard."

They headed out together through the conservatory doors and made their way across the lawn towards the outbuildings. Charly gave a brief wave before contemplating a complex set of three jumps.

"They are high jumps!" observed Abigail, who hadn't appreciated the scale from far off. "I don't think I'll be up to tackling those today."

"It's OK, we'll give you a few weeks to build up to that," smiled Sam in reply.

The stables were laid out inside a long wooden barn. It was lighter and more airy than Abigail had imagined. Some of the stalls were empty, whilst others had horses looking over inquisitively. An overpowering aroma of bark chips and hay filled the air.

"So, how does the yard operate then?" asked Abigail, remembering what a fool she'd made of herself by asking Callum where he kept his horse. "I don't know anything about this whole world."

"Well," Sam paused, wondering where to start. "Imagine this yard is like a boarding school. All the horses are the pupils, and my Dad is the head teacher. So the horses have parents – that's the owners – and they pay my Dad to look after them; it's my Dad's job to make sure all the pupils do as best as they can. He'll decide what the horse's strengths are and whether to put them in for say - GCSE geography or A'level physics."

It was all quite straight forward when put like that. Abigail took up the metaphor to check she understood. "So your Dad decided that the Black Banana should be put in for the GCSE drama at Exeter today?"

"Exactly!" replied Sam with a wide smile, pleased that his analogy was working. "Because he tried the A'level last month and did appallingly; it was obviously a step too far, so we're trying him at something simpler today. Less prize money and glory, but if he does better then we know where his level is at."

A tall girl in a hurry jogged past them with a brief wave on her way towards the driveway. "So, all the grooms here are like the teachers?" ventured Abigail.

"That's right – we employ around thirty staff and they take care of all the horses needs. They take them out for exercise and schooling and report back to my Dad."

He paused by a stable where a jet-black horse's head peered inquisitively out over the door. Sam freed an arm from his crutch and lovingly rubbed the horse's ears.

"This is Abigail's dream," he introduced. Abigail opened her mouth to make a comment about the coincidence of the name, but stopped herself in time. "We just call her Ab for short. She's our star pupil at the moment and will be heading to Ascot in May to make her debut. She's something of a dark horse – literally and otherwise, aren't you girl?" Sam rubbed the end of Ab's nose and the mare began to nod her head in appreciation.

"Come - she won't bite," Sam promised, and Abigail felt obliged to venture closer and touch the horse. Reluctantly she took a step forward and reached out to the spot between Ab's wide nostrils where Sam had been rubbing.

"Wow – that feels like velvet," she observed. "Black velvet, eh?" she was talking to the horse now, and could suddenly start to understand Sam and Charly's adoration for the creatures. It was just standing there, lapping up the attention, and appreciating the company.

They waved cheerio to Abigail's dream and Sam continued the tour, pointing out the star pupils, those that needed to get a bit fitter and the youngsters in training to become the stars of the future. Abigail was fascinated by the horse foot spa to cool down injured equine feet, but even more astonished that the horses had their own swimming pool area where they were exercised frequently.

By the time they worked their way back towards the outdoor school where the impossibly high showjumps lurked, Charly was now standing holding a stumpy fat cream coloured pony.

"April. Can I introduce you to Grace? Grace is a senior citizen now, and was my first pony – my eleventh birthday present." Sam explained. "We don't ride her as much as we used to – as she's kind of retired – but she is a hundred percent adorable, reliable and kind. You'll be as safe as anything on her."

Grace eyed up Abigail as she approached, that suspicious horse's eye flashing a warning to her. She could probably sense Abigail's mounting apprehension at having to get on her.

"I'll keep you on a lead rein," promised Charly, indicating the rope that was already hanging from Grace's bridle.

Abigail suddenly felt very self-conscious as Sam showed her how to stand and put her left leg into the stirrup. It seemed so far off the ground; Abigail hadn't had to stretch her inner thigh muscles that much since having an over enthusiastic lover three years previously. Sam was pressed up close to Abigail's back with Charly standing on the opposite side of Grace, pulling on the stirrup to stop the saddle slipping.

Oh please God don't let me make an utter fool of myself, prayed Abigail silently to herself, as she tried to rise herself as femininely as possible into the saddle. She was careful to avoid digging her left toe into Grace's side as instructed by Sam, and managed not to boot Charly in the face as she swung the right leg over Grace's back. So far, so good.

"Excellent!" praised Sam and Charly in perfect unison.

Abigail looked down onto the tops of their heads. Bloody hell, the ground seemed a dizzying distance to fall. She gripped the front of the saddle instinctively. Grace seemed to sigh heavily and shift her weight from one foot to the other, either bored already, or exasperated to feel a wobbly beginner perched nervously in the saddle.

Sam showed her how to hold the reins, but as soon as his attention was diverted she grabbed back onto the saddle as extra protection.

"OK, let's walk," sang Charly and pulled Grace forward. The old mare began to plod reluctantly forward, and Abigail gripped tighter to the saddle, trying to relax and not look petrified. Not easy.

"You have a good seat, you look good," called Sam from his viewpoint at the side of the arena, resting up his leg as Charly took charge of the lesson.

"I don't feel it!" Abigail called back truthfully, but Charly looked up at her and grinned.

"It'll feel weird to start with, but you'll get into the rhythm in a bit."

Abigail looked down Grace's long neck and through her mud covered ears and tried to imagine what it must feel like to be going at a gallop on one of these things. And staying on over those jumps. How on earth did Charly do it, she didn't even grip on to the saddle!

"I guess you've been riding since an early age," she said to the top of the brown curls below her. Charly looked up at her with a smile.

"I don't ever remember not being able to ride," she replied. "You can't really grow up on a place like this and not be thrust into the whole equestrian world."

Charly led Grace in a leisurely clockwise circle around the edge of the sawdust strewn jumping arena. Abigail tried to stop glancing at the ground, wondering how hard it would be to land if she fell. Maybe talking would distract her.

"So, you must be really busy at the moment, with college and things?"

"Oh don't!" gasped Charly melodramatically. "It's a nightmare at the moment, with Badminton horse trials only four weeks away. I'm competing for the first time – I'm really nervous! But my A'levels start the same week, so my days are just stupidly manic at the moment trying to revise and get in as much practice on Oscar."

In reality, Charly was spending a disproportionate amount of time honing her equestrian skills rather than laboring over boring, thick textbooks. Her Dad was barely around to notice her skipping tutorials and lectures; her mother was gullible enough to believe that she had an awful lot of free study periods and didn't realize that she was spending most of the time out of the house rather than sitting at the desk indoors. Charly's A' levels didn't seem relevant to her future, she had managed to resist being sent to university, and her skills on horseback were far more likely to give her gainful employment than any qualifications in maths and business.

"Oh, and for my sins," Charly continued, "I'm on the social committee at college and we're arranging the end of term ball in June, so I need to find a dress to wear, and book a band. I might even find a date to go with if I'm lucky."

"I could always make you a dress," Abigail offered, spurred on by the enjoyment of starting on Penny's dress. It was rewarding to see the designs coming off the pages of her sketchbook and becoming a reality in material form. "If you wanted. You'd just need to choose the material and a design from my collection and I'll make it for you. Free of charge," she added hastily.

"Really? That sounds fab!" enthused Charly.

"And I don't know what sort of band you're after, but I have some friends in London that are in a band. They do a lot of rock covers, ballads, music you can have a good dance to. They're pretty adaptable too, so can come up with a set list from the 60s right through to modern music."

"Would they come all the way out here though?"

It was a good point. Abigail wasn't sure that Blue Steak's fees would even stretch to cover the petrol on their van, but they were always saying that they wanted to achieve a greater geographical spread. And secretly, Abigail hoped that if it came off and she was still in the area on the run, it would be a rare opportunity to see Nadine again. She gave Charly the band's website address to take a look at some clips of their gigs, and suggested she sends them an enquiry message through the site.

"You're doing really well by the way," Charly said encouragingly after they had been circling for fifteen minutes. Abigail was starting to relax – just a tiny bit. She felt that Grace, as promised, was reliable and not likely to take off, or skip to the side, rear or buck, and all those other horrible things she'd seen horses do in films. Her plodding gait was as rhythmic as a metronome.

"How was that?" asked Sam, as Charly led her back over to the entrance of the arena after half an hour. "It looked like you got the hang of that quite quickly."

"Not bad," admitted Abigail, with a rise of panic about how to get off. "Not sure how my legs are going to feel though."

Once they'd helped her get down from Grace, she discovered exactly how her legs felt. Like jelly. They didn't feel as though they would ever fit back together again, and her bum was as numb as the time she'd gone for the ten-mile bike ride. She glanced down at her leggings, which now had large patches of brown saddle grime on the insides of her thighs and knees, and she realized that the hunt for a washing machine or launderette would soon become a priority. Charly led Grace back to her paddock, whilst Sam and Abigail headed over to the garages to get the pushbike.

The property and the grounds were amazing; Abigail couldn't stop fantasizing about living in a place like this. It must have been amazing for Sam and Charly to grow up here, surrounded by nature and fantastic countryside.

Sam left Abigail standing by the wooden garage door, whilst he went inside the house to fetch the key. Mrs. Ashington flanked him as he reappeared again, looking anxious. "I hope the bike's going to be OK," she began apologetically. "It's not come out the garage for a long time, so it may be a bit grimy."

Sam unlocked the padlock and swung open the doors to reveal a sight common to most garages up and down the country. Amidst the gloom and cobwebs was a dumping ground of family knick knacks; boxes, bikes, a surfboard, more boxes, a workman's bench; a rusty bar-b-que, a chest, piles of shelving stacked up, old carpet, a defunct computer monitor, more boxes and a pink ladies pushbike with a basket on the front.

Mrs. Ashington headed into the garage, and wheeled the bike forwards into better light, but then gave a wail of disappointment.

"Oh, it looks like the tyre's got a puncture." The front tyre was indeed as flat as a pancake.

"And the back one too," pointed out Sam.

Abigail didn't know whether to be relieved or frustrated. She hadn't relished the thought of pedaling seven miles each way into Cheltenham, but on the other hand, her choices were now back to square one. Nobody seemed to know what times the buses ran, and a taxi would be pretty costly each way, especially as she only needed a bit of ribbon and some small bits and bobs.

"Can you mend it?" asked Mrs. Ashington. It wasn't clear whom the question was directed at, but Sam took it.

"Possibly, but I don't know where I'd find the puncture repair kit. It could be buried anywhere in amongst all this junk. We'd probably have to drive into Cheltenham just to buy a new puncture repair kit, which kind of defeats the object of having the bike to use."

"If you have your own insurance, you're welcome to take one of our cars?" offered Mrs. Ashington. "My beetle or Sam's Porsche?"

Abigail's jaw dropped. The Porsche belonged to Sam? How the hell did he afford to buy and run that? At his age, the insurance alone must be eye watering. But of course, Abigail reflected, Daddy must be playing a large hand in funding his childrens' assets; their horses, the cars, the upkeep on the accommodation. Abigail could understand that all their lives, they had grown up not needing to worry about how to get the things they want. Daddy obviously has a generous chequebook at the ready. Thankfully, Sam and Charly seemed to be so grounded and affable that she couldn't resent them for their upbringing. It was just that she had always been taught the value of money, and if she wanted the latest handbag, CD or hair straighteners, she had to earn the money herself.

For a moment, it was tempting to get herself insured; she'd love nothing more than to drive that sports car, especially around the country lanes. She'd only ever driven sensible city cars around the southeast. But it was far too risky to get her driving license out a second time for any official business. She'd be asking to get caught in an instant.

Abigail realized that she'd paused for too long, thinking it over and Mrs. Ashington stepped in again.

"Or if you don't have to go to Cheltenham straight away, you can get a lift in with us on Thursday?" she continued. "We're going in to have a look over some flats, aren't we Sam?" she ruffled his hair fondly, making him cringe.

"Well Thursday would be fine," agreed Abigail, "If you're sure that's OK?" That was settled then, and the pink bike was shoved back into the garage for another session of abandonment.

Wish for something more

The energy of students never failed to amaze Craig as he looked out at the crowd through the haze of flashing lights and dry ice. They'd been on the cramped dance floor of the student union bar for an hour, bouncing up and down incessantly whilst Blue Steak ran through their upbeat repertoire of classics that included 'baggy trousers', 'mamma mia' and 'rocking all over the world'.

He never tired of having crowds of drunken guests yelling the lyrics back at him, waving their arms carelessly in the air and clearly having the time of their lives. These were often better gigs than the wedding packages they did, where the guests start off quite self conscious and sedate, the empty dance floor taking a while to start to fill, nobody quite ready to make a fool of themselves in front of family members.

Spring term student gigs were the other end of the riot scale though. Everyone having a last blow out before exams start, or returning back from a couple of week's confinement at home for the Easter holidays. He thought back briefly to his student days and remembered not even needing the excuse of terms starting or drawing to a close – most nights were alcohol or weed fuelled. That's probably why he got a third class degree.

"Do you want me to do a couple of acoustics?" Fish asked Craig, as the final chord of "Living on a Prayer" resulted in thunderous cheering and applause. "Whilst you get a couple of beers in?"

Beers – and water to drench the poor vocal chords – sounded like a great idea to Craig. They were coming towards the end of their first set and should take a short break soon anyway, but if Fish wanted to calm things down with a couple of his acoustic ballads, who was he to object?

"We're almost at the end of part one," Craig explained into the mic to the crowd, who didn't look ready to stop the party quite as readily as he did. "But before we have a break, I'm going to leave you in the hands of our guitarist Fish to play you a couple of slower songs. Hope you enjoy them."

"Yo – fishy, woooo- hoooo!" yelped someone from the back of the crowd. Nadine glanced up from where she had been working on the laptop in a quiet corner behind the sound desk. She'd managed to hook up to the free student wifi and was alternating between updating the Blue Steak website with upcoming gigs, to scrolling through Facebook updates. The gig requests were really starting to take off now, and the band needed her organizational skills more than ever. She wondered whether they might even have to employy someone properly when she goes off on the voluntary work overseas again. It would be a shame to lose work over poor organization, and she couldn't see Craig, Dougie or Fish keeping on top of the bookings, the logistics or the invoicing. It wasn't just more gig requests either; the enquiries were starting to come in from beyond London. Helped by word of mouth of guests, and the informative website, she'd received emails from Oxfordshire yesterday and even one from Gloucestershire today. It was probably time to sit the band down and talk strategy and pricing.

Fish changed his guitars around and pulled a stool up to the mic in the centre of the stage. He secretly enjoyed a few minutes of the spotlight now and then.

"Good evening – are you all having a good time!" he asked, receiving a cheer in reply.

"Play some Bryan Adams!" yelled a voice from the middle of the crowd.

"Good call!" Fish responded, untwisting his multicoloured guitar strap and beginning to strum the opening of 'Summer of 69'. It hadn't been his planned opener, but on reflection it was still a good song the crowd could participate in, whilst slowing the tempo from the madness of earlier. It would pave the way into his next planned tune, which would definitely wind the crowd down a notch or two.

Nadine knew exactly what Fish had planned to sing next, and she wasn't proved wrong as he began the opening. It wasn't such a well-known song, and correspondingly the crowd seemed to deflate a little, with many taking opportunity to drift off to the bar, head outside for a fag or make off towards the loos.

"Oh the sun is shining far too bright, for it to still be night," he began to sing, at least an octave lower than the original. Despite herself, Nadine's foot began tapping of its own accord to the beat and she raised her eyes from the laptop to meet Fish's bearing down on her.

"Let's take a walk outside, see the world through each other's eyes," he continued soulfully, not taking his gaze from her. She smiled back at him before returning her attention to the laptop. This song always reminded her of Abigail. Minimizing the Outlook calendar she'd been working on, she returned to the Facebook, where she went straight over to Abigail's profile page. Her gorgeous profile pic smiled back at Nadine and once again she was filled with anxiety and sadness for her best friend. The picture had been taken last summer at a free gig in Hyde Park. It had been a pleasantly warm day and Nadine and Abigail had taken along a twelve pack of cider and spent four hours on the grass with a small gang of acquaintances that they'd known from university, listening to the bands, chatting and joking. One of the friends had taken the photo of Ab, showing off his photography skills by capturing the sun on her face in sharp focus with tendrils of her hair falling around her face with a soft blur. She'd been caught off guard, laughing naturally and freely at some shared joke when the shutter captured the moment. And now it was for all to see on her Facebook profile. The last posting on Ab's feed was from over a week ago, when she'd posted a photo of her and Nadine splashing around in muddy puddles at Glastonbury three years ago. The caption read *"This has made me so happy, I love coming across old photos xxx"*.

There had been no reply to the message Nadine sent Ab; it was so unlike her not to have used Facebook for so long.

Fish was now halfway through the song. "I wish for long lingering glances, fairytale romances, every single day." It was quite a girly song for Fish to be serenading the crowd with; dreadlock haired Fish with his ripped jeans and inky black tattoo of a skull on his forearm. But the song choice was related to Abigail, Nadine mused sadly, remembering back to the time they'd all been together, driving along the M1 in the early hours of a balmy summer morning, playing a game of "What song suits you the most".

"Wish for something more," Abigail had announced as the song she felt summed her up most. "I'm never satisfied with what I've got – I always want that little bit more."

"Good song choice," enthused Fish. "And a brilliant song to sing. In fact, I'm going to learn it and put it in my acoustic set."

"You can't sing that!" gasped Nadine in horror, "It's a gay song about a girl who wants to become more than just good friends with a boy. It'll ruin your street cred."

Fish got his way though, and at most gigs, set about teasing Nadine by singing it in his set, catching her eye and making a point.

Nadine's fingers hovered over the keyboard before typing onto Abigail's wall. "Miss you Ab – hope you're OK". She added some kisses with a sigh. Closing down the web browser, she slammed the laptop lid shut and stood up.

Fish's eyes were still clamped on Nadine from across the dance floor as he sang the key line, "And I love you like a friend but let's not pretend, that I wish for something, wish for something more."

Nadine blew him a kiss, smiled kindly and made to head outside. She needed a fag.

If she could have seen Abigail that evening, she'd not have believed her eyes for an instant. For the past eight hours, Abigail and Mrs. Angel had been keeping each other company, and they were now watching Back to the Future, and dunking chocolate hob nobs into their Ovaltine.

It had been a productive eight hours as far as Abigail was concerned. She'd arrived early afternoon, having excused herself from Ashington Yard to come and scrub down Mrs. Angel's filthy patio slabs. Mrs. Angel tried to protest at first, but Sam had said it was going to pour with rain tomorrow, so Abigail wanted to get them looking sparkly clean in case she didn't get another chance for a while.

Once she'd worked her way up the front path with a bottle of bleach, a hosepipe and a scrubbing brush, she then repeated the exertion on the back patio. On top of the wobbly legs from riding Grace earlier, she was now exhausted. And hungry. As predicted, Mrs.. Angel was ready to feed Abigail. She just happened to have a lamb casserole in the fridge that was too big for one, so Abigail happily munched her way through a generous portion with creamy mashed potatoes that Mrs. Angel knocked together.

Whilst the food went down, Mrs. Angel had dug out a set of old photo albums and she poured over them with Abigail, describing who was who, what they were doing, what the year was, and there was usually an anecdote or two to accompany every image. They'd started out with the black and white album, where the small square prints dated back to the 1930s; a couple of photos of Mrs. Angel's parents, and of her as a child, growing up in Liverpool before the war broke out.

"It's a shame we didn't have the access to cameras that people do now," she sighed, "otherwise there would be a much better record of our lives. I don't think I've got any pictures of my friends from Liverpool. I used to be best friends with Lily Escott – she lived next door and we used to get up to all sorts. I wonder if she's still alive even. I haven't seen her since 1940."

They moved through the 50s, a few photos of Mrs. Angel with friends from music college once the war had ended, and a photo of the school that she taught at.

"No pictures of boyfriends then?" asked Abigail, flicking through images of places and colleagues, houses and landscapes.

"I didn't have a boyfriend until 1960, can you believe it? I was 32 and beginning to think that I would never meet anyone and remain a spinster for the rest of my years. Then I met Andrew. He was the nephew of the head teacher at school and we were introduced because he was like me, you know, getting into his 30s and going to be left on the shelf if he wasn't careful."

"But did you fancy him? You didn't go out with him just because you were feeling left behind, did you?"

Mrs. Angel was smiling at the memory. "I thought he was the most handsome man I'd ever clapped eyes on," she confirmed. "I was amazed that he seemed interested in plain little me. We had tea at his aunt and uncle's house as our first date – that was a bit awkward because Mr. Angel senior was my boss of course. After that, he took me to the pictures for our second date and kissed me in the back row. I can't remember what the film was, but I can still remember the kiss. There I was, 32, and being kissed for the first time." She lowered her voice conspiratorially even though there was no-one around to hear. "I lost my virginity on the third date. He took me over to Margate for a long weekend, and we stayed in a tiny back street guest house, pretending to be Mr. and Mrs. Angel. I loved being referred to as Mrs. Angel, so I suggested we should get married and start to have a family before it got too late. We married two months later."

"You weren't already pregnant?" asked Abigail, remembering Kate's horrific incident with Callum.

"No," she laughed, "In fact, it took me three years to conceive in the end – despite lots of trying, we were beginning to give up hope, but finally in 1965 Carol came along. Look," Mrs. Angel closed the current photo album and skipped to the next where she had images of Andrew, and then baby pictures of daughter Carol. Andrew was a good-looking chap, Abigail discovered. He was tall and slim, with a quiff built into his wavy hair that made him seem a lot like Elvis. In every picture he was dressed impeccably. Through the 70s the photos gradually turned into colour, although they were often blurry and badly shot. Access to brownie and polaroid cameras had turned everyone into photographers, without the luxury of being able to delete the bad ones like youngsters did today on the digital cameras and phones.

"I never wanted Carol to be an only child, and we kept trying for a brother or sister for her, but it just wasn't to be."

Through the 80s, images of family Christmases spent together, Carol's marriage to Mark in 1984, with a huge disgusting merengue of a wedding dress, and guests wearing jackets with enormous shoulder pads. The tight curly perms on the women were as laughable as the porn star moustaches on many of the men. There were then more baby pictures, as Mrs. Angel became Grandmother to Isabella. There were proud smiley school photos, snapshots of family celebration dinners, and images that catalogued a variety of pets. Then the photos seemed to dry up around the year 2000. Carol had left Mark, met Graham and he'd taken her and the teenage Isabella up to Edinburgh to start a new life. The last photo of Andrew Angel was also around the same time, looking frail and swathed in a blanket in a wheelchair in the garden.

The faraway look in Mrs. Angel's eyes hadn't gone unnoticed by Abigail. She found herself hating Carol for just abandoning her mother like that, and depriving her of easy access to her only grandchild. She didn't want to ask what had happened to Andrew.

"Anyway," Mrs. Angel, pulled all the albums into a pile and Abigail helped to carry them back over to the sideboard where they had been stowed. "I've told you all about my love life, where's the young gentleman in yours?"

"Oh, I'm single still," she admitted. "I haven't quite found Mr Right yet."

"People can leave it a lot later these days, can't they? There are so many more opportunities for girls with careers, and they can have their families later in life. So you're not seeing Sam then?"

Abigail was taken aback and pulled a face. "Not in that way, I just went up there this morning to see if I could borrow his Mum's bike."

"And you spent time with him yesterday. So today was technically your second date. Look what happened to me on my third date!"

Abigail laughed it off. "He's a lovely lad, and I get on really well with his sister Charly too. And I met his Dad this morning and he's also very sweet. But I wouldn't think about trying to find a boyfriend in Sloth. Anyway, Kate seems to think Sam's gay."

Mrs. Angel mulled it over. "Could be, I suppose. I can't say that I've ever seen him with a girl or a boy – in that way. Mind you, I haven't seen him for a long time. Once upon a time, he'd be in the village quite a lot with the other boy scouts, running errands and helping out people like me. He's just too busy with the horses these days."

She got up from her chair and waddled across to the TV. It was time for another dose of "Where in the World" that saw Abigail and Mrs. Angel screaming answers in frustration at the TV screen, as the dim contestants shook their heads at the most obvious questions.

"We ought to go on this show together!" Mrs. Angel remarked, although it wasn't clear whether she was being serious. "We'd be a good team together, what with you being good at unscrambling the anagrams and me knowing all the older things."

"Just think if we won that jackpot!" replied Abigail, who had no intention of applying to go on television. She was a wanted criminal on the run; hardly conducive conditions for an appearance on national TV.

"What would you do with that money?" asked Mrs. Angel, and

Abigail stopped to think. Her first impulse had been to describe the most amazing Gucci bag that she'd buy along with not one, but two pairs of identical Jimmy Choos but in different colours. A week ago that answer would have been straight out of her mouth before she could stop herself, but it seemed a complete waste of money now. There was nowhere in Sloth that a Gucci bag and Jimmy Choo shoes would be appreciated.

"That would set me going with my own dress making business," she replied thoughtfully. "I guess I'd need a website, a business plan, a really good sewing machine and bulk quantities of haberdashery. I've got the designs and the ideas, I just need money for the practicalities to turn it into reality." Abigail nodded, pleased with the answer, and fleetingly wondered why she hadn't bothered to think about saving money in London, instead of frittering it all away on designer bling. "What about you," she asked Mrs. Angel. "What would you spend it on?"

Mrs. Angel screwed up her nose dismissively. "Oh, there's nothing I need money for at my age. I'd just want to win the trophy. Buenos Aires!" She blurted out at the screen in response to a question about the tango. "Although," she began hesitantly, "It would be good to pay someone to cart a lorry load of groceries from the supermarket to my house. You know – all those heavy tins and packets and things. Shopping is one thing I do struggle with, I've got the drag bag to take to and from the shop on the lane but they haven't got the widest range of things in there."

"That's what online shopping is for!" exclaimed Abigail, before realizing that the World Wide Web was one thing Mrs. Angel didn't have access to either. "All the big supermarkets offer the service – you just tell them when you want it delivered, order the goods, pay with a card and it'll turn up on your doorstep at the allotted time. Well, nearly always," she added, remembering a few occasions when she'd been hanging around on behalf of her Mum, waiting for the weekly shop.

This was obviously news to Mrs. Angel, who got as excited as a small child on Christmas Eve. Before long, they were both going through the cupboards in the kitchen making a long list of large, heavy imperishable items that Abigail could order on Kate's computer for her. Washing powder, tins of vegetables, bulk buy toilet rolls, flour, rice, potatoes.

"Here –" Mrs. Angel handed Abigail a debit card in pristine condition. "I've never used it so I hope it will work OK, especially after all that banking mess recently. And be careful using that thing on the Internet. You hear such terrible stories of people getting their life savings taken from some scam or other."

Abigail reassured her that the supermarket systems were as secure as anything, and the card details could be stored so when she wanted to repeat the order, she could simply ask Kate or Callum to do it for her.

"Oh I can't wait!" Mrs. Angel cried. "So you'll order it tomorrow and it will come later in the week. How exciting. Let's celebrate by watching the Tuesday night film with a big mug of Ovaltine! Oh Ovaltine – stick that on the list – the biggest jar they do."

Wednesday

Sam was right. The fine weather had come to an end and Abigail was woken in the early hours of Wednesday morning by the pitter-patter of raindrops on canvas. In her hazy wakefulness, she remembered leaving her shoes and book outside the tent, and with a curse, had to drag herself out of the sleeping bag, unzip the door and fumble around, dragging her items into the dry safety of the tent's interior.

The rhythmic pounding continued relentlessly through the night, but after a while, Abigail must have managed to doze back off, as it was light when she next opened her eyes. The soundtrack of rain on canvas continued, and Abigail remembered that she'd promised to walk the dogs for Kate today. Of all the days to pick. She was hardly awash with wet weather gear.

She arrived at Kate's house just as little Aidan was being bundled into the car seat to leave for nursery.

"Help yourself to stuff in the cupboard under the stairs," Kate instructed, taking one look at Abigail, who was coatless and already beginning to feel the damp seeping into her trainers. She went inside to the excitement of the beagles, Eddie and Jeremy, and hunted around in the cupboard. There she found a pair of wellies and a roomy waterproof jacket. Perfect.

The rain was set in and persistent, and Abigail had no idea where to walk. She was hoping that the beagles had a set route and would lead her, but they simply buzzed around from smell to smell, pulling Abigail on a wonky directionless course, and tying her up in knots with the leads. Her feet took her towards Upper Maisey, the one place she did know, the dopey dogs enjoying the smells along the way, and Abigail secretly relishing the freshness of the air now that the dusty heat had broken. The green shades on the trees, grass and hedges appeared more vibrant, the blossom on the trees was bursting to life and it felt as though nature was sucking up every raindrop into its parched roots. She passed meadows where daisies and dandelions poked their heads through lush overgrown grass, and another endless field full of deep yellow rape plants.

Ashington Yard appeared on her left before long, and she slowed to take some lingering looks towards the property, wondering if Charly or Sam would make an appearance. But the residence itself looked silent. There was no doubt activity further down the driveway, at the stables where the grooms would be going about their business, but from the road, the pulse of the operation couldn't be seen.

She carried on a little further and came to a T-junction. The beagles were no help, but she figured if she kept turning left, eventually she would find herself back in Sloth. The lanes were so blissfully quiet. Free from traffic and lonely, with no-one around. Well, except for a drenched jogger that was heading towards her. As the runner came into view, Abigail realized that the slender figure and the brown tangle of hair that had become a dripping mass down her back were familiar.

"Ah – dog walking duty eh?" Mandy greeted her, still bouncing from foot to foot as though stopping would cause her to seize up.

"Just doing my bit to help out Kate and Callum," replied Abigail evenly. She could never be sure whether Mandy was going to be pleasant, playful, make snide remarks or perhaps all three. "You're very keen, jogging in the pouring rain."

"Ah – got to," replied Mandy, checking the oversized gadget watch on her wrist. "I'm running the London marathon in a couple of weeks, so need to get in the training."

"Wow – the London marathon," was all Abigail could manage in reply. As someone who had never run, with the exception of a short dash for the bus, it was inconceivable. "Have you done it before?"

"Once. A couple of years ago, I finished in four hours two. Can you imagine how gutted I was not to break the four hour mark?" Abigail made a sympathetic face, not having a clue what it felt like to run more than four minutes, let alone for four hours. "So I am determined to do a sub four hour time this year. Looks like I'm on course to do it, if my training times are anything to be going by. Anyway, must leave you, got another six miles to squeeze in."

"Go ahead, er... good luck!" she called after Mandy who bounced off like a baby deer trotting after its mother. She started to think about the exercise she did at home – or the lack of - and was being put to shame by Mandy. She had a gym membership because one of the girls at a previous temping placement had got her a good deal through the "Introduce a friend" incentive. But she barely got her money's worth from the membership. An occasional swim; a slow saunter up and down the pool for twenty minutes followed by fifteen minutes sitting in the jazuzzi watching the shadowy figures of men lifting weights through the frosted glass. Once she went to a yoga class that concentrated on deep breathing techniques and relaxation. She nearly fell asleep on her mat at that class. Then there was step aerobics. That got her heart rate elevated, but she only went once and ended up stuffing her face with a latte and a muffin after the class and undoing any calorie loss. Maybe she should take more exercise. Perhaps daily dog walking would be a good start.

By the time she found her way back to Kate and Callum's house, the appeal had worn off. She had been walking for over ninety minutes, as the turning left idea was a solid one, except that the roads were very long before they conceded any opportunities to change direction. The rain was also still beating heavily and Abigail felt soaked through, despite the waterproof coat and wellington boots. Horizontal blasts had pummeled her leggings with spray, soaking through to her cold skin, and the droplets on her coat had dripped a course down onto her bum, with the result being sodden knickers.

She tried to dry the dogs off as best as she could with a tea towel and stripped down to her underwear, hanging the dripping coat over the back of the utility room door. On close inspection of the washing machine, she discovered to her delight that it was a washer and dryer, perfect for drying off today's wet gear, and she could also bring her dirty washing over at some point to wash and dry in return for more dog walking. Just maybe on a drier day.

She crept up the stairs to find a dressing gown to wear whilst her clothes were in the dryer. She felt guilty as though she was intruding into parts of the house that she hadn't been invited into, but she couldn't stand around the house shivering in the nude whilst the clothes spun around the dryer. The upstairs was as untidy as the lounge, with a small box room that was floor to ceiling with junk. The room next to that was clearly baby Aidan's room, with more toys, nappies, dummies and miniature clothes strewn over most surfaces. Across the landing from the bathroom was a master bedroom with king size bed, the marital quarters thought Abigail, padding on tip toe into the room, paranoid that she was being watched. There was a black silk dressing gown hanging on the back of the door, so Abigail was grateful she didn't have to wade through the ankle deep tide of discarded clothing on the floor to try and find something to wear. She slipped on the dressing gown and still couldn't tell whether it was Kate's or Callum's.

Once the clothes were spinning happily she made a "to do" list for the day. Her mind felt calmer if she had some structure to work against.

1.	Tidy Up
2.	Ironing
3.	Hoover

Computer jobs
| 4. | – Finish Wits End survey (print?) |
| 5. | – Write Blog |

6.　　　　– Order groceries for Mrs. Angel
7.　　　　– Set up Facebook site for April Smith clothing + message Nadine
8.　　　　Watch "where in the world"

After 5pm
9.　　　　– Dress fitting for Penny

She looked at the mess in the lounge, pulled up the sleeves on her dressing gown and made a start. The downstairs was transformed in no time, with toys tidied away, newspapers folded and stacked, the ironing completed and now piled neatly in a basket, and the carpet vacuumed clear of crumbs, dog hair, and pieces of unidentified grime. It wasn't going to stay that clean for very long, but Abigail was pleased with the end result. She felt she'd earned the session on the computer.

Firing up the internet browser, she navigated to her blog page and let her fingers type away once more.

One girl and her tent – Part Two
April Smith
Wednesday 10ᵗʰ April

There is another picture in the boardroom of the office that is also an inspirational image, designed to motivate employees. It shows a wild sea crashing against rocks with a quote from Mark Twain that reads, "The worst loneliness is not to be comfortable with yourself."

I have now spent several days in the small village, and I feel I am working hard to overcome the things that put me out of my comfort zone. I have befriended an elderly lady in the village; I've yet to learn her Christian name – she is from the era where respect for your elders dictates that she is referred to as "Mrs." - but I will call her Angel. She is in her 90s but seems to have little help or support from family or friends, so I embarked on an afternoon of gardening for her. I've never used a lawn mower or pair of secateurs in my life, but what's to fear? The sense of reward I felt from tidying up her modest piece of garden in an afternoon was immense.

My next achievement was getting on a horse for the first time. I started off by plucking up the courage to stroke the beast and then actually sat on its back and let myself be led around for twenty minutes. OK, I wasn't galloping or jumping jumps, but baby steps, eh? Today I have walked dogs for the first time. They clearly loved it, and although I got soaking wet (and I'm a bit exhausted because I'm not used to exercise!) I got pleasure from taking the time to look at the beauty of the countryside around me.

So what does this all have to do with Mark Twain? Well, over the past few days I've been looking back more and more at the previous me; the girl who left London as a selfish, narrow minded temp who was only happy in the confines of her comfort zone, only bothering to do what she knew she could do. And I'm really not comfortable with being that girl now I taste the other riches of life. I'm embarrassed to think that my mantra for life was to sit and wait around for a rich man to come and fall in love with me; look after me so that I wouldn't have to take any risks to survive. I always wished for something more, yet never bothered to think about how I was going to get it.

I'm not sure that this makes me lonely, either now or before, when I was blissfully unaware that I could change as a person. But it does make me question what loneliness really is. I would have said that Angel is a lonely lady. She lives alone; her family lives a long way away and never makes the effort to visit. Whilst everyone in the village knows Angel, they all have busy lives and don't take the time to check she's OK. If there's one thing I'd like to achieve before my time here runs out, is to change that.

I may need to take some action out of my comfort zone to achieve that, but I'll let you know how I get on…

Abigail only had to click one icon and the blog was live. She saw that three people had read her blog from Sunday night, picking up some of the keywords from search engine results. She wondered who those three people were. Who had the time to find her needle in the haystack that was the Internet?

Eddie and Jeremy were both quiet for once, sleeping at her feet in the study. Abigail wasn't sure if they were allowed in the study, not with Kate even being banned from the room for being "a dozy mare". But Callum wasn't here, and they were thankfully worn out from the walk that morning.

She barely registered that it was lunchtime, tenaciously finishing the work that she'd promised people. The questionnaire for Dan's Mum, printed off for her to review and saved on a datastick that Abigail always carried around in her handbag. Next, she took Mrs. Angel's shopping list, set her up an account with the only supermarket that would deliver out to the Sloth area, and in twenty minutes had placed all the items into a virtual basket, checked out and made a mental note to visit Mrs. Angel on Saturday afternoon when it would arrive.

She was so engrossed in her task that she hadn't registered that Eddie and Jeremy had stirred, and left their sleepy spot on the floor beside her. The faint sound of playful growling and the thump of canine bodies jumping on and off the sofa drifted in from the lounge, but Abigail remained dedicated to the tasks in hand.

The final task on the computer had purposefully been saved for last as something to look forward to. Using her webmail address, Abigail set up a new Facebook site with the intention of being able to message Nadine from it. She set it up under the name "April Smith bespoke fashion". It may come in handy one day, she figured, if she could ever make a career out of her designs.

She thought long and hard about what image to use. It would need to be something recognizable to Nadine, so that she would pay attention to the message and realize it was from her. But she couldn't use a picture of her own face; it was too risky that the police may pick up on it.

She glanced down and remembered Callum softly stroking her wrist and the gentle way he ran a finger over her bracelet. The bracelet – of course. Using the built in webcam on the computer, Abigail made several attempts to capture an image of the bracelet depicting the word "Ab" in colourful rainbow threads. When she was happy with the picture, it was deftly uploaded onto the Facebook page and Abigail felt pleased with her efforts.

From her newly created site, she looked up Nadine's limited profile and clicked the link to send a message. She would have to word this very carefully, she figured, in case the police were monitoring poor Nadine's account in the hope of tracking Abigail down.

Hi Nadine,

We were at uni together on the same course - I hope you remember me. Just to let you know I'm doing fine and living over in Gloucestershire at the moment. I'm just about to set up and launch my own clothing range and wondered whether you'd be kind enough to like my Facebook page so that you can keep up to date with the latest designs.

Hope all is well, it would be nice to hear from you.
April

She clicked the send button and prayed that Nadine would realise that April Smith was of course her. Abigail smiled at the thought of her friend and reasoned that there was no way she wouldn't recognize the bracelet and put two and two together. Nadine was switched on at the best of times.

An almighty crash and the unmistakable sound of smashing glass from the lounge drew Abigail's attention back to the current time and with a sinking heart she rose from the office chair and went to investigate. The beagles, completely oblivious to the fact there was a large pool of water and hundreds of scattered shards of glass strewn across the lounge floor, were still chasing each other around the sofa.

Abigail took in the sight to ascertain what had happened and concluded that one of the excitable beasts must have launched himself at the window sill to try and escape a nip from the other, bringing down the hefty vase of largely dead roses, which smashed quite conclusively on the edge of the coffee table.

"Come on you two," she ordered with as much authority as she could muster. "Get in the kitchen while I clear this up."

It was a textbook example of distraction. How that one clumsy canine event caused a chain of other events that took Abigail's attention away from everything she'd just done in the study and kept her distracted until it was time to leave to head off to Fry's farm.

Shutting the beagles in the kitchen made her remember that she was still wearing the dressing gown, so the next priority was reclaiming the warm laundered clothes from the dryer and getting dressed again. Then tracking down old newspaper to wrap the broken glass in, and clearing up the spilled water and combing through every inch of carpet to check that each shard of glass was reclaimed and binned.

She had just about finished that task when the sound of Kate bustling through the back door further distracted her. She had Aidan in her arms, a Tesco carrier bag swinging from each wrist, both stuffed full of groceries.

"Hiya!" she called cheerily, crashing in to the kitchen. Abigail stepped forward to take Aidan from her arms so that she could put the carrier bags down on the kitchen counter top. Five o'clock already, Abigail observed. Time flies.

"Plop him on the sofa and stick the telly on – there should be a cartoon or something to keep him occupied. I'll put the kettle on. I'm gasping," she said, sliding out of her coat and hanging it in the cupboard under the stairs. She glanced around the lounge, taking a while to work out what was different. "You've tidied up, thanks."

Her fleeting lack of gratitude was slightly deflating for Abigail compared to the amount of effort that she felt she'd put in, but Abigail remembered that above all, she was still very much in her debt. Abigail explained about the vase as Kate fussed around making tea, glancing through the lounge door now and then to check Aidan was OK. Fully engrossed in some fast moving noisy cartoon, he was fine.

"That old vase was a pain anyway," she replied dismissively. "Callum brings me back flowers every time he rides a winner – if he remembers. It's become a bit of a tradition, but secretly I find it a bit of a pain because I forget about them and they wither and drop petals everywhere and the water goes a yucky colour and stinks and they generally end up looking awful."

Abigail recalled that the flowers she had cleared up within the past hour were indeed skanky and well past their best, and wondered how long it had been since Callum last rode a winner. She also explained that she had enjoyed walking Eddie and Jeremy and she was happy to help out anytime.

"Oh, that's great. Actually, Friday would be a big help," concurred Kate. "I start a bit earlier on a Friday, so that'll save me half an hour."

"Would you mind if I brought a few smalls over and used your washing machine?" Abigail asked.

"Of course not," Kate breezed. "Help yourself."

Kate handed Abigail a cup of tea and indicated to go through to the lounge, where they could keep a better eye on Aidan. Kate sat next to her toddler on the sofa and pulled him onto her lap, securing him around the waist with one arm, the other nursing her cup of tea. Abigail winced, visioning the cup slipping and scolding hot tea all over the little man, but she remained silent. Kate's child, Kate's house, Kate's rules.

"Do you get lonely with Callum being away all the time?" Abigail asked. It was a question that she'd pondered a lot since meeting the couple. Kate took a sip of tea and screwed up her nose.

"Not really. I find myself so busy that I barely notice when he is here. And he's pretty useless anyway, so when he is here, he's not much help."

Abigail hadn't expected that reply and thought that it must be sad to be in a marriage that you were both too busy to appreciate. It struck Abigail that Kate never seemed to be proud of Callum. Even Mandy had expressed more admiration for his achievements than Kate seemed to do.

"You don't ever go to watch him race?" Abigail questioned.

"I can't bear to watch him race," she replied decisively. "It's such a dangerous profession that I can't bear to see him fall. Which he does quite often. I just wait for the phone call from the ambulance or hospital. Saturday will be the worst day of the year for me; he's riding in the Grand National, so the chances of him suffering a fall are quite high. There's no way I can watch the race, not even on the telly."

"But what if he won?" Abigail challenged. "You'd miss his glorious moment!"

"Oh if he won they would replay the scene over and over on the news channels, so I'd get to see it then. Can you imagine if he won? He'd have the biggest head in the village."

She leant forward and to Abigail's relief, put her mug of tea on the coffee table in front of her and sat back more comfortably on the sofa. The movement seemed to break Aidan's trance from the TV screen and he turned his head towards the two girls as if seeing them for the first time.

"Bunny gone," he blurted out, waving a chubby finger in the direction of the TV screen.

"Yes, bunny gone," confirmed Kate, ruffling her son's curls affectionately. Aidan seemed satisfied that his assumption was correct and turned his attention back to the animated action.

"He's great isn't he?" Kate said to Abigail, and it took her a moment to realize that she was referring to Aidan rather than Callum. "When I look at him, he's a complete blend of Callum and me. His hair is most definitely Callum's," she tousled the dark locks again, much to Aidan's irritation as he squirmed in protest. "I can't get my hair looking this silky, and mine would never curl like that. But his eyes are mine."

Abigail looked between mother and child and noticed that the eyes were the same soft almond colour, with beautiful silky eyelashes framing them. Callum's eyes were much darker, dangerous and piercing as they looked straight at you. "And there's no doubt where he gets his cheeky little smile and laugh from." Kate tickled Aidan around his waist and he wriggled and squealed in pleasure. As she stopped tickling, he looked around at his mum with a wicked grin. Yep, that's a carbon copy of Callum, thought Abigail. Aidan, quickly forgetting the tickles, turned back to the TV and was quickly transfixed again by the animated bunnies running across the screen being unsuccessfully chased by a fat cartoon fox.

"So do you worry about Callum around other girls while he's away?" Abigail asked, getting back to the original subject in hand. She remembered his flirtation in the study on Sunday night. She may have simply misread the signals, but it seemed overly forward given that they'd only just met. Unless it was the Southern Irish way.

"Nah, it's very much a man's world," she replied dismissively. "He spends far too much time with other naked jockeys for my liking, and God knows what filth they talk about amongst themselves." She leant forward and drained her tea before putting her empty cup on the coffee table – the first piece of mess that would surely multiply by Friday. "There are a few female jockeys around and quite a lot of girl grooms, but he generally keeps male company when he's away."

Abigail unconsciously stroked her bracelet and hoped for Kate's sake that was the case.

Thursday already

Nadine adored people watching. It was a muggy Thursday in London, and with nothing better to do, she had wandered aimlessly from her flat in Tower Hamlets and strolled west with no particular destination in mind. She'd joined the canal at Limehouse Cut and as she ambled alongside the canal she wondered idly whether to see if she could browse some funky t-shirts at Spitalfields market, or lose herself in some books at Canning town library. A BBC2 documentary on Captain Scott a few nights previously had fuelled her interest in the Antarctic expeditions and she pondered taking some books out of the library to read up further about these fascinating trips.

She was too warm to be bothered to make many decisions about what exactly she should fill her time with today, and after two hours her feet had led her to the leafy tree lined avenues through St James Park where workers were munching shop bought sandwiches out of plastic packaging on the benches alongside the lake. Groups of Mums sat on the grass on blankets with pushchairs and a mountain of paraphernalia that accompanies any trip with young children, surrounded by home made food in tupperware containers, flasks, plastic cups and toys to keep the youngsters entertained for a couple of hours.

Spying an empty bench and scanning it to make sure its surface was clear of bird poo, she sat with a contented sigh, happy to take the weight off her feet for a few minutes. It was the perfect spot for people watching and she idly tried to guess which couples were grabbing a few illicit minutes together. A lot of the people passing by were tourists; every skin colour, age and nationality, cutting through the park on their way to or from seeing the surrounding Royal hotspots. A visitor's itinery to London wasn't complete without ticking off Buckingham palace, the Mall and maybe St James's Palace. Horseguards Parade and Downing Street could also be included at the same time.

There was one! She spied a couple sat on the grass about fifty metres away. They were both dressed in suits, although he had shed his jacket for her to sit on, her legs tucked beside her, as her tight pencil skirt didn't afford much opportunity to sit cross legged as he was doing. She was slightly leant into his body, his protective arm wrapped around her waist, and every now and again he would lean down and plant a loving kiss on her temple. Nadine's eyes scanned down to the lady's left hand. Wedding ring. And his left hand, curled around her ribs? Wedding ring. If they were married to each other, they wouldn't be making out in a public park in the middle of the working day. Would they? Nadine was cynical.

"Excuse me, do you happen to have the time?" A young tanned man wearing casual jeans and a t-shirt, passing by the path in front of her, broke Nadine's attention. Nice, she thought, I could make out with him in the middle of the day any time.

"Er...yeah," she pulled herself together and fished her phone from the depths of her scruffy corduroy bag. "Just gone half twelve," she replied.

"Cheers," the man smiled, and made off on his way towards the Mall, leaving Nadine watching his departure in disappointment. Obviously not a chat up line then, he did need to know the time. She sighed and went to put her smartphone back in her bag, when she spotted a small notification mark on the Facebook icon on the screen. Half past twelve and I've not even checked Facebook today, she marvelled at herself. It was often the first thing she did when she woke up.

Usually the notification was something dull, often somebody had tagged her in a post or a photo, or there were bonus points to be had on one of the addictive games you can play through the Facebook login, maybe someone had checked in nearby to her? So she was chuffed to see someone had sent her a friend request. She clicked into the icon. Somebody called April Smith. She frowned, the name meant nothing to her, but as soon as she saw April's profile picture a lump rushed to her throat and tears pricked at her eyes.

There was Abigail's bracelet, bold and colourful, the word "Ab" stitched clearly across the centre of the photo.

"Oh you clever girl," murmured Nadine to herself, realizing instantly that Abigail had set herself up as a fictitious person on Facebook to make contact. She read the message with her heart bursting, grateful that Abigail was safe and well. Gloucestershire? What an odd choice of location.

Nadine instantly accepted the friend request and went to send a message back. There was no way she was going to play along with the fictional April Smith rubbish though.

"Abigail, So grateful that you've been able make contact," she typed, her ugly bitten fingers speeding over the keys in haste. *"Please come home, you're not in trouble and we're all really worried about you. We miss you like crazy. XXX."*

She was just about to click to send the message when she wondered whether Abigail was stuck without cash and had no way of getting home. Maybe this was a cryptic call for help. As an afterthought, she added *"PS : If you need the guys to come and get you, they'll come and pick you up in the van. Are you really in Gloucestershire??"*

She clicked the send icon and felt rejuvenated. Abigail was safe after all, not laying dead and rotting in a ditch somewhere, or living off the street being abused by pimps and drug addicts. The thought made Nadine smile to herself. A celebratory scout around Spitalfields market was just what she'd treat herself to she decided, rising from the bench and heading off in the direction of the sexy stranger.

Yes, Abigail was fine, and had been in her element that Thursday morning, helping Sam with his quest for flat hunting. The rain of the previous day had vanished, and Thursday was warm and exactly how spring should be; bursting with optimism and full of blue sky with fluffy white cotton wool clouds. Abigail had been gazing at the sky as she stood at the end of the driveway of Wits End, waiting for Sam's mum to come driving along from Lower Maisey as arranged to pick her up. Like many people across the generations, it had been a childhood game to make shapes out of the clouds. That one looked like a spiky dragon, dragging toilet roll on his back foot. And that blobby one looked like a map outline of Wales.

"What's she waiting for?" asked Mandy, twitching the lounge net curtain.

"Who, April? Dunno, she didn't say," replied Dan with a lack of interest. He was fitting new laces to his football boots after the old ones snapped at last Sunday's evening practice.

"Say? When? When did you speak to her?" Mandy's receptors stood to attention and she turned away from the window to study her boyfriend's face.

"Ten minutes ago. She came in to drop that survey thing off for Mum. She's done a pretty good job." He flicked his eyes to the dining table and Mandy instantly made her way over to inspect the work that Abigail had prepared. She scanned her eyes over the printed page. It was certainly neat and precise. She read through the questions, and to her irritation, couldn't find fault with any of it.

"Hmm, she only dropped off one copy then. That's not much good, is it?"

Dan put down his boots, which were now fully laced. New laces always looked odd against the worn leather and dried remnants of mud.

"She's left a datastick with the document on so Mum can alter anything she doesn't like, and print off as many copies as she needs."

Mandy made a 'humph' sound and tossed the paper back onto

the table. Typical girly swot, she thought, she seemed to think of everything. She wandered back to the window and peered back out over the lane.

"She's a bit dressed up isn't she? And what's with her hat? Doesn't she realize this is sleepy Gloucestershire, not the Chelsea High Street?" Dan was clearly ignoring her. "Oh, she's getting a taxi."

Abigail had not expected a taxi to turn up and was still therefore watching a Sherman tank shaped cloud roll lazily across the Sloth sky as the black Nissan Sunny slowed to a stop before her. She'd had the forethought to pull her hair up into a tight plait and hook it up inside the beany hat that she'd bought before fleeing London. There would be far more CCTV cameras in Cheltenham than in Sloth, and she didn't want to take the risk of being identified.

She glanced up, expecting the driver to wind down the window to ask for directions, and jumped to see Sam waving at her from the passenger seat. She settled into the back seat with a polite greeting.

"Mum's not coming after all," Sam explained, craning his neck awkwardly to regard her in the back. "She's not feeling too well, so it's just you and I."

"No problem, hope it's nothing serious," she replied.

"No," Sam responded with a sigh. "Just a headache and stuff. You look nice by the way." He turned back to look where they were going. Abigail had made an effort with the little clothing choices left available to her. It felt like an adventure to be heading to the City after the trappings of the village, and so she had paired up one of the prettier floral tops she'd bought at the jumble sale with her tight black work pencil skirt and heels. Sam wore a plain white t-shirt and mouldy green capri shorts. She guessed his clothing choices were limited with plaster on his leg.

She watched the taxi meter climb over the five pounds mark before they'd even passed the "Thank you for driving carefully" sign to signal the end of the village. She was glad she wasn't paying, and prayed that Sam wasn't expecting her to fund the return trip. She mulled the etiquette over in her mind as they travelled along the lanes in comfortable silence. The Ashingtons had definitely invited her to join them, and it was Mrs Ashington that was ill and thus creating the need for a taxi. Surely there was no expectation for her to pay. She reversed the situation in her brain; a trick she's learnt to try and see things from other people's perspective. If she'd been driving and invited Sam along and then hurt her foot and couldn't drive, would she expect Sam to offer to pay for the taxi? No. But then that was her. Not everyone is like me, she figured.

"Is there anywhere in particular you need dropping?" Sam asked, breaking her train of thought. He consulted a piece of A4 paper in his lap. "I'm starting at Wellington Square, but we can let you out anywhere."

Abigail shrugged. "I really have no idea where anywhere is in Cheltenham." She leaned in further between the two front seats. "Are they the details of the flats you're going to see?"

"Yeah, Mum got them for me. There's four different places here, but they all look pretty similar to me." He held the paperwork out towards her, which she took as an invitation to take from him to glance over. Oh my God, these were posh flats. Brand spanking new, posh, high-end penthouse flats. She just had to see these!

"I'm happy to come with you to look over these if you need some female input," she suggested, trying to sound nonchalant when every fibre of her body was aching to nosy around these bachelor pads. These were the homes of premier league footballers. She glanced at the price tag of the Wellington Square development. Half a million pounds. Good grief. That wouldn't get you much in London, but it wasn't exactly the typical first time buyer price tag either.

"If you don't mind," replied Sam gratefully. "I have no clue really what I'm looking for."

"It's going to be costly to move out of your parents you know," she began. "You've got to think not only of the initial outlay of buying, but there's all the costs associated with moving, then all the bills you'll have to factor in; council tax, water, gas, insurance..." she stopped as she realised Sam was grinning at her.

"What?"

"There was me thinking I'd left my mother at home."

She hit him with the papers playfully and handed them back to him. "I'm just trying to help. I was hoping to move out, but when I sat down and did the sums I just couldn't even scrape together the deposit, let alone make the living costs work out for me." But then, I haven't got rich old daddy to bank roll me, she thought enviously. "Don't forget you're also going to have to buy the furniture to go in all these rooms."

"Well, just leave the finances to me," was all he offered in reply, as the taxi pulled into the kerb. Considering they were less than a mile or so from the town centre, the leafy street was quiet and snaked around a large green square. All the houses overlooked the square, most of them imposing white regency buildings with steps up to the grand front doors, and vast windows that would allow the sunlight to pour in. The location reminded Abigail of areas of Kensington, although the tall terraced properties of South West

London were nearly all guesthouses these days.

Sam paid the taxi fare, which had risen over the fifteen pounds mark, and wrestled his leg out of the front seat.

"This is it." He indicated a dominant white block that stood alone in the corner of the square, a black railing fence guarding it protectively from the pavement. Once upon a time this would have been an amazing family home, like something out of the costume dramas Abigail liked to watch on TV, with servants below stairs and spoilt children playing with vast dolls houses in their well stocked nurseries. In the 21st Century though it had been carved into several flats – or apartments as the literature described them. The American term probably meant they could charge an extra £50,000. Developers had clearly stripped out the history from the core of the building and replaced it with trendy modern living.

They walked into the sales office, tucked in one of the downstairs front rooms. A short, plump lady leapt up from behind the desk, immediately offering a neatly manicured hand to shake.

"Well hello there," she gushed. "You've come to look over our amazing show flats have you?" Abigail studied her make up critically, as she had a tendency to do. The foundation was flawless, but she'd overdone the blusher slightly and the greys in the eye shadow were probably a little too heavy for daywear. "I'm Sally, and you are...?"

"Sam."

"April."

"Lovely! Well, welcome to Wellington Court. We have a range of apartments on offer, from our 2 bedroom inner apartments, to the 3 bedroom apartments that have terraces and views over the square. We've got a show apartment of each. Were you interested in the 2 bedroom?"

Although her voice was light and bouncy, Sally was used to young couples coming purely to nose around the show flats, with clearly no budget to be in a position to buy. Unless she could smell the money, she tried to put youngsters off at the first hurdle by offering them the bottom of the ladder.

"I think I'd like to see the 3 bedroom," replied Sam. He waggled the paperwork in his hand. "I understand you have a top floor penthouse."

A flicker of irritation crossed Sally's face for the briefest of moments. "Right. Well, let me start by taking down your details." She returned to her side of the desk and opened a leather binder and took up her fountain pen. So it is Mr and Mrs....?"

"Mr Ashington," replied Sam, who seemed oblivious to the power play that Abigail could sense Sally was playing. "April's a friend that's helping me today."

Sally's pen paused in mid air and she suddenly regarded him with a look of recognition. "Ah, Sam Ashington, you're the..."

"Yes, one of the Ashingtons from up the road," he interrupted her abruptly. Her face beamed as she suddenly realized that these people weren't time wasters after all. She abandoned her plan to take down their details and fished around in a key cabinet for the corresponding bunch to the penthouse flat.

"Right, well I'll take you up to have a look at the penthouse flat. It really is amazing, and I'm sure it's going to be snapped up very quickly." She regarded Sam's leg in plaster. "Luckily it's accessed by a lift, so come with me..."

Obediently they followed her across the shiny laminated floor back out into the hallway as she described how the ground floor would also be converted into 2 flats once the upper floors were sold, and this would become the communal entrance hallway to all properties. The lift was already waiting for them on the ground floor and they stepped in, and stood in awkward silence for a few seconds as it made its gentle ascent.

"Can I just say how sorry I was to hear about your uncle," Sally said in a muted tone, touching Sam briefly on his forearm. Abigail tried not to frown as Sam mumbled his thanks. "So tragic," Sally sighed and looked at Abigail for agreement. Politely Abigail nodded, wondering what had happened to his uncle. She only remembered one uncle being mentioned and that was the one that ran the Carpenter's Arms. As far as she was aware, there was no tragedy there.

The lift doors serenely opened with a gentle ping, and the moment was broken. They stepped out into another large hallway, with only one front door leading off from it. Sally opened the door, and stood aside to let Sam and Abigail enter ahead of her. Light poured into the apartment through the glass windows that stretched the full length of the open plan lounge from floor to ceiling, stretching right through to the kitchen and diner. It was the most amazing space Abigail had ever seen in real life.

"I'll leave you two to explore on your own," said Sally. "Just bring the keys back on down when you're ready. Take your time."

She retreated out of the apartment, her four-inch heels clacking on the gleaming oak floors. Sam and Abigail stood in silence in the middle of the space, drinking it all in. The glass dining table was neatly set up for a dinner party, complete with a vase of fresh roses and candelabra. Tiny spotlights in the ceiling needlessly illuminated the glass and silverware further.

"Wow." Abigail didn't know what else to say. This was the

sort of place she could settle into with Raul Delgado and hold dinner parties for the premiership hot shots and their wives and girlfriends. She wandered over to the kitchen area and ran a finger over the polished marble countertops.

"This is amazing. Do you cook?" She asked Sam.

"I can do a mean beans on toast," he replied with a grin. Her heart sank a little. This was a kitchen for cooking in. There was so much space, and the oak cupboards went on forever.

"Would you really need something this extravagant?" she questioned. It was bothering her that as a first time buyer, he would be moving into a three-bedroom place with nobody to share the space, nobody to cook in the amazing kitchen. "It seems a waste to have just little old you rattling around in here, making your beans on toast with one tiny saucepan on the stove."

"I do them in the microwave actually," he replied. Great. Abigail's heart sank further. She opened and closed a few cupboard doors just to feel the softness of the way they melted back into position with none of the crash and bang with which her parents' kitchen units snapped shut.

"Ooh, a built in wine fridge!" she enthused.

"It's the ultimate party pad, don't you think?" he replied, swinging himself over to the brown leather sofas in the lounge area. "Can you imagine what wicked parties I could hold here? I'd have MTV blasting from the large plasma screen here, and I'd invite some of the lads from the yards, people from the village, Charly and her friends. Shame there's no hot tub on the patio, she's got some hot friends."

Abigail moved over to join him at the sofas. "So you're spending all this money in the hope you'll get laid?" Her tone was confrontational, and Sam was momentarily taken aback. He blushed.

"Callum says that I should be getting a lot more lady action given my...uh.. connections, so it's not the *only* reason, but I'm hardly attracting the fairer sex living at home, am I?"

"Any girl that sleeps with you just because she's impressed by the apartment really isn't worth sleeping with at all."

Abigail realized the hypocrisy of the statement, given her thoughts about Raul Delgado a few moments earlier, but when she reversed the situation to apply to Sam, it seemed all wrong. He was lovely enough to warrant a girlfriend without the showy trappings.

Peevishly Sam moved over to the sliding patio doors that led out to the terrace. From the fourth floor, the views over the sleepy square below and the skyline of the City beyond were breathtaking.

"I'm sorry, I shouldn't have said that. I've upset you now," she apologized as he slid the doors open. He paused and looked at her. She was looking down at her feet.

"No you haven't," he replied quietly. "I'm just going out here to have a think."

Abigail decided to leave him alone and padded off to look around the bedrooms. Aside from the showy master bedroom with the oversized mirror and walk in wardobes, the other two bedrooms were small and disappointing by comparison. Bedroom 3 was an odd shape; long and thin, so would have to be used just to store junk, as it was barely large enough for a single bed, nor square enough for a study.

Surprisingly there was no ensuite, just a family bathroom for the occupants of all bedrooms to share. It was spacious and gleaming, but Abigail found her enthusiasm for the apartment was waning. She'd gatecrashed Sam's morning, and then upset his plans by throwing a spanner in the works. She hated herself for it.

She crossed back over the expanse of the open plan living area and hovered at the patio doors. Sam was sat on the bistro style chairs that circled a small glass table, staring out into nothing.

"The bedrooms are a bit disappointing," she clarified, wandering over the balcony and taking the seat next to him. He glanced up at her and managed a feeble smile. "Don't pay any attention to what comes out of my mouth," she continued, "It's your money, your investment, and you're free to buy whatever you like. If you want a party pad, you buy a party pad."

They sat in silence for a few moments, Abigail feeling slightly awkward. "Do you want to go and see another one?" she asked.

Sam shrugged. "I guess they're all going to be much of a muchness," he conceded, flicking through the estate agents details. "They're all oversized, showy and come with a sickening price tag."

"Well, tell you what, do you fancy going to have coffee instead? My treat?"

Sam nodded and seemed to shake himself out of the dark mood that had descended over him. Telling Sally that they may be back with Sam's Mum for a second opinion, they left the building and drifted off towards town. It was slow going, with Sam swinging himself along on crutches and Abigail's tight skirt limiting the length of her stride, but it wasn't far enough to warrant calling another taxi.

"I can leave you in the coffee shop whilst I go and get the ribbon if you like," Abigail offered, "rather than dragging you around boring shops on your crutches." They were taking the short cut that Sam knew through the quiet back streets as the residential gave way to commercial properties.

"Nah, I need to fetch a few bits for the party on Sunday, so we could split up for an hour and meet back somewhere."

Abigail stopped dead and was gaping through the window of a small back street boutique. "Oh my God, that is gorgeous." A skinny mannequin wore a floaty emerald green silk dress. Tiny diamante beads decorated the halter neckline and the swaths of fabric flowed down to the knee. Abigail knew that the dress would swish when worn.

"Oh, I like that," conceded Sam, following her eyeline. "That would look great on you at the party on Sunday." Yikes, Abigail hadn't realized that the party was that dressy. She had planned to wear jeans and a t-shirt. It was only a bar-b-que after all. But the dress was to die for.

She looked around the rest of the window display. Designer jewellery dripped off a soft velvet cushion, there was a shelf of trendy handbags and a feature on Jimmy Choos. Nothing was priced. That meant only one thing. There was no way she could afford anything in this store.

"Ah, this is the Betty Boo Boutique!" observed Sam. "I've heard people talk about this. Why don't you try the dress on?"

Abigail hesitated. She really wanted to see how that dress would feel on her, the silk caressing her skin, hugging her curves, making her feel sexy and special. But what was the point; she couldn't blow that much cash on something she didn't have the need for. She sighed. "I've got lots of dresses at home, I don't need another one," she replied, fighting the urge to cave in.

"Girls always need more dresses, come on, just try it on. You know you want to." Sam was already pushing the door to the boutique open. Had he not made the comment about getting "lady action" earlier, she would have been convinced this was the action of a gay man. No straight man wants to hang around a boutique waiting for girls to try on dresses, do they?

She grinned and acquiesced, following him into the Betty Boo Boutique. It was empty, save for a female shop assistant who was around their age who smiled in greeting as they entered. It was embarrassingly quiet too, just a Simon and Garfunkel track being played on pan pipes coming out from a small CD player on the shelf near the till. Abigail felt self-conscious as her footsteps clopped around the laminated floor.

"Here," Sam's radar spotted the dresses on the rack first. "What size do you need?"

"I'll try a ten," replied Abigail coyly, watching as he deftly flicked through the hangers before pulling out the right size. "Shame it's not St Patrick's Day on Sunday," he joked. "It'd be the right colour."

She took the dress and disappeared into the cubicle positioned by the till, wriggled out of her skirt and top, and realized that she'd have to shed the hat too, as that would spoil the effect. She removed her bra; the halterneck not being designed for bra straps to show on the shoulder.

"I want a fashion show," called Sam from beyond the curtain. There was no mirror inside the cubicle anyway, she realized, so she would have to step out onto the shop floor. She slid the silk over her head and could already feel the transformation taking place as the dress unravelled itself around her curves. The side zip pulled the bustier tighter around her chest, nudging her boobs up and pulling her waist in. The skirt was so lightweight it felt as though she had nothing on below the hips.

She stepped out from behind the curtain and Sam's jaw dropped. The bored sales assistant raised her neatly plucked eyebrows.

"That looks amazing!" she said. "There's a mirror here, look."

Abigail sashayed to the mirror, loving the feel of the material as it swung in time with her footsteps. She regarded herself and had to admit it looked every bit as good as it felt.

The door to the shop clanged opened and a young couple bustled in. It was typical, thought Abigail that there probably hadn't been a customer in here all day and now there was a rush on. The shop floor was barely big enough to accommodate them all.

"Hey it's ginge!" The man greeted, giving Sam a friendly shove on the shoulder. "Or should I say 'hop along ginge'? How are you doing Buddy?"

"All right, how are you?" Sam looked genuinely pleased to see the friend. Accompanying him, Abigail observed a carbon copy of her London self. A petite blonde, with designer sunglasses pushed up onto her forehead. Abigail glanced down to see a neatly tailored trouser suit, designer handbag and ballet pumps. She was stunningly pretty, not a thick eyelash out of place, and on the surface, way out of the league of the rough and ready lad she was with.

"This is my friend April," Sam introduced. "April, this is Luke, and his fiancé Harriet. Luke's one of the jockeys that occasionally rides for my dad."

Before they could even shake hands, Harriet was running a dainty manicured hand down the silk skirt of the dress that Abigail was wearing. "That's the dress in the window," she breathed in admiration. "It looks like it was made for you. Are you going to get it for the party on Sunday?"

Shit, pressure. "Oh I'm not sure. It seems a bit extravagant, and I need to save all my pennies at the moment," Abigail replied.

"Well get Mr Gingernuts here to buy it for you," suggested Luke, ruffling Sam's hair. Sam squirmed as he tried unsuccessfully to duck from Luke's touch. Abigail sensed that he was probably used to this sort of banter, but she felt a protective wave sweep over her.

"Oh, he's barely ginger," she replied, trying to divert the conversation away from the purchase of the dress. "I'd say it was more a shade of Moroccan sunset."

It was a phrase that she'd heard Nadine use once before to describe a redhead friend, and thought it was quite sweet.

All three of them stared at her, and Sam raised an inquisitive eyebrow. "Very apt, I didn't think you knew anything about horses." Abigail frowned in confusion, but Harriet was already tugging Luke away towards the racy underwear in the back corner.

"I'm looking for wedding day undies, we'll see you on Sunday," she called in farewell.

Abigail retreated to the changing cubicle and reluctantly unzipped the dress, relishing the feeling as the silk slithered over her bare skin as she pulled it up over her head. She had a credit card for emergencies in her purse, and it was achingly tempting. The scenario ran in her head though, the police picking up the transaction and coming to ask the skinny shop assistant for details of the girl that made the purchase. She'd overheard everything that had just transpired, Abigail realized, so she'd be able to recall that the purchaser was with a ginger lad with a broken leg, who knew Harriet and Luke – a jockey that rode for the ginger lad's Dad. The police would add two and two together before you could say "silk" and the Ashingtons would have a line of police cars on their impressive driveway by morning. She couldn't afford the risk, let alone the dress. She checked the price tag. Fuck. £175.

"I'll think about it," she sighed, reluctantly hanging it back in its place on the sparse rack.

"Let me get it for you," Sam offered in a whisper. "Seriously," he added, seeing the dubious look on her face. "To say thank you for helping me out this morning."

"Don't be silly, I was no help at all. It's only a dress, and you can't be spending your hard earned pub wages on me like that."

Sam shrugged and backed down, suggesting that they split up now for an hour and then meet up once they'd done their separate jobs.

"Oh," Sam said, hesitating as they began to make her way out of the boutique. "You go ahead. I'll just ask Harriet if she's going to the bookies, she can place some bets for me. Do you want her to put anything on the Grand National for you?"

Abigail shrugged. "I have no idea who's running, so you'd better choose." She rummaged around in her bag and pulled a ten pound note loose from the wad in her purse. She'd seen people hand over ten pound notes in the bookies in the soap operas, so hazarded a guess that she wasn't overdoing it. "Ten pounds on whatever you think." He grinned and took the note from her.

"I know the perfect horse. As long as you don't mind me going on its name rather than the form."

"As long as it's got four legs, I'm happy with anything," she confirmed, and headed off in the direction of the high street. A ten-minute trip to a large department store allowed her to scoop up all the sewing materials she needed to finish Penny's dress, as well as a packet of sensible pants so that she would have some to wear the following morning. Along the road, she spotted the library that she'd gone into on her first arrival in Cheltenham just a week ago, and found herself wandering in once again. A bank of PCs buzzed away in the corner under a sign that read "Public access computers". On closer inspection, she realized that she'd need to have a library card to access a machine, so there was no hope of checking April's fake Facebook page today to see whether Nadine had replied.

To waste a little more time, she wandered into a charity shop to see whether there were any knockout dresses that she could buy for Sunday's party. There were a few contenders with decent labels, but in the wrong size. Everything in a size ten would suit her mother or a fourteen year old.

She was still ten minutes early returning to the coffee shop, so was surprised to see that Sam had already beaten her back and was flopped into one of the banquette seats at the back of the café, nursing a black coffee.

"I was going to treat you to coffee," she scolded, placing her tray down on the table. She decanted her large caramel latte with a double chocolate muffin onto the table and took the seat beside him. Heaven. "Did you want something to eat?" she asked. "It's lunchtime."

"Nah, I'm not hungry," he replied, sipping at his drink.

"Oh, I am." She took a large bite from her sticky muffin and relished the feel of the chocolate melting into her gums.

"If you're hungry then you should be eating something nutritional, rather than that crap. It's full of empty calories."

Abigail stopped chewing and put her muffin down in disbelief. Was he really lecturing her on diet? "It's tasty though," she replied defensively.

"When your body tells you that it's hungry, it's asking for

nourishment, not something that simply tastes good. You're a typical comfort eater, aren't you?" His tone was accusing, and deep down Abigail knew he was right. Her defensiveness kicked in.

"What would you know about my eating habits anyway?" she retorted. She looked back at the muffin and it suddenly appeared far less appealing. It was just a blob of sugar and fat.

"I saw you had sticky toffee pudding at the pub on Monday, you've told me about all the crap that Mrs. Angel shoves at you, and about the bacon butties you've been making each morning for breakfast." Put like that, Abigail realized that the stress of the last week *had* led her straight into the arms of comfort food. She pushed the half eaten muffin away from her.

"And there was me thinking I'd left my mother back in London," she reflected back the words he'd spoken to her that morning. "You just leave the calories to me."

"I'm sorry," Sam's tone softened. "I just spend so much time making sure the horses get the right nutrition to match their performance needs, I'm a bit of a diet fanatic. I just don't want you to reach your thirties and wonder how you ended up like Fatty Em."

Abigail managed a smile. Fatty Em was a young character on a popular comedy show, with blubbering rolls of fat as her trademark joke. Sam reached into the backpack he'd been carrying around all morning, now bulging with purchases for Sunday's celebrations. "Want a banana?" He offered.

She took the fruit gratefully and put the remainder of the muffin back on the tray with some finality. "So did you get everything you needed for Sunday?" she asked, indicating the backpack.

"Yes, and I've asked Harriet to put your ten pounds on a horse called Moroccan Sunset."

"Moroccan Sunset - Seriously? I had no idea!" Abigail confessed. "Is he a favourite?"

Sam chuckled. "Erm, well, out of the forty horses running I'd say there are thirty eight or so that have a better chance than him, but the great thing about the Grand National is that it's anybody's race really." Mentally Abigail waved goodbye to her ten pounds. Glumly she realized that would have bought her a few days' worth of food in the shop, healthy or otherwise. "You get your ribbon?"

"Yes, I can get Penny's dress finished later and take it up to Fry's farm."

"Temping's going to seem a little bit dull after all this sewing," Sam observed. "Do you have anything lined up for when you go back?"

Now there was a question. A life behind bars maybe? The

agency she was signed to would certainly not be offering her any gainful employment anytime soon.

"No, there's not much out there at the moment," she lied in reply. "In fact, I may stay on in Sloth just a bit longer than I originally planned."

Sam seemed to brighten at this news. "That's great. And even when you do go home, I hope you'll keep in touch with us all."

"Of course!" She took a sip of her sweet latte and noticed the outrageous sweetness of the syrupy flavor for the first time. Maybe tea would have been a better choice. "I can't imagine going back to office work," she mused.

"Well you're lucky, at least you're educated, you've got a lot of skills, you can pretty much do anything you want to do. In fact, if I can be perfectly honest with you, I think you've wasted a lot of time in the temp world." Deep down, Abigail agreed with him. There were things she could have been doing that would have been more satisfying than temping, such as setting up her own business, or going abroad on voluntary schemes like Nadine.

"I guess I have just drifted since I graduated," she admitted. "But I wanted to save up money, to stay in my comfort zone I guess."

Sam was nodding, reflectively. "Drifted." He let the word roll around the space between them for a moment. "I feel like that too. I left school with no real qualifications that were any use, and relied on my Dad to put work my way. I'm going to be twenty five next month. I feel I should have a plan to do something more meaningful."

"Well, whatever you've done up to now seems to have worked; you're the one with the Porsche and looking at apartments that will set you back half a million pounds."

"But life's not just about money, is it?"

A week ago, Abigail would have disagreed, arguing that money can buy things that make you think you're happy, and that's better than not having money. Sitting here now, she had learnt that the value of money was different in Sloth.

Sam sighed heavily and flopped back in his velvet banquette seat. "Sorry if I'm on a bit of a downer today," he needlessly apologized. "I'm tired and my leg's throbbing, the painkillers are making me drowsy and more grumpy than usual."

The opening bars to a song come over the speakers, instantly recognizable to Abigail as the tune Fish liked to perform acoustically in Blue Steak gigs. She was instantly transported back to the time when they were arguing over which songs summed them up best. Nadine, Fish, Dougie and Craig. Just thinking about the group and the friendship between them made the coffee shop in Cheltenham feel a million miles from them. This must be what homesickness feels like, she decided, wanting nothing more than to have her parents or the Blue Steak gang walk in that door and give her a hug. It had only been a week, but it was the emptiness of the future, the uncertainty that stretched out before her that scared her most.

"It's OK, I understand," Abigail replied, realizing that she hadn't acknowledged Sam's apology. "I'm pretty tired too. I don't sleep great on the ground, then the early light and the birds tweeting at a silly hour wake me up."

Abigail thought back to Sally's words earlier that day, giving Sam sympathy for his uncle. She was aching to know the story but didn't know whether it was any of her business. It just felt as though now was a time when they were both being open and honest with each other. She drained her latte and decided to be brave.

"Sam, what happened to your uncle?"

He glanced at her in confusion momentarily, and then obviously remembered Sally's comment from that morning. He took a deep breath. Over the speakers, the lyrics were still lamenting and mournful.

"My Mum's brother, Robert. Although everyone called him Buddy. He was a pretty successful jump jockey, he rode a lot of winners for my Dad, he even won the Cheltenham Gold Cup three year's ago." Sam paused to smile proudly at the memory before continuing. "Last year, on Boxing Day he was riding in the King George at Kempton. He was out in front by at least a length when he had a horrific, crushing fall at the last fence." Sam paused again, remembering the moment in his mind. "Well, he was rushed off to hospital, airlifted, and was in a coma for days and days."

Sam's eyes had misted with tears, and Abigail instinctively reached over to place her hand over his. Without looking at her, he squeezed her fingers gently in acknowledgement. "He just never woke up. He couldn't survive that level of brain injury. He died ten days after the fall."

"That's awful," muttered Abigail.

"It may have been a blessing that he didn't survive. If he'd come out of the coma he'd probably have been brain damaged, maybe paralysed too. Mum's devastated, of course. She's not really been herself since. She doesn't sleep very well, she drinks too much and she hasn't been back to work since it happened."

"What did she do?" asked Abigail with interest.

"She worked in a small garden centre just outside Cheltenham. It's a family run place so she mucked in and did all sorts from working on the till, repotting seedlings, even helping out in the café. I think she should go back, get some routine back in her life."

"Well, I guess different people have different ways of coping. She probably just needs a bit more time." The track on the speakers had now changed to a Wham hit from the early 80s, changing the atmosphere in an instant. Abigail had been taken into a dark place listening to the lyrics that she'd heard Fish sing time and time again, but now the music choice was like a deliberate ploy to pull them both out of their morose moods. Abigail realized she was still holding Sam's hand, and she pulled it away decisively.

"I've got an idea. If we've finished in Cheltenham, why don't we go back to yours, flop on the sofas and watch some afternoon rubbish on the telly. There may be a film on, or we can shout at the dippy contestants on 'Where in the world'."

An hour later they were back at Lower Maisey, via a stop at Abigail's tent so that she could pick up Penny's dress to finish by hand whilst they watched the telly. Thankfully Sam reached for his wallet before the taxi slowed to turn into the Ashington's driveway, so Abigail presumed he was happy to pay the fare again.

"You feeling better?" Sam asked his Mum, who met them in the hallway. Abigail regarded her in a different light, armed with the knowledge of her recent grief. Dressed in a crumpled cotton dressing gown, she looked as though she had only recently got out of bed.

"Yes, thanks," she smiled, pecking him on the cheek. "Hello April. How were the flats?"

They gravitated into the kitchen, where Sam dumped his backpack on the island and started to make cold drinks. Abigail stood a little foolishly in the corner.

"Er.. nice," Sam replied hesitantly. "But I need to do a bit of thinking before I rush into anything." He poured orange juice into two glasses and Abigail stepped forward to carry them for him.

"Oh," was all Mrs. Ashington responded. Abigail couldn't make out if she was surprised or disappointed. "So we don't get rid of you that easily," she joked.

They retired to the lounge, leaving Mrs. Ashington unpacking the goodies from Sam's backpack in the kitchen. The two border collies came scampering up to them, their tails wagging madly and thumping every item of furniture in their wake. One shout from Sam for them to "get on their beds" and they retreated, tails lowered between their hind legs to go and lie on the blankets in the corner. Heads resting on their outstretched front paws, the two pairs of brown eyes stared at Sam, awaiting any next command from their master.

It was bliss to flop into the giving fabric of the sofas. Abigail missed a lot of home comforts; collapsing into the soothing embrace of a couch was one of them. Being entertained by moving images on the TV was another.

Sam made himself horizontal as soon as he'd drunk the orange juice, gratefully resting his plastered leg, and propping his head onto the scatter cushions. Abigail stayed upright to sew, resisting the urge to tickle his exposed toes that peeked through the end of the plaster.

This is nice, she thought contentedly. She reflected on the therapeutic nature of sewing and how it made her feel relaxed happy. A surrogate family who seemed welcoming and friendly surrounded her.

As if on cue, Charly returned from school, flopping on the single armchair as she greeted the pair. "How were the flats?" she asked.

Abigail waited for Sam to respond, but when he didn't, she glanced at him and realized he'd fallen asleep. She smiled at him fondly. Sleeping beauty.

"Amazing," she confessed. "Swanky and swish, with fantastic views over Cheltenham...but not sure if that's really what he's after." She lowered her voice. "I think he's a bit confused now."

"Really? I thought he had his heart set on them." Charly kicked off her shoes and tucked her legs underneath her. "But I'm glad. Personally I think he should fast forward over the playboy lifestyle and go straight for the country cottage where he can bring up some kids and teach them to ride on Grace."

"Oi, I can hear you," muttered Sam sleepily. Without opening his eyes he grabbed a spare cushion and aimed it in the direction of Charly. She caught it with lightening quick reaction.

"Well, go back to sleep and we can talk about you again," she challenged, launching the cushion back at his head. Abigail loved to see Sam and Charly bounce off each other. As an only child, she was envious of people that had great friendships with their siblings.

With Sam gently snoozing at her side, Abigail explained the concept of 'Where in the world' to Charly, who normally wasn't home from school this early. "And Mum wouldn't normally let me put the telly on anyway without doing homework or revision. But she won't tell me off with you here." Abigail hoped she hadn't started a habit for Charly after she clearly enjoyed the episode.

"Right, before I go, I'm going to entrust my sketchbook to you," Abigail said. "Have a look through and see if there are any particular dress designs you fancy for the ball dress. If not, have a look through some magazines and cut out any pictures that take your fancy. I can easily plagerise designs; I don't think Vera Wang's going to sue me."

"Cool," Charly replied, rising from her seat to see Abigail to the door. As there were gentle snores rising from Sam's lips, Abigail decided not to wake him to say goodbye. "I'll return it to you Saturday afternoon."

"Saturday?"

"Are you not coming to the Carpenters Arms to see the Grand National? Practically the whole village turns out to watch the race on the big screen there, and this year with Callum riding, it'll be a phenomenal atmosphere. It gets so busy that both Sam and I have been roped into helping out behind the bar..."

"Oh, I've got a date with Mrs. Angel I'm afraid," Abigail apologized, remembering the shopping that would be arriving. Shame, it sounded like a great party. "But if I can get away, I'll drop by. If not, I'll see you at the party on Sunday and you can give it back then."

Abigail couldn't put her finger on the reason, but she felt disloyal as she walked away from the Ashington's. The afternoon had clouded over now and she wished she had a jacket on. She thought back seven days and remembered the night at the backstreet bed and breakfast in Ilford. The sky had been grey and savage then too. It felt much longer than a week ago, so much had happened. She'd made a dress for one thing!

"It's amazing!" Penny screeched. "That extra ribbon makes the difference!" She had seen a draft of the dress the previous evening and tried it on for size, but now the finished article did bring it all together.

"Oh, that's fantastic," agreed Mrs. Fry, as Penny did a twirl in the kitchen. It was the first time that Abigail had met Penny's Mum. She was a larger version of Adam and only slightly more feminine. She had a large boil on her chin with a long wiry hair growing from it, and a West Country accent that made her appear a caricature of the farmer's wife. "You'd better go and take it off and hang it up so that it doesn't get spoilt before Sunday." Looking around the kitchen, Abigail couldn't agree more. It was the filthiest kitchen Abigail had seen in a long time, and that included Fish's flat. Cats appeared to be laying everywhere, on the table, on the clothes in the washing basket (Abigail had no idea whether the garments were dirty or clean) and there was even a grimy looking tabby in the sink licking the drips from the tap.

"How much do I owe you?" Mrs. Fry asked, opening her purse hesitantly.

"Oh, nothing, Penny bought the material."

Mrs. Fry hesitated, torn between wanting to insist out of social convention, and not being able to afford to do so. "But your time must be valuable…"

"No, seriously," Abigail waved her off, and Mrs. Fry closed her purse again, relief evident on her chubby face.

"Well, let me make you a cup of tea or coffee at least," she persisted, shooing the tabby from the sink and filling the kettle from the spot that the feline had been lapping seconds earlier. Abigail longed to say no, but shrugged, which Mrs. Fry took as agreement. She motioned for Abigail to take a seat, so she pulled out the only wooden chair that didn't have a cat curled up in it, although it was covered in fur regardless.

"I'm not much good at sewing," confessed Mrs. Fry, placing a couple of mugs of steaming dark brown liquid on the farmhouse table. Abigail wasn't sure if it was tea or coffee, and there had been no offer of sugar. "I like doing other creative things, like baking, and when I do get a bit of spare time I make greetings cards." She shuffled over to some shelves on the back wall, where there were a few scruffy looking cookbooks that had seen better days, a leaning tower of pots and pans, and a few large square metal storage tins. She reached for one of the tins and brought it back to the table.

"I make up packs of five and sell them on eBay. I don't get much profit, but I enjoy doing it and it's relaxing."

She handed Abigail a pile of cards, which were all unique. Featuring relief patterns made from images cut from magazines, fabrics, and wrapping paper, there were cards for a variety of occasions from thank you, get well, congratulations, driving test passes and many were simply blank. Considering Mrs Fry came across as a brash clumsy farmer, the cards were surprising delicate and elegant.

"These are great," agreed Abigail. "I'll buy a pack from you. I'll need some thank you cards when it's time to leave Sloth."

"You can take them, I can't charge you after you made that dress and everything. Here, there's a load more in here," she fetched a shoebox from the shelves and placed it on the kitchen table.

Abigail pretended not to have heard Mrs. Fry's last comment and fetched a five-pound note from her purse and left it on the table. She selected five blank cards with various scenes on the front, and tucked them into her bag. She sipped at her drink and winced. She was still unsure whether it was tea or coffee, but something didn't taste right.

Penny had returned to the kitchen, armed with several pairs of shoes and a handbag to seek Abigail's opinion of which would best go with the dress. Spotting Abigail's face as she drank the drink, she began to giggle.

"We have our milk straight from the cows, none of this pasteurizing nonsense for us," she explained. "That's why the milk will taste funny to you."

"Oh no, it's fine, really," lied Abigail, struggling to force the last few sips down. She could still taste the wretched sourness on her tongue for hours after she left Fry's farm and, despite Sam's scolding about comfort food earlier, decided she deserved a Thursday night treat at the Carpenter's Arms, if only to take the lingering taste from her mouth.

Something in the air

There was definitely something in the air. An atmosphere of anticipation, a collective excitement rippling throughout the villagers of Sloth. Two pensioners were discussing the going at Aintree in the village shop as Abigail went to buy a cereal bar for breakfast. They glanced at Abigail once or twice, silently inviting her to join in with a comment, cajoling her to dive into their discussion. Having nothing of note to add, Abigail paid for her bar, nodded cordially at the customers and left the shop.

As she passed the Carpenter's Arms, bunting was being strung around the front door and across the downstairs bay windows. A chalkboard replaced the A board advertising posh coffee, with colourful stick horses drawn on by an amateur hand, galloping across the board. "Watch the Grand National here. Saturday 4pm. Good luck Callum!!" read the wording underneath.

Eddie and Jeremy were also excited, although Abigail doubted it was a knowledge of the forthcoming steeplechase that was making them frisky, and more to do with them seeing her take their leads from the hook. Kate had already left for work and Abigail was torn between checking Facebook straight away, or saving it until she'd come back with the dogs. The whirlwind of paws and yapping as soon as she entered the front door with Kate's spare key made her mind up for her.

She walked briskly, dragging the dogs away from smells they would no doubt prefer to linger longer at. Eager to get back to check the computer, she rushed the dogs around the circuit, nodding at villagers that greeted her like a local, stopping only to bag up the poo.

Back at the house, she left Eddie and Jeremy slurping water noisily from their bowls, slopping water over the edge, whilst she took up her place at the computer. She was already logged in as April Smith from her last session on Wednesday and her heart leapt as she saw there was a new message waiting for her to read.

"Abigail, So grateful that you've been able to make contact. Please come home, you're not in trouble and we're all really worried about you. We miss you like crazy. XXX. PS : If you need the guys to come and get you, they'll come and pick you up in the van. Are you really in Gloucestershire??

Abigail read the message over and over. The first line sounded a little bit formal, as though Nadine was being told what to write. Was it a message that the police had given her to type? Was it a trap? "The guys" could mean anything; it could refer to the boys in blue, and the van could be the police van, trundling into Sloth to cart her off to the station for questioning. She was obviously fishing for an address at the end by asking if she really was in Gloucestershire. If Nadine thought she was going to write back with an address for the police to come and find her at, she had another thing coming.

She read it through again. Maybe Nadine didn't have the police telling her what to write. It could all be straightforward. Nadine's worried and wants me home, she reasoned, and Blue Steak would come and get me if I have no money. Tricky, tricky, tricky.

Unsure how to respond, Abigail left the computer and decided to sort out the washing that she'd brought over. She could mull over a response as she undertook some menial tasks around the house. The lounge was a bombsite once again, but at least the dressing gown was flung over the sofa. Abigail stripped off and wrapped herself in the dressing gown, adding the clothes she'd just been wearing into the washing machine with her other clothes that had all been worn to death over the past eight days.

The washing machine gave a deep gurgle and began to fill. It was a satisfying noise, accompanied by the sight of the water level rising on the opposite side of the glass window as it gently began to agitate the clothing inside. She flicked on the kettle and began to pick up stray items in the lounge to tidy away; dirty coffee cups, newpapers, Aidan's toys, a pair of boxer shorts. Abigail winced as she retrieved the pair of black pants from the edge of the sofa. Not knowing quite what to do with them, she hovered in the lounge, the pants dangling from her hand.

All of a sudden, a noise came from the staircase beyond the lounge. It couldn't be the dogs, who were still snuffling around in the kitchen, and with apprehension, Abigail concluded it was definitely human footsteps descending the stairs. Maybe Kate had overslept and was just getting up...

"Ah there's my dressing gown!" greeted Callum, entering the lounge stark naked, completely lacking any shame or embarrassment. Abigail yelped and turned away to stare at the wall. "It looks much better on you than it does on me."

"I thought you were at Aintree!" Abigail protested, not daring to turn back to face him. The one second glimpse of his black hairy chest and his cock bouncing away in the nest of wiry pubic hair was all it took for the vision to burn itself onto her retina.

"Nah, change of plan. I had a non-runner yesterday so came home for a flying visit. I'm heading up there in a bit. Now, is there any chance I could have my boxer shorts please?"

Abigail realized she was still clutching them, and without turning her body, she flung them over her shoulder in the direction of Callum's voice. She heard him pull them on, and felt it was safe to turn back to face him.

"It's only the second time we've met, and we're already both nearly naked," joked Abigail to fill the silence that she found awkward. Callum had his hand down his boxer shorts adjusting his tackle, and had no such qualms.

"I know," he replied. "It doesn't normally take me so long. I must be losing my touch." He flashed his wicked grin at her and she blushed. "Did I hear the kettle on?"

Without waiting for an answer, he made his way through to the kitchen, and Abigail followed. A coffee would be good. She hovered near the table and watched him as he made the drinks in his underwear.

"If Kate walked in right now, do you think she'd get the wrong impression?" she asked. It was said lightly, meaningless conversation to fill the empty air. If Nadine were here, Abigail reflected, she would accuse her of wasting words.

"Believe me, Kate would not notice. I'm always walking around in my pants anyway."

Callum set the drinks down on the kitchen table and Abigail took that as her cue to sit down. He reached for the Racing Post newspaper and began idly to flick through. He even had hairy hands and fingers, Abigail observed, masculine black fuzz reminding her of an ape.

"So, are you nervous about tomorrow?" Abigail asked. She was acutely aware that she had to do all the probing. Although they'd not been in each other's company very long, he'd not yet asked a single thing of her.

"I'm excited, I'm also pretty hopeful. I'm riding the Wise Professor, you know, the horse that I won the Gold Cup on?"

Abigail nodded as though she was an expert now.

"Although he's a bit of a careful horse," Callum continued. "Cautious, you know? He'll get round safely if all goes well, but he lacks the power to really go for it at the end, which is when it really matters. So whether he can outrun some of the more gutsy horses, we'll have to wait and see."

Abigail could see a picture of one of the fences in the newspaper, and shuddered. One of the Aintree officials was standing by the jump in the photo, brushwood rising over his head to show that the fence was over six feet tall.

"Do you worry about injuring yourself?"

Callum folded the newspaper and set it to one side. "You can't think like that," he replied, taking a slow sip of coffee and regarding Abigail thoughtfully. "I know the odds of falling are high, you see the guys getting really bad injuries all the time. What happened to Buddy is always in the backs of our minds of course, but I'm young, I'm naïve, I think I'm invincible. Stupid really, but it's been a lifestyle for me since I can remember, and the kick you get from racing can't be found doing anything else."

He followed her gaze to the picture. "Ah, The Chair. It's like the scariest but most exhilarating thing when you realize you've landed safely over that beast. Such a buzz." He smirked at a thought. "You know, horse racing is the only profession where you're followed around by an ambulance as you carry out your job. Can you imagine if there was a team of paramedics in your office following you around in case the photocopier blew up in your face of something?"

"Those photocopiers can be really dangerous!" she replied in jest. "And death by filing cabinet is a common risk we office workers face."

They sipped at their coffees in silence once more. Abigail willed him to ask her a question. Nothing came, and she caved in.

"You didn't even feel differently when little Aidan was born? I had a friend who was into abseiling – the taller the building or rock face or canyon the better. Then his son was born and the next time we went up to slide down a tower, he couldn't do it. He kept thinking "What if" and never abseiled again."

"It was even more important to keep racing when he was born," he countered. "Somebody needed to keep the money coming in, put food on the table, clothes on his back, a roof over his head… and I'm not going to make it as an astrophysicist anytime soon, so I have to stick at doing what I'm good at." Callum's face softened. "He's a gorgeous kid though, ain't he? I remember the day he was born, he had a head of black curls from day one, and these tiny little fingers and toes. I've never loved anything as much, and I was amazed that I actually made something as gorgeous as that. Most things in life I do arseways, but you know, I'd finally done something right."

He drained his coffee and checked his watch.

"What have you got planned for the next day or so?" he asked. Bingo! He did understand the art of conversation was a two way process after all.

Abigail gave a non-committal shrug. "Nothing much, this and that, you know."

"Well, why don't you come up to Aintree with me?"

What? It was a serious question, but Abigail couldn't quite compute his intention. Did he mean just as a friend?

The washing machine struck up on its noisy final spin cycle, breaking the tension of the moment, leaving Abigail trying to formulate a response in her mind. Before she had chance to work out what to say, Callum stretched out his leg under the table and slowly ran his bare toes seductively up the inside of her calf.

"I've got a double suite booked at a really swanky hotel tonight, and nobody to keep me company. It can be a lonely life for a jockey you know…"

His foot had reached the top of her knee, and she pulled her chair back in disbelief and stood up. His intensions were now totally clear.

"I don't think so Callum." She grabbed at the empty coffee cups and took them haughtily over to the sink to wash up. With all her clothes contained in the washing machine, she was completely trapped in the dressing gown for the time being.

"Ah, no worries," he shrugged it off, as though it were nothing. "It was just a thought. I'd better get dressed."

He rose from the table and disappeared towards the stairs. Abigail realized her heart was pounding. She couldn't fathom out this brazen man. One minute he pours out his love for his son, and in the next breath he'd just asked her to go away to commit adultery with him. She could hear him crashing around upstairs singing 'Rock around the clock' and shook her head in disbelief.

She busied herself washing up the dirty crockery she'd rescued from the lounge and kitchen, and turned the washing machine into dryer mode. She flicked through the abandoned Racing Post that lay on the table and paused over an article about ladies' day fashion. Hmmm. Possible inspiration.

"Right, I'm off." Callum dumped a holdall in the hallway and fetched a bunch of keys from the hooks above the fireplace.

"Good luck!" Abigail called back.

"Thank you. Cheerio Abigail."

The front door slammed in his wake and it wasn't until she heard the throaty roar of his car vanish from the end of the drive that it registered. Abigail. He had definitely said Abigail. She played it back in her mind. Maybe she was mistaken. April, Abigail, no they couldn't be muddled, not in his Irish lilt. He had definitely said Abigail. That could only mean one thing. Fucking Mandy had blabbed.

Grand National

"This is amazing," marvelled Mrs Angel for the third time since the supermarket's delivery van had drawn up outside the cottage, partially blocking the sleepy country lane for ten minutes. The polite driver had greeted her with a cheery hello, and offered to carry the bulging bags through to the kitchen on Mrs Angel's happy agreement.

Abigail didn't feel she was being a great help after he departed, taking an item out of the carrier bag, then opening cupboards to see where it would live. Invariably, it was always the last cupboard she came to. Mrs Angel was on fridge duty, rearranging the opened cans of condensed milk and ship paste to squeeze in oddments of ham, tongue, luncheon meat and tripe from the meat counter.

"This should keep you going for a while anyway," observed Abigail, finding the cupboard pertaining to hot drinks and condiments and attempting to squeeze in the oversized jar of ovaltine.

"Well you'd think so," replied Mrs Angel wistfully, glancing up to look out the window onto the garden beyond. "But time has a habit of passing by frighteningly quickly. Look how much those bushes have grown since you cut them back on Monday. And that grass is growing at the rate of knots again."

Abigail had to admit that the downpours mid week and the glorious sunshine that followed was a recipe for ensuring that nature fought back.

"I was thinking," Mrs Angel continued, shutting the fridge door and joining Abigail by the sink to view the garden better. "I could get something like a wooden arch put in by the garden gate and have some sort of climbing plant to grow all over it. I think that would make that part of the garden look a lot prettier."

Abigail seemed to recall that her Dad had put something similar into their garden back in Richmond but she'd barely paid any attention as usual. Before she had chance to brood over not being able to see her Dad or his garden in the foreseeable future, another thought popped in her head. Mrs Ashington!

"I could ask Mrs Ashington's advice if you like; Sam told me she was working in a garden centre and so she might be able to advise on what sort of plant we should have." Abigail barely noticed that she'd said "we". The amount of work she'd put into the garden so far almost gave her possession rights anyway.

She glanced at the clock. It was only a quarter of an hour

before the Grand National was due to start. Her mind wandered to Callum and she wondered how he must be feeling. Beneath his bravado, he must have a pit of butterflies in his stomach.

"Are you sure you don't want to go to the pub to watch the race?" she asked hopefully. It was a lovely warm afternoon and the atmosphere would be lively by now.

"Oh, I don't think we need to be surrounded by those drunken louts," replied Mrs Angel dismissively. "We've got all the cake and coffee we need right here. In fact, let's put the kettle on and get the telly warmed up, it's nearly time."

Abigail put the last can of peeled plum tomatoes into the cupboard that housed an assortment of tins ranging from processed peas, canned peaches and Devon custard. She balanced it precariously on a tower of tinned sweetcorn and squashed the door shut before it all collapsed. She took her place in the armchair; it had come to feel like her personal sitting place as she'd spent many afternoons watching 'Where in the world' there.

The TV was already showing images of the horses parading around the ring. In the background, Abigail could see scores of people watching, dressed up in their finery with fascinators, hats, high heels and glitzy handbags. She could have been there she mused, although dressed in what she had no idea. She'd already raided the jumble sale leftovers upstairs to find a dress for the Ashington party tomorrow, and could only find a plain white dress that was vaguely suitable. It wouldn't make her stand out or feel special, but it would do. It would have to.

"Right, here we are." Mrs Angel shuffled in from the kitchen to the lounge and placed a tray on the coffee table. Two mugs of steaming milky coffee, two slabs of battenburg cake cut and presented on bone china side plates, plus a two thirds full bottle of Harveys Bristol cream and two empty sherry glasses. "If one of us gets a winner, we both get to go onto the hard stuff," she joked conspiratorially.

Abigail smiled at her fondly. Her own grandmother had passed away a couple of years back and she'd never spent quality time with her like this.

"I've got some money on Moroccan Sunset," explained Abigail, although omitting the full story of why that particular horse was chosen.

"I haven't got any money at stake, but I'll bet a glass of sherry. Now then..." she picked up the newspaper that had been resting on the footstool, already folded over onto the page that listed the runners and riders. "I always go for a name. Hmmm. There's The Wise Professor of course, which is the horse that Callum's riding, but I prefer Bad Teacher. Yes, Bad Teacher it is."

They scrutinized the screen to see whether they could spot their choices, but it was all a blur of mainly chestnut horses with their identical skinny jockeys on board. The pack circled a few times, the horses jiggling with anticipation and excitement; the expectation oozing from the crowds packed into the Aintree stands. Mrs Angel studied the remote control momentarily before increasing the volume just in time as the male voiced commentary began.

"And they're off, for the most important steeplechase in the calendar, the Grand National. The forty runners hurtle their way to the first with Zippy and the grey Fresh Prince prominent, Haydon Harbour, Solway Sting, Wild Cat and Houston on the inside with In the Light, Fat boy slim and Bad Teacher in the centre and Poster girl chases them as they prepare to rise."

Both Abigail and Mrs Angel stared transfixed at the screen as the first fence loomed and Abigail realized that she was actually holding her breath. A different voice took up the commentary, still calm and measured.

"And it will be Haydon Harbour right out in front with Carmen as they got over the first fence, and they are all safely over the first fence. Lost hope was last, along with Houston at the back of the field as they prepare to go over the second. It's Carmen, with Bethleham King on the outside; the first two safely over the second fence and again, they are all safely over...."

Two fences safely jumped but no mention of Callum's horse yet, or Moroccan Sunset. Abigail tried to scan the jockeys on the screen to see whether she could spot Callum, but it was an impossible task as the forty horses all flocked together in a dangerous huddle. Mrs. Angel was leaning forward in her seat, flicking her eyes between the newspaper in her hand and the screen. "Apparently Bad Teacher is in orange colours, so he should be easy to spot," she murmured. "Oh, there he is!" Towards the front running horses they could clearly see a jockey wearing shimmering orange; looking like the silky wrapper of a quality street chocolate.

"...And now the back marker is Willy Darko," continued the commentator, "and the canal turn is coming up. Carmen will take off in front of the Canal turn, from Bethlehem King, Bad Teacher, Joie de Vivre and The Wise Professor, Moroccan Sunset and Burnt steak just tucked in behind, and now they're coming up towards Valentines.."

At last, a mention for Callum on The Wise Professor, as well as noting Bad Teacher and Moroccan Sunset. Abigail watched in horror as the camera view pulled back to show the full pack and several had just fallen, the coloured blobs of jockeys curled into tiny balls on the ground, whilst the horses scampered back to their feet and continued the chase. Their reins and stirrups flapped in time to their hooves as though being ridden by invisible ghost jockeys. Abigail couldn't make out who they were, and found herself nibbling her thumbnail; something she never did.

"Sugar has come down at the Canal turn, Mustard man was also another faller, and Penalty time is getting tailed off.."

It was only 2 minutes into the race, and the commentary continued in a steady voice. Abigail had no idea how much further they would have to go but knew that commentators would get animated and excited as the race started to hot up. It wasn't happening yet, although the pack of runners was starting to spread out. Another wide angled shot from the camera and Abigail became aware of the row of ambulances moving along ominously alongside the track, keeping pace with the race. The jockey-less loose horses were galloping on, weaving in and out of the other horses. Are they enjoying it, wondered Abigail, or was it just a "fight or flight" pack mentality?

"As Carmen leads them over the fourteenth, Bethlehem King still sitting in second, then a couple of greys; Fresh Prince and Joie de Vivre alongside Bad Teacher and Burnt steak in black and white silks on the outside there. Next Katie Conrad on Kipper, riding next to her brother Ron on Lonesome as they go to the Chair, Carmen leading from Bethlehem King, Solway Sting was impeded ...."

The pair could feel the commentary starting to speed up, as another horse falls, and a few horses at the rear being pulled up, the pack thinning further. They sat in silence and continued to watch for a further minute.

"There's Moroccan Sunset," pointed out Mrs Angel, consulting the newspaper to check that the colour of the silks matched. He was still OK, still running strongly and gradually appeared to be nudging his way towards the front-runners. Two of the loose horses went around the edge of the water jump and rejoined their mates on the other side. Abigail managed a smile to herself. Maybe they weren't that stupid after all.

"As they head towards the one before Becher's, it's Carmen leading by around three lengths, followed by The Wise Professor and Moroccan Sunset. Zippy has been pulled up, and Kipper made a mistake there, and as they approach Becher's Brook for the second time, it's Carmen who leads the field, with Callum O'Casey aboard The Wise Professor in the mix with Moroccan Sunset drawing closer, and then behind them it's Kipper.

Abigail could barely watch as they went to jump Becher's.

She remembered the photo in Callum's paper yesterday demonstrating the sheer size of those jumps. Her eyes flitted between Callum, who was wearing a striking black and white striped jacket and Moroccan Sunset running gamely up the inside of him. She was holding her breath again and silently willing them on, please get over safely. No wonder Kate can't bear to watch Callum ride, she realized, her own heart was pounding away.

They all rose and got over Becher's in one piece and the commentator carried on listing those in the midfield and then towards the back of the pack. There was such a great distance between the front running pack, which included Callum, Moroccan Sunset and Bad Teacher, and those at the rear, that surely they had no hope of catching the leaders. Abigail guessed that the jockeys would just want to get around the course to prove a point.

The commentators started to get more animated, their speech speeding up and raising half an octave.

"As they go over the third from home in the National, it's Carmen on the outside of The Wise Professor, followed by Bad Teacher, and that's the first three as they go over the Melling Road. That leading pack is being followed by Moroccan Sunset, and Bethlehem King as they go towards the final two fences."

They had to change the commentator more frequently at this stage as the first one was running out of breath.

"Kipper is being driven along in about seventh place, as they race towards the penultimate fence, The Wise Professor in the striped jacket being driven along on the outside of Bad Teacher, and they're followed by Moroccan Sunset with three to four lengths to make up.."

Was it possible that Callum was actually going to win this? Abigail wasn't sure where her loyalty lay, as she prayed Moroccan Sunset would be able to find the energy not to fade and prove them all wrong. Thirty-eight better horses indeed!

The camera panned out again and the stands come into view, lining the home straight up to the finish line. The euphoric punters screamed encouragement as the leading pack jostled to be first to the line. Abigail could have been one of them, she realized with a faint twinge of regret.

Towards the last fence they went, Abigail leaning forward in her seat and jigging slightly with nervous anticipation. Carmen still led, but only by a whisker, with The Wise Professor being urged on with all Callum's might. Moroccan Sunset chased close on their heels in third. In seconds they were all safely over the last fence and started to head towards the finish line.

"The eleven year old Moroccan Sunset is running the race of

his life on the outside, as they race towards the elbow in the Grand National, and it's Moroccan Sunset taking the lead for trainer Sean Redcar with the young Scot Mac Ryan aboard, The Wise Professor is chasing, Bad Teacher is third, with just a furlong to go in the National. It's Moroccan Sunset with a loose horse for company, he's stretching four lengths clear from The Wise Professor, and the gap is widening, it's a win for Moroccan Sunset, with first time National run for Mac Ryan for Sean Redcar, as they cross the line.

Abigail jumped up from her chair with a whoop, still not taking her eyes from the screen. In the packed stands, betting slips were flung up in the air, the jubilant race goers in the crowd bouncing up and down and waving their arms around maniacally. Abigail knew how they felt.

Despite Callum's efforts, The Wise Professor was flagging over the last hundred yards and Carmen beat him into third place, with Mrs. Angel's Bad Teacher crossing the line fourth. She had earned her sherry after all. The camera stayed on the finish line for a respectful few seconds as the stragglers claimed the remaining places, exhausted and barely managing to canter to the finish line. Then a close up of the jockey on Moroccan Sunset, clearly amazed and delighted that he had actually done it.

The commentators were far from speechless, gabbling ecstatically about the fifty to one shot that had just beaten all the odds, and dissecting every move, every jump, and every mishap. Mrs. Angel snapped at the remote and the TV died with a defeated whine. "Sherry?"

Abigail had forgotten how easily sherry slipped down, and it was three generous glasses later that she headed for the Carpenters Arms. She heard the drunken singing emanating from the pub garden before she'd even got to the end of the Mrs. Angel's front path. As she got closer, she could see that customers had spilled out of the pub onto the lane, standing around in groups, pints in hand, in various states of inebriation.

Sam observed her coyly from his spot behind the pumps as she pushed her way in through the crowd and nudged between two elderly gentlemen who were propping up the bar.

"Well, Mrs. Moneybags!" joked Sam. "I guess you want a double to celebrate?"

"Oh, no," replied Abigail, realizing that the last thing she felt like doing was mingling with this drunken rabble of strangers. "I'm not staying long. I've just popped in to pick up my sketch book from Charly."

A flicker of disappointment crossed Sam's features momentarily, but Charly appeared from the back, hurried and flustered. It had clearly been a manic shift.

"Here you are," she handed the precious sketch book over the bar to Abigail. "I've miraculously managed *not* to get any mayonnaise or ketchup on it, and I've marked some designs I like with post it notes. They're great, you know, I'm surprised you haven't started this off as a business. There are so many opportunities for bespoke dresses, what with balls and galas, race meetings, weddings..."

"Stick another pint in there Sam," a ruddy faced regular interrupted, leaning over Abigail to hand his glass over. "Drowning me sorrows after that awful performance from Willy Darko. Did you see the race?" he asked Abigail, drawing her into the conversation as if they'd known each other all their lives.

"I did. Great ride by Callum."

"Pah!" the man snorted, "That Irish twat will have a head as big as a melon when he gets back."

"Well Frank, April here had money on Moroccan Sunset," Sam told the customer with a tone of pride in his voice. "I take back everything I said, and now bow to her superior knowledge," he smiled at her warmly, conspiring their shared knowledge of his hair being the inspiration behind her bet.

"Ah, it was just beginner's luck," Abigail replied dismissively. "What about you two?" She directed the question at the siblings behind the bar, deducing that Frank had not profited from the afternoon. "Did you win anything?"

"I had an each way on Bad Teacher," replied Charly, "but at ten to one, I've made about two quid profit. Better than Sam here though." She tousled his hair playfully whilst he grimaced.

"I backed Callum," he said with a sigh. "To win. I should have known better than to trust bloody Callum. Let that be a lesson, April. Don't trust Callum!"

His words sent a shiver down Abigail's spine as she remembered that Callum knew about her real name. Sam's words suddenly seemed very ominous.

The Ashington Party

All hands had been on deck Sunday morning at Ashington Yard, where grooms had been relieved of their normal duties riding out, mucking out and cleaning tack in favour of hanging bunting, dressing trestle tables on the lawn and rigging up the sound system. Tim the head groom had overseen the erection of the bouncy castle and installation of the bucking broncho on the lawn, whilst Sam and Charly took up their duties that they had overseen year after year; food and drink.

Kate had dropped Aidan off with her neighbour Val, who luckily preferred the company of a toddler to eating, drinking and socialising with nearly everyone else from Sloth. Kate had tried on a variety of dresses that lurked in the depths of her wardrobe, but wasn't satisfied that any of them did her any favours, and opted to wear her smart jeans paired up with a new top that she'd bought after work in Cheltenham on Friday and some heels that came out on special occasions. She knew that her feet would be killing by five o'clock but hoped she could get a seat for the evening and have everyone run around after her for a change.

Callum couldn't care less what he wore or what he looked like, much to Kate's exasperation. He was the Great Callum O'Casey; everyone should be honoured to be in the presence of the third greatest jump jockey in the UK.

"What do you look like?" Kate scolded, as he emerged from the bedroom wearing his baggy flannel shorts with a golfing t-shirt. Lowering her eyes to his feet she saw that he'd put on flip-flops. At least it was better than socks and sandals - a fashion faux pas that was not uncommon with Callum.

"I want to be comfortable," he retorted defensively. "It's a drink fest, not a fashion parade."

Kate's heart sank. Every year Callum kept the Monday clear of any racing so that he could take advantage of the well stocked free bar. He was normally tiddly by five, loud by six, insulting by seven and either passed out or having to be put to bed by eight, cutting her evening short. Most years she nagged at him not to go too mad on the alcohol, but despite promises, he was as predictable as clockwork. "Having said that," he continued, "I bet that Mandy will be looking mighty fine in something tight and clingy, and April's bound to be looking good enough to eat." He grinned lecherously at Kate who threw a wet flannel at him from where she was applying make up in the bathroom mirror.

Abigail did not feel she was looking her best as she surveyed herself in the long mirror in the toilet block. The dress she'd picked

146

out at Mrs. Angel's was the best of a bad bunch, but it looked dull and uninspiring. White didn't suit her pale skin, the square neckline needed to be enhanced with bold jewellery that she didn't possess, and the chunky belt around the middle felt old fashioned but couldn't be done away with. No dress would ever match up to the beautiful green silk dress she had tried on in Cheltenham, and she was now silently cursing the fact she hadn't bitten the bullet and bought it. Too late now, she reflected. She'd just have to be little miss Top Shop rather than little miss classy boutique.

Her trusty kitten heels were deployed for the first time since her arrival at Sloth. They had dried out from the rainfall of that first Friday night, but if you looked closely you would be able to see faint tide marks where the water had badly damaged the suede.

Callum opened the door to her and welcomed her in.

"Well done on the race," Abigail congratulated him as she stepped into the lounge, which once again resembled a bombsite despite her tidy up on Friday.

"You should have been there," he replied, choosing his words with care as Kate descended the stairs to join them in the lounge. "The atmosphere was absolutely electric. Amazing. I plan to get very drunk tonight to celebrate, as I haven't been able to yet."

There was certainly no incentive not to drink, Abigail noted, as the taxi dropped them off at the Ashington's driveway. A waiter in a penguin suit stepped over to the taxi with a tray of champagne flutes as soon as they stepped out, welcomed them and pointed out that the drink was laid out on the back lawn and they were welcome to help themselves. The food would get underway in a few hours.

The party was advertised as starting at 2pm, and was in full swing by the time the trio arrived at 3pm. A swarm of well-wishers descended around Callum as they made their way towards the action, patting him on the back, offering congratulations and shaking his hand. He lapped up the adoration, and had soon peeled away from Kate and Abigail to join in the technical horsey talk with those in the profession.

"As a general rule," said Kate in hushed tones, "you can tell the racehorse owners by their hideous fashion sense. Salmon coloured trousers are a giveaway." Abigail sniggered as she spotted a group chatting together on the lawn wearing large trilby hats, trousers in various shades of pink and mismatched sweaters. "Jockeys are obvious," she continued. "They're all the ones under ten stone. The trainers are pretty much ruddy cheeked and pot bellied. With the exception of Mr Ashington of course, he's not eaten quite enough foie gras dinners to get the belly yet, but I dare say he could work on it."

"And the wives and girlfriends?" Abigail enquired, thinking of the glamorous selection of top league footballers' wives and girlfriends that adorned the trashy weekly magazines that she read religiously. Maybe this was the perfect platform for finding her Mr Right.

"Pretty normal, thankfully!" Kate replied after a moment's pause. "Successful jockeys, owners and trainers are usually pretty minted, but don't like to splash it around too much, so they don't attract the gold digging crowd." Kate quickly surveyed the gathered guests with an expert eye and began to point people out. "Emma over there is a nurse; she's married to Jake. That's Felicity, the thirty-year-old wife of sixty-year-old Charles Hillier, she teaches French at a comprehensive school over in Gloucester. And then there's yours truly - hard done by dental nurse married to the third best jockey in the country." She smirked, mocking Callum.

They made their way down the lawn to a long trestle table that held an array of alcohol. An impressive speaker system blasted out hits from the late 70s. Abigail recognised songs from Blondie, Bowie and the disco sounds of the era. Robin had chosen the music. His party, his music, and it seemed to be going down well with the gathered crowd; many jigging their hips unconsciously as they clustered in groups together. There was even a gang of preschool children jumping up and down wildly to the beat, working off the hyperactivity caused by the excess of orange squash that afternoon. Abigail had been raised listening to the same tunes, thanks to her Dad's large vinyl record collection. As the CD age ballooned, Abigail still loved to get out his black discs and carefully position the needle on the album and enjoy an afternoon at 33rpm. Many of her friends had never played records, nor heard of the Ramones or the Jackson 5, so she felt an air of superiority over her peers for being word perfect on most of their hits.

Abigail had no sooner swapped her empty champagne glass for a full glass of white wine, when Penny came hurtling across the lawn in excitement.

"April, April, April," she shrieked breathlessly. "I was talking to Felicity a minute ago and she loves my dress. Adores it! She wants you to make her a dress for a fundraising do she's got coming up in June, and then she remembered that her sister has a wedding to go to in the summer, and said she's looking for something amazing to wear to show off to an ex boyfriend and make him jealous, and ..."

"It's probably easier if I go over and have a chat with them myself," she proposed, interrupting her, having the feeling that she was in danger of bursting with information if she wasn't careful. Twenty minutes later, Abigail had discussed designs and swapped details with Felicity, having actioned two firm commissions. Smiling like a Cheshire cat, she realised that this was just the start. Charly was right, there seemed to be an untapped market in these circles and networking was the key.

She found Kate sitting with a small group on a blanket alongside the bucking broncho. Abigail vaguely recognised a few of the faces as being grooms and stable lads from Ashington Yard, enjoying the freebie that their employer had laid on. Kate had her shoes already kicked off; she'd lasted an hour before she felt the familiar ache.

Abigail sat with the group and tuned out of their chatter as her brain began to speed away with itself, planning ahead as always. She couldn't run a business from a tent, relying on Mrs. Witts sewing machine, but could she set herself up in Sloth and live out her design career here? She'd need a place to stay, which would mean ID and references. Wouldn't it?

She did some rough financial calculations in her head; set up costs were minimal - a sewing machine and a computer so that she could have access to her email and Facebook site. Then there was rent and living costs on top, but she'd found her living costs to be minimal this week by the reciprocal arrangements that she'd managed to put in place. She calculated that if she could rent a spare room from one of the friends she'd made so far, there was less likely to be questions asked, ID required and the rent would surely be lower than market rate. Her eyes scanned lazily around the gathering; there was Robin enjoying a joke with a man wearing a hideously oversized paisley patterned cravat. Ashington Yard was a possibility. But then Mrs. Angel may be more generous with rent and Abigail would be able to keep her company in return. Her eyes fell on Penny; there was a family that could use some extra income, but then Abigail remembered the cat fur everywhere and decided that she had to draw a line somewhere to meet her basic hygiene standards.

A group cheer brought her back to her senses and she realised that Kate was getting up to have a go on the bucking broncho. Kate could certainly use some help around the house, and maybe the company too with Callum being away so frequently. The computer was already there. There were plenty of options to think about.

"Go on darling, wrap your legs right round him and give him the ride of his life," jeered Callum, weaving his way unsteadily across the lawn towards the group. He was clutching a can of cider; certainly not his first that afternoon. He plonked himself down in the circle, taking the space next to Abigail that Kate had recently departed.

"Ride him hard cowboy!" He screeched with laughter thinking his act was the funniest thing, but most of the group ignored him. Kate pulled a face as she gripped onto the front of the saddle with one hand and raised her left hand in the air, waiting with trepidation for the operator to flick the switch to start the plastic steed. It started to move slowly, making jerky circles clockwise whilst Kate tried to get a grip on the slippery surface. With a shallow buck it suddenly reversed its direction and Kate landed spread-eagle across its neck momentarily before a final swing clockwise caused her to fly off the broncho and land with a thud on the inflatable surround. Eight seconds.

"Eight sodding seconds," laughed Kate, making her way back over to the group and squishing back into the circle on the other side of Callum.

"Abigail, you should have a go," Callum announced, far too loudly for Abigail to be comfortable.

"No - April really doesn't want to have a go," she replied through gritted teeth to him, reminding him with her tone and pleading look not to use her real name.

"Oh go on spoil sport," he persisted, sounding like a bratty kid in the playground. He lowered his voice conspiratorially and leant into Abigail. She could smell sweet cider on his breath. "Otherwise I might accidentally keep referring to you as Abigail. And anyway, I want to see how well you can cope with a mighty beast between your legs." He roared with drunken laughter again, causing Kate to catch Abigail's eye with an apologetic gesture. "And when you fall off I want to see if I can see your knickers."

"Callum!" Kate shrieked in horror. "I'm sorry April, I did give you warning what he's like after a few. And mind your language you - there are young ears around."

She indicated Penny, who hovered within earshot of the group, watching with fascination as one of the grooms had now managed to stay on the broncho for nearly thirty seconds. The trick appeared to be the ability to tuck his long legs up around the bull's ears and seemingly cling on with the tips of his toes. The bull was getting increasingly agitated, and at around the 40-second mark, it gave a final buck and top speed jerk that sent the groom flying into the padded ground. The audience gave an appreciative cheer in recognition of his efforts.

"You lot are boring," Callum complained, getting back up onto his feet again. "I'm going to leave you to your boring dull games and go and get another drink. Then I may go back to the pool where Dan, Adam and Craig are telling the filthiest jokes without getting any grief about their language from their other halves." He belched loudly and smiled thoughtfully. "And that Mandy is looking verrrry sexy, she's got this tight dress that scoops down by her big bouncy boobies and shows off her cleavage and..."

"Go away Callum!" instructed Kate, waving her hand at him, shooing him off like a rabid dog. He shrugged in surrender and staggered his way off unsteadily across the lawn towards the house. Abigail had been wondering where Dan and Mandy had got to, and she'd not seen Sam or Charly all afternoon either. She was still quietly seething inside every time she thought about Mandy telling Callum her real name, and she remembered that she needed to have a few stern words with that little madam. Still, she consulted her watch and realised that this party would run for hours yet. More and more people had been arriving as the afternoon wore on, it seemed that the event was notorious for miles around.

The hog roast was underway by six o'clock and Abigail drooled as she scanned the trestle tables loaded with warm rolls, salads, and pastas. The slab of pork rotated over a fierce heat, dripping fat into the embers and creating a smell that drifted over the Ashington campus like a bisto wave. Despite having seconds, the food didn't seem to be soaking up the white wine that Abigail was consuming. It was a problem in social situations where Abigail wasn't totally comfortable around everyone, she clung to her glass like a lifeline, lifting it to her lips whenever there was a pause in the conversation or she felt someone's gaze fall on her. Whether she liked it or not, Abigail was the sort of girl that got people of both sexes gazing at her a lot. Which meant this afternoon her glass had been raised to her lips a lot more frequently than it should have.

Kate on the other hand wasn't even holding her glass. It was set on the grass in front of her while she chatted easily to the group on the rug. Occasionally, she would pause and take a tiny sip of the amber liquid, then set it in front of her again. It was getting embarrassing the number of times Abigail had gone over to the bar to get a top up compared to her friend, and she decided that it was probably best to take herself off for a walk. Water, she decided. A glass of water would be good.

She wandered up the lawn and stepped into the tranquility of the house via the conservatory doors that had been left wide open, inviting the partygoers to spread wherever they liked on the property. The lounge was deserted and it was tempting to sink into those squashy sofa cushions and just lay for a moment listening to the slightly muffled sounds of laughter, activity and the chirping of Brotherhood of Man coming from the PA system. Fearful of Callum discovering her, she decided to stay vertical, and made her way through to the kitchen.

Despite the glorious sun outside, the kitchen blinds were drawn closed and the kitchen was in darkness. The stillness of the empty house made her feel like a trespasser, but she could still hear merriment emanating from the pool area beyond the side door and knew that she wasn't far from the action. Fumbling for light, she found a small rocker switch by the cooker hood, which she flicked and the units became bathed in a soft glow from tiny spotlights under the cupboards. One by one, she opened each cupboard door in turn hunting for glasses.

"If you need a glass, there are some clean ones on the draining board," came a voice from the gloom. Abigail turned, startled, to see Mrs. Ashington sat slumped alone at the breakfast bar. She made for a very sorry figure, sat miserably in the darkness nursing a large glass of red wine in front of her. She wore a plain black Lycra dress, and once again, she wore make up like a car crash on her gaunt face. A chunky orange bead necklace provided a brash splash of colour, but otherwise the look was of someone having no interest in enhancing her appearance.

"I didn't see you there," replied Abigail needlessly. "Are you not enjoying the party?" Abigail found a large tumbler glass on the draining board as promised and filled a glass of water from the tap. She hovered, momentarily torn between standing by the sink or joining Mrs. Ashington at the breakfast bar. As if reading her mind, Mrs. Ashington pulled out the stool next to her and patted it.

"I don't really enjoy these things anyway," she confided as Abigail slid into the stool next to her. Close up, she could she how red and puffy Mrs. Ashington's eyes were. Whether this was from tiredness or crying Abigail couldn't be sure. It may even have been another disastrous make up attempt. "But this year it's even worse."

She paused, peering into her glass as though it would provide an answer. She was like a small child, lonely, miserable and vulnerable. Instinctively, Abigail put an arm around Mrs. Ashington's bony shoulder and rubbed it gently, encouragingly.

"Sam told me about what happened to your brother," she said softly. "It must be very difficult...to be surrounded by all this." Abigail was referring vaguely to the yard, the horses, the grooms and riders, daily race meetings and all the paraphernalia that would remind Mrs. Ashington on a daily basis of the industry that killed her brother. She regarded Abigail neutrally for a second and then turned her attention back to her glass.

"So many people here knew him," she replied quietly, "and all they can say is they're sorry. As if it's their fault. As if that will make me feel better, as if that lets them off the hook somehow." Abigail wasn't sure what to say and remained silent as a small tear escaped from the corner or Mrs. Ashington's eye and tracked a slow hesitant course down the side of her nose. Abigail watched in fascination. She envied people like Mrs. Ashington and Nadine who could get upset, have tears roll down their cheeks yet carry on talking normally. When Abigail got upset she had two settings; misty eyed or full on blubbing, the latter rendering it impossible to get any sensible legible words out between sobs. She'd witnessed Nadine in the past deliver a lengthy monologue – the one about being at her grandmother's bedside as she passed away for example, or finding a distraught mother in Cameroon cradling her dead baby that had died from malaria – tears rolling freely down both cheeks but her voice remaining steady and calm as though she was simply regaling her with an every day tale.

"I'm fed up of being told people are sorry," Mrs. Ashington continued. "I'm fed up of rattling around in this stupid place while everyone else is merrily getting on with their lives. I just..." She stopped abruptly. "God, I'm sorry," she roughly wiped the solitary tear from her face with the back of her dress sleeve. "I'm being silly, pouring my heart out to a stranger. I barely know you."

Abigail didn't remove her hand from Mrs. Ashington's shoulder and observed her kindly. "Don't worry, you can tell me whatever you like." I'm pretty good at keeping secrets, thought Abigail, like the fact I'm being hunted down by police for bringing down the banking system. Yes, you tell me anything. "Have you told Robin how you feel?"

Mrs. Ashington met her eyes briefly before looking back down with a sad smile. "No. When is he ever here to sit down and listen to me properly? He talks all day long to everyone else but me - owners, jockeys, grooms, suppliers, from the time he gets up to the time he crawls into bed in the early hours, he is a hundred percent preoccupied with everything that goes on at this yard. He's either in the study wading through paperwork, away at a race meeting, down on the gallops, out in the yard. Everywhere I'm not."

"What about Sam? He's quite concerned about you."

She gave out a long sigh and drained her glass. "He's a sweetheart, but I think deep down he's just worrying about me turning into an alcoholic."

"And do you think there's a risk of that happening?" Abigail was surprised that she was being so bold with her questions. It rang a vague bell from some training seminar that she'd attended that the best way to get people to admit things is to turn the questioning to reflect back on them.

Mrs. Ashington gave a small laugh. "I've always had a

relationship with alcohol. We're probably seeing a bit more of each other at the moment, but it's just a temporary blip. Maybe I should take a lead from you and have a glass of water," she added. The atmosphere had suddenly lifted, and Mrs. Ashington gave her eyes a final decisive wipe, smearing mascara down her cheek.

Grateful for the distraction, Abigail got up from her stool and fetched a glass of water for Sam's mum, which she drank gratefully.

"I understand you work in a garden centre." Abigail was careful not to use the past tense. "I've been doing a little bit of gardening for Mrs. Angel in the village and I could really use your expertise actually. We were thinking of getting some kind of climbing plant to cover an archway, but don't know what sort would be best."

"Oh, er..." Mrs. Ashington suddenly looked baffled at this change of topic. She hadn't had to think about the world of the clematis or hydrangea for several weeks. She crumpled her face up in thought. "Well it would depend on whether the arch is in a sunny or shady spot, how quickly you would need it to climb, whether you can keep on top of the pruning, if you wanted a flowering one, and if so, what colour flowers would you want..."

"Well, maybe we could all go out to the garden centre together and take a look. It would be a real treat for Mrs. Angel to be able to get out and do something different." Abigail also realized that Mrs. Ashington could also use a change of scene too. "I'll leave you to think about when you're free."

"Yes, that would be good. There's a nice little café up there," Mrs. Ashington smiled at Abigail. "I'd like that. Now then," she rose from her stool. "Shall we go out and see what's happening around the pool?" she suggested.

"Well, rumour has it that Dan and Adam are telling filthy jokes, and Callum is very drunk," replied Abigail, rinsing the two glasses at the sink and placing them back on the draining board to dry. "But you might want to touch your face up first."

The area around the pool was a sun trap, protected from the breezes that had been sweeping across the lawn, and Abigail wished she'd come out here sooner. The house provided a protective barrier from the noise of the party on the lawn, and the walled pool patio felt like an exclusive club by comparison. A separate ghetto blaster had been set up, this time emitting Latin beats to the crowd; salsa, mambo, with the bold brassy trumpet sounds mingling with relaxing chilled percussion section. There was a male female split, with Dan, Sam, Adam and an older scruffy man that Abigail presumed to be Adam's Dad sat around one table whilst Charly, Mandy, Mrs. Fry and Penny sat to the other side of the pool area.

Abigail observed Mandy for a few moments, mustering the courage to take her aside to challenge her about shooting her gobby little mouth off. She was holding court, regaling the group with an anecdote about a duathlon that she was training for, the others hanging on her every word. Abigail took a deep breath and tried to recall her assertiveness training. She had to be direct, non judgmental and open to listening to what Mandy had to say in her defense, whilst also not wanting to make too big of an issue about the name change. Above all, she mustn't draw attention to herself.

With Mrs. Ashington at her side, they approached the table. Seeing their arrival, Mandy immediately broke off from her tale and greeted them with a wide smile.

"Hey, Mrs. A, it's great to see you! I wondered where you were and April; oh my God, you look fabulous," she jumped out of her seat and motioned to Abigail's dress, as mercurial as ever. One minute making snide asides, the next moment making Abigail feel like the most adored friend she had. "I just love your dress, it really suits you, you look amazing." There was so much gushing, Abigail wondered whether she was taking the piss out of her, but it seemed genuine and knocked the wind right out of her assertive sails.

"You look lovely too," replied Abigail truthfully, before lowering her voice. "Could we .. er... Have a little chat in private?" Abigail flicked her head to motion over towards the deep end of the pool.

"Oh, sure." Unfazed, Mandy shook her glossy dark mane back off her shoulders and headed off in front of Abigail to the quieter end of the pool and away from the ears of the others. "What can I do for you?" she smiled. Nice as pie. Glamorous and open in her body language. Shit. Abigail had rehearsed a few lines in her head, and struggled to remember which one she opted for that sounded the most reasonable.

"Well, it's just that Callum has started to refer to me by the name that appears on my driving license and I don't want it getting any further really. I'd rather people just call me April."

Mandy looked unsure what was being asked of her. "Well, I call you April..." she responded, her eyebrows furrowing in confusion.

"Yes, but I didn't appreciate you telling Callum that wasn't my real name...".

"Oh hang on," Mandy interrupted, her facial expression suddenly changing. There was a flicker of aggression starting to appear, the anger flaring to the surface. This was exactly what Abigail didn't want to happen. She'd made the textbook error of throwing the accusation out there too early. So much for listening to what Mandy had to say.

"You think it was *me* that told Callum that you're not called April. For God sake, I don't give a flying fart whether you're called April or Eric, in fact, I can't remember what your real name is." Although she wasn't raising her voice, Mandy was becoming animated and Abigail glanced to the seated groups to check that attention wasn't being drawn their way. They appeared to be ignored so far, but Abigail was struggling to keep the conversation under control.

"I'm sorry," Abigail began, "but somebody must have told him, and you are the only person that knows, so it was a natural assumption to make."

"Well it wasn't me, and if I'm perfectly honest April, I'm disappointed and offended that you think I would gossip about you to the likes of Callum, when the truth is, I really don't give a shit."

"I'm really sorry," Abigail repeated, "let's just forget it."

In an instant, Mandy's face had switched back to being friendly again and she took a small step closer, smiling slyly. "Forget what?" She gave a small chuckle and gently shoved Abigail on the shoulder.

For days after, Abigail would play the following few seconds over and over in her mind, trying to work out whether it was an intentional push, or a friendly gesture to draw a line to the end of their discussion. Either way, there was no changing the outcome as Abigail took a step back, and in the split second of her foot leaving the ground and gravity taking over, she realised her mistake, and the consequences that were to follow. There was no ground for her foot to connect with, and in slow motion she felt her body falling backwards until the water engulfed her. Totally, fully, the momentum of her fall back into the deep end of the pool was met with a satisfying splash and water embraced her, claiming her entire body, head and all. Abigail's horrified gasp was met with a mouthful of icy chlorinated water.

Her first thought was to blame herself. She'd stepped back, such a stupid thing to do. But then she recalled the shove, and anger welled up briefly. She'd actually been pushed into the pool!

By the time she surfaced, spat out whatever water she hadn't swallowed, and was treading water, taking stock of the situation, Mandy had long vanished. Now everyone's attention had been caught, with Charly nearest to the deep end, rushing up to help her climb out of the steps. With mounting horror, she realised that her Faith shoes were sodden for the second time since arriving in Sloth, maybe completely ruined this time. Worse still, her beloved handbag was still on her arm, pool water soaking both it and the contents, including her precious sketchbook. Fucking Mandy.

A dozen concerned faces watched as she clambered ungracefully out of the pool, her white dress now virtually see through and dripping a massive puddle poolside.

"What happened, did you slip?" asked Mrs. Fry.

"It's a good job you can swim," chipped in Penny. "That's the deep end and if you couldn't swim you would have been in a right pickle."

"It's OK, I just stepped back. Stupid me." Abigail tried to give a casual laugh but it wasn't exactly convincing.

Somewhere from the assembled crowd there was a stifled chuckle. The chuckle grew louder, before transforming into a giggle. Like a tidal wave, the rising laughter couldn't be stopped. Embarrassed, everyone looked around the crowd to spot the culprit, no-one knowing what to say.

Abigail scanned the faces and saw from the back of the assembled crowd, Mrs. Ashington with her hand over her mouth, desperately trying to stop the sounds escaping from the depth of her belly. She couldn't help it, and the giggles became ever more forceful.

Abigail's anger towards Mandy melted away, and she met Mrs. Ashington's eyes and smiled back. Seeing that the tension of the moment had been broken, a few other people in the crowd seemed to exhale and relax.

"That was....just...so funny!" shrieked Mrs. Ashington between gasps of air. She was virtually bent double.

"God, April, you're soaked!" said Charly, stating the obvious. "I'll go and find you a towel and then maybe you can find something else to wear from my wardrobe." Charly was around the same height as Abigail, but had a stockier frame to the point that she would be at least a dress size larger. But she couldn't hang around in sodden clothes all night.

She waited, shivering in the shower room whilst Charly went to the airing cupboard to dig out a dry warm towel. She kicked off her heels and opened her precious handbag to survey the damage. All the banknotes in her purse would need to be dried out, as well as the pages of her sketchbook. Tentatively she thumbed through the damp mass and was relieved to discover that most of the contents were intact and legible. Her make up was ensconced in a waterproof case, and there wasn't much else of worth in the bag; a tampon, biro, and some old receipts. Her phone had been stowed away in her tent out of temptation's way, and in this case, harm's way. She doubted whether there would be any charge left in it, but found there was little call for it in Sloth, especially as the GPS signal would send a beacon to the police if she were to switch it on. Her watch - a delicate gold face on a dainty bracelet style strap - was still ticking. It had only had a two second dunk so Abigail was hopeful it would survive OK.

"Here you go," Charly came back to the shower room with a gloriously warm, dry fluffy towel and a soft long dressing gown that felt like it was made from a shag pile rug. "Come on upstairs when you're ready and we'll see if there's anything in my wardrobe that you want to wear."

Abigail peeled off her dress and underwear and spent a few glorious moments under a hot shower. It was a far cry from the shower block at Wits End, which, despite the addition of the new curtains, still remained a depressing experience. The Ashington's shower room was light and airy, roomy and the water was piping hot. Baskets of expensive smelling toiletries lay at the guest's disposal. Maybe Mandy had done her a favour.

Ten minutes later she was clean and dry, with the exception of her hair, which she couldn't dry without having a hairbrush to use. She made her way out of the shower room and towards the staircase with eager anticipation. She hadn't yet seen the upstairs of this fantastic residence.

"Psst, April, come here." Before she got to the staircase, Sam was beckoning to Abigail from the doorway of the study and obediently she followed him in and shut the door behind her as instructed. Sam swung himself across the room on his crutches to his makeshift bed and turned to face her. He looked uncharacteristically ill at ease, and a feeling of dread flooded over Abigail. What had she done wrong now?

"Are you sure you're OK after that fall?" he questioned. "I know you're too polite to make a fuss, but if there's anything I can do, anyone that needs to be blamed.."

Abigail wondered whether he'd seen the full extent of Mandy's shove, but quickly shrugged it off. "No, seriously, just me being clumsy, I stepped back and forgot I was on the edge of the pool. Put it down to me being blonde. Charly's going to fix me up with something to wear."

"Ah, no, well, that's really why I called you in..." he was back to being shifty again, and Abigail began to feel uneasy. "You remember when you gave me your driving license in the pub..."

Oh shit. Abigail's heart began to pound again.

"Yes," she replied hesitantly as it looked like he'd stalled.

"Well...I happened to notice that your birthday's coming up quite soon..." Abigail breathed a small sigh of relief. Not the name then, that was something. "I hope you don't think that's creepy, but it stood out because it's the same day as mine. Except that I'm a year older. Anyway, I hope you won't think this too forward of me, but I felt compelled to get you a birthday present in Cheltenham, and it would probably come in useful now, so I thought I should give it to you early."

Ooh, thought Abigail. Some underwear would be really useful right now, but it would be borderline inappropriate for him to have bought her underwear. Maybe that's why he was so nervous. With some difficulty, he discarded his crutches and bent down to pull a brown paper carrier bag out from under his camp bed, and Abigail instantly recognised the dainty blue logo of the Betty Boo boutique. No, surely not.

He handed her the bag sheepishly. "I would have wrapped it if I'd known it would be needed tonight, so I'm sorry for the poor presentation."

Abigail peeked inside and saw a flash of emerald green silk, and snapped the bag shut again. "Oh my God, Sam, seriously, you shouldn't have. I can't accept this, it's too much." Her protests were waning.

"Don't be silly," he insisted. "That dress was made for you, it would have been criminal not to get it." He reached out to her hand that was still dangling the bag in mid air, and pushed the bag back towards her chest. "You deserve this, please accept it."

There was a moment's awkward silence. Abigail wondered whether it was now customary to get Sam something of the same value for his birthday, now that he had made it known when it was.

"Well thank you Sam," she accepted graciously, "you know how much I love the dress. It's perfect, thank you." She leaned forward and pecked him on the cheek and he drew her into a bear hug. She wondered briefly whether he was going to make a move to kiss her properly, and she prayed that he wouldn't. Not because she didn't feel any affection for Sam, but she felt that it would cheapen the gesture by doing so. A kiss in return for the dress. She wasn't ready to prostitute herself that badly, no matter how special she felt the dress was.

They remained holding each other, with Sam's warm steady breaths blowing gently against her ear. They stayed that way, silent, for several moments and there was no move to kiss her. Maybe he was gay. Abigail thought randomly about how many men she knew that would take the opportunity to be holding her in a dressing gown as invitation to dive right in.

The door suddenly crashed open and Charly came falling into the study with Penny in tow. Abigail and Sam instinctively jumped apart like guilty lovers caught in the act.

"Sorry," apologised Charly, realising that she'd interrupted a moment, "I didn't know anyone was in here."

"Don't mind us," sang Penny, "we're just here to get those Sylvia Downton books."

Abigail and Sam shuffled about awkwardly, not looking at each other as Charly and Penny raided the bookcase, animated with excitement for the next Sylvia Downton installment.

Abigail motioned that she would go and get dressed, and made her way back to the shower room, where she put on the dress once again. It felt as sexy and amazing as it had when she first tried it on in the boutique a few days earlier, the silk skirt shimmying around her thighs and the hem caressing the tops of her knees. It felt strange to wear the dress without underwear, she felt particularly vulnerable with the air circulating between her legs. Her loose breasts would just have to sway, support-less and voluptuous without a bra to cradle them into place.

Everyone cooed and admired the dress when she reemerged into the party half an hour later, having finally been upstairs and found some shoes to borrow from the depths of Charly's wardrobe. The shoes didn't exactly match as perfectly as Abigail would have liked, but they seemed to fit OK.

She hadn't appreciated how quickly the sun had sunk behind the horizon and it was suddenly dusky outside, and anticipation was starting to build for the firework finale. Some of the crowds from earlier had left; there were no longer small children bouncing on the castle, nor running riot across the lawn, but others had replaced them. New revellers were arriving after taking part in the day's race meetings, or just having been at the pub most of the afternoon.

If Abigail had realised then how the rest of the evening was going to pan out, she would have taken her leave before the fireworks. Hindsight is a wonderful thing, but Abigail had no such luxury as she mingled with new friends, not aware of the chain of events that awaited her.

Going home

"The train now arriving at platform 2 is the 11.54 to London Paddington," the crackly announcement came across the waiting room, where Abigail was sat in the corner, trying to hide her tear dampened face from the other travellers that wandered in occasionally to shelter from the savage winds outside.

She felt like she'd barely stopped crying in all her woken hours over the past twelve hours, ranging from childlike snivels to sorrowful sobs. There were several trigger points that had started all this off, starting with Dan evicting her from the campsite. The decision to throw in the Sloth towel however, was finalised following Callum's behaviour later that evening; a catalyst for the realisation that all she wanted was home, familiar surroundings, a non judgemental hug from her Dad and to be able to enjoy friendships that weren't based on lies, false names or hidden secrets.

Weighing up on the other side of these benefits came the uncertainty that returning to London brought. Could she make it home without being intercepted by the police? What would happen when they finally caught up with her; just how much trouble was she in? It was certainly worth leaving Sloth to find out. Dan had sidled up to her during the firework display at the Ashington's and expressed his displeasure that she had upset Mandy with her accusations and said that he thought it best she "move on" in the morning. That was his exact words, she reflected, as she boarded the train that was now awaiting passengers to carry them back to their lives. "Move on". To start with she saw this as an opportunity. Given the contacts she had made to inspire her dressmaking venture, she realised that by "moving on", her hunt for a place to stay would have to be ramped up.

She'd needed some space to think through her plan of action, away from the noisy whizzing, popping and banging of the colourful explosions from the fireworks exploding in the night sky above her.

In the gloom, she drifted away from the crowd, wandering away from the house, lost in her thoughts, and found herself heading towards the stables. If only she'd stayed put, she reflected, things would be a lot different this morning. She could have wandered back to Sloth, called in on Mrs Angel and asked if she could lodge with her for a bit. Or gone to find Kate and tell her of the predicament over her living arrangements. Now, she didn't know whether she'd ever see Kate again. Hindsight was a wonderful thing.

She truly thought that she'd be alone as she wandered into the stables. She was pleased to see that the black face of Abigail's Dream was peering inquisitively over the stable door, and she approached the horses with far less caution than when she'd been in this position earlier in the week.

"Hello girl," she murmured, rubbing the velvety patch between her nostrils. The horse eyed her up silently. "You're not bothered about the fireworks then?" she asked her equine friend as a particularly fierce crack shattered through the night air. If horses could shrug, Abigail would swear the horse responded with a nonchalant reply.

"Me neither," came a familiar Irish drawl. Abigail's heart sank as Callum appeared from the tack room next door. "I found Mr Ashington's secret stash of whisky, much more enjoyable." He held up a bottle of whisky that was three quarters empty. It was a good brand, a single malt that her Dad usually got given at Christmas to enjoy on special occasions. "Shame it's Scottish, the Irish make it much better, but one can't be choosy with a freebie. Want some?"

"No, it's OK."

Callum put the bottle down on the ground and joined Abigail at the stable door. Wordlessly he stretched his hand up to slowly rub the horse's ears, a tender gesture that showed a return to the gentle Callum that she'd witnessed on Friday. Before he'd ruined the moment and asked her to join him at Aintree. His right arm was resting on the top of the stable door, touching Abigail's left arm, skin to skin. He turned his head to face her, his eyes dark and dangerous, but hypnotically thrilling.

"So, what are you running from?" he asked slowly. "What's your big secret?" His drunken state seemed to have vanished and apart from the smell of whisky on his breath, his thoughts were clearly focused and sober. Abigail's heart started pounding. He clearly knew more than he should.

"What's Mandy been saying?" Abigail stammered.

"Mandy? Mandy's not said anything, but you have!" Callum started to chuckle at a private thought and clamped his hand over Abigail's wrist. "You left yourself logged in on Facebook you daft cow. I couldn't help but read the message from your friend. 'Please come home, you're not in trouble,' he quoted from Nadine's message in a mock woman's voice. "'We all miss you.'"

He took her by surprise and tugged her by the wrist away from the stable and dragged her into the darkened tack room next door. He had surprising strength for someone with such a small frame. Abigail's heart was thumping hard and fast in her chest now, an ominous feeling sweeping over her.

"So," he continued, half throwing Abigail in front of him and standing in the doorway, blocking her exit. "It seems that you have a dirty little secret that I know, which means that you will need to be very nice to me to make sure that I don't accidentally pass that on to anyone else. Hmmm?"

Abigail's thoughts were racing, trying to recall any training courses that she could draw on to help diffuse this situation. Callum was advancing on her. Her mind was blank. Nothing to draw on. Then again, the assertiveness training course when tackling Mandy hadn't ended well.

"How about starting with that kiss that you've been dying to give me?" He clamped his whisky drenched lips onto hers with passionate force; wet, desperate kissing that reminded Abigail of her first kiss at school. Aged nine with a scrawny ginger kid called Alan, who had to kiss her because his friend was busy getting off with her friend Lisa. They'd been like a couple of goldfish, trying out the kisses they'd seen on TV. This was different though; Callum's intentions were far less honourable than Alan's had ever been.

She managed to wriggle her head free and shoved Callum away from her. "Callum, you're a married man and you really don't want to be doing this," she scolded in a shaky voice. "You've had too much to drink." Her rebuttal seemed to fuel him up more, and he began to beam.

"Ooh, a frisky filly!" he exclaimed. "I know how to handle a misbehaving little filly, they just need to be shown who's in charge." He glanced around the tack room and in a swift movement grabbed a riding crop that was laying on the dusty floor. "We use the whip in several ways," he explained, moving closer to her once again. "Firstly to make the horse focus on the job in hand." With a snap of the wrist he brought the crop down sharply onto her bare shin with a loud crack, making her yelp. It was more the shock that he'd actually just slapped her with the whip than any great physical pain. She took a step back but felt that she'd reached the wall on the far side of the tack room. Totally trapped.

"And secondly to make the horse do what we want it to do." A second slap of the crop, this time across the thigh. "Understand?" He now looked angrier, more menacing. It took all her strength not to nod in reply.

He clamped his mouth back onto hers, pressing her body back against the wall. She tried to push her hands against his chest, but he fought them off, grabbing her wrists and forcing them down to his crotch. There was no mistaking where he intended this to lead, she realised with rising panic. Every negative emotion rose in her; despair, humiliation, helplessness, panic. And then anger. Only a small glimmer of anger, but it was enough to enable her to send a knee straight up into his crotch. The only defence, taught to girls from an early age.

He recoiled in pain temporarily, doubled over, cradling his wounded parts. That was the moment. That was her chance. She had replayed the scene over and over in her head since that time and could not explain to herself why on earth she didn't run. She stayed, rooted to the spot, surprised that he'd let go of her. In a split second, her chance was gone, and Callum looked up at her from his crouched position. "You bitch," he spat venomously. "You bloody bitch, you're gonna pay for that."

This time his grip on her wrists with his left hand was tighter, rougher, and he quickly thrust a knee between her legs to force them apart. His right hand still clutched the riding crop, which he used to raise the silk hem of her dress.

"Callum, please get off me," she wailed, feeling defeat seeping through her veins. It was ironic; the years she'd spent in London, wandering around the streets after dark with rape alarms in her handbag, and here she was about to meet her fate in sleepy Sloth. She tried to give his shoulder a final shove with her free left hand, and to her surprise his body peeled away from her with surprising momentum.

"You heard her, get off her." Callum fell backwards across the tack room and into a stack of empty buckets. Through the gloom of the tack room, Abigail saw Mr Ashington's shape looming in the doorway. He grabbed Callum by his collar and shoved him roughly out of the tack room. "Go and get Kate to take you home, you pathetic piece of shit."

Satisfied that Callum had been shooed away like a rabid dog, Robin turned his attention to Abigail, standing like frightened Bambi in the shadows. She had never been so relieved to see anyone in her life, an uncontrollable shaking now rising up from her knees through to the tips of her fingers as the adrenaline took hold.

"Are you OK?" He stepped forward, engulfing Abigail in his arms as she crumpled into tears. Within seconds, she convulsed with hot, salty, snotty sobs racking through her body, the relief and despair pouring out of her in equal measure. He held her, strong and silent until the sobs slowly subsided. Abigail felt safe cocooned in Robin's arms; it brought back fond memories of being cuddled as a small child. Falling off her bike and scraping her knees raw, the time she stepped on a broken glass bottle on the seabed, all times that her Dad had scooped her into his arms and let her cry until there were no more tears to come.

He handed her a tissue and she wiped her eyes and blew her nose. No doubt she looked a mess now, but she was beyond caring. With a protective arm around her shoulder, Robin led her over to a chair in the corner and sat her down, perching his own buttocks on the edge of the desk alongside.

"Thank you," Abigail muttered, feeling that words were necessary. "I don't know what would have happened if you hadn't come along."

"I think we can both imagine," he replied grimly, to which Abigail shuddered at the thought. She was having trouble shaking the memory of the hardness of Callum's crotch pressing into her and the heat of his disgusting whisky stinking lips on hers. Like an image burned onto a retina, the mind couldn't blot out the horrors of the last ten minutes. "I usually do a quick nightly check of the horses about this time, and saw the whisky bottle outside. Has he hurt you?"

Abigail glanced down at the red line that had appeared across her shin from the slap of the whip, and inspected her wrists where she could still feel the burn of his rough grip. "I'll live," she replied flatly.

"April, I think we should call the police to report this."

"No!" Abigail yelped, a little too quickly than she'd intended. "I mean, there's no harm done."

"That's not the point, though, is it," Robin replied, the sensible voice of reason. "I mean, you said yourself, if I hadn't come along...". Abigail struggled to think of a response that would convince. "And if we let him get away with this, then he may try it on the next girl that comes along. The little shit," he added with uncharacteristic venom.

"I don't want the police involved," she replied quietly "If only for the sake of Kate and little Aidan."

"Well, it's your call," he sighed, obviously disappointed in her. "But you may be doing Kate a favour longer term. Maybe sleep on it, see if you change your mind in the morning."

Abigail nodded slowly, already knowing that she was doing nothing of the sort in the morning. She was going home. Her mind now made up, she couldn't stay in this stupid village any longer. Robin offered her his hand, sensing the talk had concluded, and pulled her gently to her feet. "Talking of sleeping, I don't like to think of you alone in that tent tonight. Do you want to stay here? Sam's bed is available - with him sleeping downstairs," he added to prevent any confusion.

Abigail didn't need to think very hard about it. The prospect of a soft warm bed with clean sheets and a nice hot shower in the morning was far more tempting than going back to Wits End, where she wasn't wanted, where the ground was rock hard and her sleeping bag was beginning to smell of onions from her night time sweats.

With a protective arm around her shoulder, Robin led her up

the shady side of the hedgerow towards the house so that they wouldn't be spotted. Abigail didn't want to see anyone she knew, and Robin didn't want to be seen with his arm around a girl half his age. The gossip in the village could be vicious. They went into the house through a side door that brought them into the corridor opposite the shower room. As they reached the base of the stairs, Robin peered into the open door of the study, and cocked his head. He indicated silently for Abigail to look in, where she saw a fully dressed Sam slumped face down on his makeshift bed. He looked like a rag doll, discarded by a child, his good leg dangling off the edge, his right arm flopped over his head.

"It doesn't matter if they're twenty four months, or twenty four years, you never tire of watching your children sleep." Robin regarded his son fondly for several seconds, Abigail touched by his love for his son. "Anyway, Sam's room is the one at the end of the landing - help yourself to anything you need." He leant forward and pecked her on the cheek. "Sleep tight."

"Thank you Robin." She paused on the first stair and turned back hesitantly to him. "By the way, and I'm sorry if it's none of my business, but I think your wife could do with a bit of Robin time at the moment." She paused and observed Robin's face, deep in some private thought momentarily. "Anyway, goodnight."

As the train trundled through the Gloucestershire countryside, Abigail managed a soft smile to herself as she remembered the kindness that Mr Ashington had shown. She felt a pang of guilt that all she'd left in repayment was a card - one of Mrs Fry's - that had been dried out in the airing cupboard after having a dunk in the pool with the other contents of her handbag.

She couldn't believe how well she had managed to sleep, given the dramas that had unfolded through the evening. But then again, the bed was extremely comfy, with just the right amount of softness to wrap around the contours of her body, with silky feeling sheets and a snugly duvet that she wrapped protectively around her. She'd taken a deep sniff into the pillow, expecting to smell the scent of Sam, a certain male aroma embedded into the cotton. But all she could detect was the clean fresh scent of washing powder; the bedding had clearly been changed during Sam's defection to the downstairs study.

His room was spacious and Abigail suspected that all bedrooms were of a similar size, complete with ensuite facilities and views of the peaceful countryside outside. Sam's room overlooked the pool and she could hear that the party was still continuing outside, with the babble of undecipherable conversation and soft laughter rippling through the night air. Candles and nightlights burned in glass holders on the tables around the pool, and Abigail watched the shadowy figures momentarily, unable to identify anyone in particular. She shut the curtains and felt inexplicably self-conscious, residing in Sam's private space without his knowledge.

After Callum's assault on her, she couldn't bear to sleep naked, so rummaged through Sam's drawers and found a purple rugby shirt and a pair of black stretchy trousers that may have served some equine purpose, but appeared to suit the job in hand. She resisted the temptation to rifle through any of his personal belongings, but took a long look around at the pictures on the wall. Mainly racing pictures, a football wallchart, and a framed newspaper cutting featuring what could only be his late uncle after his win in the Gold Cup. She was too tired to read the article but studied the colour photograph of the man kissing the round golden cup. *"Robert 'Buddy' Bradley celebrates his first Gold Cup triumph after winning by three lengths on Cloudy George"* read the caption. Abigail noted the traces of ginger hair poking out from beneath the green and brown silk cap, confirming that Sam had inherited the gene from his mother's side of the family. Wearily, she clambered into bed, exhaustion pulsing through her veins, and quickly drifted off to sleep to the soundtrack of party laughter rising up from the stragglers still enjoying the jacuzzi into the early hours.

The house was silent when she woke, and she was horrified when she looked at her watch and saw that it was nearly ten o'clock. Feeling like an uneasy intruder, Abigail padded into the kitchen and helped herself to a glass of juice. There was no evidence of the mess and festivities of the previous evening; somehow, little pixies had miraculously cleared the lawn of debris, of the bar, of the bucking broncho. Even the bunting and the sound system had been taken down. Nobody would know anything had taken place last night.

"Where is everyone?" she enquired of a female groom that wandered into the kitchen as Abigail was sat nursing her orange juice. There was vague recognition of each other from the bucking broncho session.

The groom looked slightly miffed to be treated like the Ashington's personal PA, and with a hurried shrug, mumbled something about Sam and his Mum having to go into Cheltenham hospital for a check up on his leg. "I guess Charly's at college and Robin's already left for Leicester."

Abigail didn't know whether to be relieved or disappointed. She had made her mind up that she wasn't staying around, but it felt wrong to just up and leave - taking Sam's clothing with her. But it seemed as though she had little choice, she had to go. She just scrawled in the blank greetings card "Thanks for your hospitality, Love April". She added two kisses and popped it in its envelope, leaving it propped up on the breakfast bar.

She prayed that she wouldn't bump into anyone on her walk back to Wits End; not Mandy, not Dan, not Kate and certainly not Callum. She couldn't bear to be confronted by a familiar face yet. Thankfully the roads were empty of traffic, and she returned to the tent undetected. She'd already decided to donate most of her goods to Mrs Angel for the next jumble sale in the village. With the exception of the dress that Sam had bought for her; she would treasure that, despite the memories it might bring back of the attack in the stables.

She reached to the back of the tent and pulled out the UGG boots. They had been consigned to the rear corner since purchasing them, as Penny had been right, it certainly wasn't the weather to be wearing them at the moment. Deep inside the right boot, a bit of white caught her eye. A small slip of paper. Curiously she pulled it out and squinted to read the scrawl. "*I hope we get the chance to meet again, call me.*" it read, accompanied by a mobile phone number. To begin with, she thought the note was left over from the boot's previous owner, but then she spotted the paper was actually a receipt from a pitch at Weird Al's car boot sale. Dated the Sunday she bought the material. On closer inspection, there was a signature underneath the number. Sam.

She stared at the paper for what felt like several minutes. The only explanation was that he'd put the note inside the boot when she'd left her box of goods in the land rover at the car boot sale. Tears pricked her eyes again, although she wasn't quite sure why. Knowing that he'd wanted to see her again from that very first meeting brought an aching sensation to her heart, made all the more upsetting that she was abandoning Sloth now. With just a poxy greeting card in the kitchen that said nothing of what she really felt. What was she feeling? She questioned herself anxiously. Well there was certainly affection towards his kindness and generosity, but a nagging guilt that she'd never been totally honest about who she was or why she was in the village. She could still remember the comforting feeling of his warm breaths on her ear as he hugged her unconditionally in the study last night.

She sighed, and realised that if she managed to get back to her parent's home in London without being intercepted by the police she could charge her phone and contact him. Eager to get going, she tried to pull herself together and made off for Fry's farm with the UGG boots tucked under her arm. There was one destiny for these.

The farm was also deserted as she approached the house up

the rutted track that served as their driveway. Penny would be at school and she guessed that Adam and his parents were busy doing whatever farmers got up to during the day. She'd been in the village ten days and still had no better idea of country life than when she arrived. She left the UGG boots on the porch step, and left a note using a page torn from her sketchbook.

"My time in Sloth has come to an end but I'd like you to have these boots to sell on ebay. Ask Penny for ideas on what to spend the proceeds on. April. Xxxx"

She returned to the campsite and loaded up all her other bits and pieces into carrier bags before taking the tent down and trying to work out how to get it all back into the carry bags it came in. Dan would probably have packed it away in a matter of minutes, but finally Abigail had stowed it away as best as she could. Balancing everything precariously in her arms, she had one last call to make. With carrier bags swinging from her forearms and a teetering heap of items crammed into the cardboard box, she rang Mrs. Angel's doorbell.

Mrs. Angel could tell something was up instantly as soon as she saw Abigail on the step, face puffy and red eyed.

"Whatever's the matter?" she said in greeting, to which tears started leaking down Abigail's face once again. Placing all the boxes and bags into the hallway, she followed Mrs. Angel as she led her through to the lounge where they sat on the familiar armchairs. Abigail had nothing to lose now, she figured, and piece by piece, told her everything. Once she started talking, she could barely stop and everything came out. The fiasco with the password at Bartletts, the banks crashing, running away, changing her name, missing her family and Nadine, the eventful party the previous evening, about the dress Sam bought her and finding Sam's note this morning. Nothing edited, right down to the detail of the smell of Robin's aftershave as he held her while she cried like a baby. She described the hatred in Mandy's eyes as they argued on the poolside, and elaborated on the tiny sequins on the beautiful silk dress from Betty Boo Boutique.

Mrs. Angel sat and listened without interruption. Now and then Abigail would pause to take a tissue from the box on the coffee table and wipe at her sore eyes or blow her nose.

Mrs. Angel wasn't sure where to start first. "You poor thing, what a lot you've been through," she said finally, when it was clear there was no more to add. "You could have told me sooner you know."

Abigail nodded. She could have trusted Mrs. Angel with her secret. She felt she could trust Mrs. Angel with her life.

"Well, I'm sure you're not in trouble, you didn't muddle up the computer intentionally, so I'm sure when you explain that, they wont blame you."

Abigail shrugged. She wasn't sure what to think any more.

"I'll be sorry to see you go," Mrs. Angel added truthfully. "The garden's going to get in a right state soon, and who am I going to share "Where in the world" with now?"

Abigail smiled a wonky smile.

"Sam will be disappointed you've left," she continued. "I had a chat over the fence yesterday with Mary next door, and she says she's been talking to Ella - the barmaid of The Carpenters Arms – and she was saying that Sam had been singing your praises to her. He's been telling everyone in the pub how helpful you were when you went looking at flats together."

"He was probably being sarcastic," Abigail reflected, remembering the way she was critical of many of his choices that day. But then she remembered the beautiful dress that he'd bought her off the back of her biting remarks. "Anyway, he won't feel that way about me when I'm banged away for 20 years, rotting at her majesty's pleasure."

"Well, I'll write to you in prison," smiled Mrs. Angel. "I wrote to this inmate on death row in America once upon a time."

"Really?" Abigail's mind was suddenly distracted from her self-pity at this revelation. "What happened?"

"He lost his appeal. They gave him a lethal injection."

That was a conversation stopper and both women sat thoughtfully for a few seconds, before Abigail remembered that the clock was ticking and she had a home to be getting back to.

"I brought you all the things I've accumulated to put with the items for your next village jumble sale," Abigail explained, indicating the boxes and carrier bags she'd dumped in the hallway. "I'll pop them upstairs with all the other bits."

And that's when Mrs Angel must have done it, Abigail reflected, fingering the fat envelope that had magically appeared in her handbag at some point between arriving at Mrs Angel's house and the moment she went to get her purse out of her handbag at Cheltenham station to pay the taxi driver. Glancing around the train carriage to check that nobody was watching, she pulled out the wad of fifty-pound notes and fanned them out like a flamenco dancer's prop. Just feeling that amount of cash was humbling. £5000 from Mrs Angel's savings, the same amount as the current jackpot on "Where in the world". The coincidence had not gone unnoticed by

Abigail and she didn't need Mrs Angel to spell it out to her that this was a gift to start up her dress making business.

The train hurtled on through the countryside and the landscape gradually gave way to the first signs of industry. The tracks passed by semi industrial landscapes, the outskirts of towns that had grown up in the last half century as places to house the workers that would fill factories, the offices, and the call centres. The sorts of places that Abigail would have been called upon for temping placements. The old Abigail, she reflected. No more temping. If she didn't become a prisoner back in London, she would now be a self-employed businesswoman. The thought of that sounded of good.

More and more concrete buildings appeared alongside the tracks and the train made its approach into Paddington station. Automatically Abigail fled the carriage with her head low, her hair scraped up under her trusty hat, and morphed back in a Londoner again. Hurried footsteps, no eye contact, and tutting at tourists that dithered in the entrance to the tube station. Her heart pounded faster as she descended into the depths of the underground, heading for the district line platforms, anticipation as familiar noises and aromas filled her senses. She scraped a free newspaper off the seat and rattled her way around to Earl's Court, where she changed onto the spur line to head for Kew. It was almost as though she'd never been away; this felt like returning from work, hearing the place names of tube stops, and playing the announcements out in her head, moments before the automated voice did. "Ladies and gentlemen, our next station stop is Stamford Brook, Stamford Brook the next scheduled stop. Please make sure you take all your belongs with you, and take care as you step down from the train."

As the train drew away from Gunnersbury, Abigail was on the home straight. The next announcement was for her stop. She surveyed the platform as the train pulled in to check for any police officers waiting to intercept her. Nothing. It was safe to emerge. Clutching her carrier bag of leftover possessions (one green silk dress, her semi-ruined kitten heels and a pair of Kate's old jumble sale jeans that were immensely comfy. And her underwear.) she exited the station briskly, back to London mode. Head down, no eye contact.

She breathed in the air, grateful that there was no smell of muck spreading. Her strides took her on autopilot through the calm leafy suburb, straight down to the junction where she finally turned into her road and scanned up and down the kerb. There was no police car outside the semi detached property that she'd called home for a quarter of a century. Relief flooded through her momentarily; it seemed that she would at least be able to get inside the house without being detected. She doubted whether her parents would be at home; term time meant that her mother would be at school until later in the afternoon depending on whether there were any afternoon activities or meetings. Her Dad would be at work, probably in meetings or chained to his desk writing curt emails or ploughing through some dull report. Abigail wasn't entirely sure what his job entailed on a day-to-day basis. He worked for the railway industry and had the words "asset" and "management" in his job title. She'd never needed to know any more than that. He wouldn't be home until nine o'clock. Monday night was always snooker night, which he'd attend straight from work. She'd rarely reflected in the past at just how routine driven the household was.

It felt great to put her key in the front door once again. It seemed as though her adventure had taken her away from the safety of this place for months; not the twelve days since she fled Bartletts in a blind panic. Stepping into the hallway there was the sleepy silence of an empty house. The oversized grandfather clock in the corner - inherited by her father from his great aunt – provided the only movement as its pendulum swung lazily and methodically, punctuating the silence with military regularity. She looked around the hallway as if seeing it for the first time, yet everything was exactly as she left it. The phone sat on the oak wood table by the coat stand, the family diary open to display that week with her mother's familiar scribble on some of the days. Hair appt, 5pm. Pam's b'day. Parents evening.

She headed up to her bedroom and threw her few possessions onto the duvet. The first task was to charge her phone again, and once that was connected into its socket she fired up the laptop that sat on her neat desk that overlooked the garden at the back.

One girl and her tent – Part Three
April Smith
Monday 15th April

I don't have another picture in the boardroom as the inspiration of this blog – my last and final post – but I did hear a quote once that really resonates with how I am feeling about my experience over the past week:

"The saddest thing about betrayal is that it never comes from your enemies."

I know I set out to blog about the experience of coping without comforts and possessions, but I think it would be more useful to use the blog to explore what I have learnt in a wider sense.

I have now come home, back to my comfort zone, back to all that is familiar, but not because I was pulled back by a sense of duty or having completed the mission. I was pushed back. People that I thought were friends, people that I had learnt to trust over the week let me down badly, and one person in particular – a jockey that will remain nameless – betrayed me to the point where I couldn't stay any longer.

I've been brooding about this for the past 24 hours, how somebody that I would happily have called a friend, could treat me so horrifically. But then, I realized that I haven't been completely honest with the people that regarded me as a new friend. I was living a lie too, with a false name and scattering fibs around to suit my needs, so am I guilty of betraying the people that came to trust me?

It's time to put it all right. Whilst I forgive the betrayal, I'm not excusing the crime. I'm just not going to be a victim and here ends that particular chapter of my life.

It was 5pm by the time she clicked the "Upload" button to put her blog live and she felt like she had underlined her time in Sloth now. No more need for "One girl and a tent" to continue further; she had said everything she needed to say. But there was one person who needed to read it. Taking her half charged phone in one hand, and the scrap of paper with Sam's scrawl in the other, she thought long and hard about the message.

'Sam, just got your number. Sorry I didn't get chance to say goodbye but you may want to read this.' She typed in the URL of the blog post, and then signed four kisses. She didn't put her name.

There. Definitely underlined. The police could come and take her away now and she felt that at least she had explained everything that was left unsaid. The ball was now in Sam's court. It was a liberating feeling. She was about to phone Nadine, when she heard the sound of a key in the front door. In a single movement she let the phone fall back onto the desk and leapt across her room in one single stride and bounded down the stairs. "Mum!"

Mrs Daycock was shutting the door behind her, glanced up at the commotion and beamed. "Oh, hello Ab, you're back then. I wish you'd phoned to let me know as I haven't bothered to make any supper with your Dad being out tonight and ...." She was forced to stop talking as Abigail flung herself into her mother's arms.

"I'm so sorry Mum," Abigail whispered, finding tears pricking her eyes and a lump rising to her throat. She clung tight to her Mum, suddenly appreciating the impact that her disappearance could have had on her parents.

"Oh, not to worry, I'm sure I can find something else in the freezer. I think there's some of those meat pies in there from the farmers market.". It was clear that Abigail was reluctant to let go, and finally Mrs Daycock had to attempt to peel her daughter off of her. "Are you OK?" she asked, trying to make eye contact.

The mixed emotions of the past twenty four hours were engulfing Abigail and once again, she fought back the tears. "What's the matter? Did it all go wrong with that fellow you went away with? Tell you what, let's put the kettle on - I'm gasping - and you can tell me all about it."

Before Abigail could open her mouth, her mother was making her way through the hall towards the poky kitchen at the rear of the house. In confusion, Abigail followed her.

"Am I not in trouble?" she asked quietly. Her mother had her back to Abigail, filling the kettle from the tap. Without saying a word she fetched the floral teapot down from a top shelf and placed two mugs on the counter top.

"What, for running away? You're twenty three years old Abigail, you're free to do what you like." There was a scolding tone to her voice. "Although," she added disapprovingly, "you could have told us where you were, and that you were OK. I was hoping for a postcard at least". Her mother stopped fussing around with tea bags and took the opportunity to take a more dedicated look at her daughter. "Have you been looking after yourself properly, you look pretty rough. And what are you wearing?"

Abigail glanced down and realized that she was still wearing Sam's baggy purple rugby top and black riding trousers. "They're Sam's," she replied flatly without explanation. "So no-one's been looking for me?"

Her mother frowned, trying to think. "Well, the agency are mad at you and want to know what's going on. And Bartlett's want your guts for garters of course. You owe them a big apology young lady."

Bingo. Somebody *was* mad at her then. "Running off like that and leaving them with no cover. Especially just as hell was all breaking out with that computer virus thing." Abigail digested her words and watched as she swilled boiling water around in the teapot to warm it. Her mother wouldn't dream of making a cup of tea in the mug itself.

"So, this Sam, is that who you went away with?"

"Hang on, wait a minute. What computer virus?"

Her mother regarded her impatiently. "There was a virus that got into the computers of the banking system, seemed to bring all sorts of chaos with people not being able to access their accounts. Honestly Abigail, I know you were in the throes of passion, but you could have at least picked up a newspaper while you were away."

The realisation dawned on Abigail like a ton of bricks, and she suddenly felt pathetically foolish. There was never any police, she'd been in no trouble, and there was never any possibility of any lengthy prison sentences. She wasn't the next Nick Leeson after all. Humiliation burnt across her face, but the saving grace was that it was only Nadine and Mrs Angel that knew the whole truth. And she certainly intended for it to stay that way.

She took the mug of tea from her Mum and smiled gratefully. "It's good to be home."

Ascot

"So, do you think Sam will be there?" Nadine asked Abigail. The girls felt like royalty on the back seat of the Bentley that had been arranged to pick them up. Abigail shrugged noncommittally; she was sure that wasn't the first time that Nadine had asked the question and was feeling a bit peevish that she was even asking. So what if he was there? So what if he wasn't?

Deep down she knew that if he wasn't there then she had certainly offended him. Unsure of what she'd done to upset him, his silence since she'd sent him the text with the link to the blog three weeks ago made it clear that he no longer wanted anything to do with her. She hated the thought that she'd upset him. In the three weeks that had passed since her abrupt departure from Sloth, she'd done a lot of reflecting on the events that had transpired in the sleepy Gloucestershire backwater. She missed Sam. The distance from him made her realise how much she had enjoyed his company and what an influence he'd had on her. She'd filled Nadine in with everything that had gone on, and Nadine was now curious about all the characters in the plot.

"I'm looking forward to meeting Charly," Nadine chattered on, her eyes darting around the Berkshire countryside as it passed by the tinted windows outside. "We need to sort out the playlist for Blue Steak to play at the ball next month. There's only so much you can do by email, it's much easier when you can meet someone and discuss things face to face."

It was thanks to Charly that the invite to Ascot had come through. Having liked April Smith's Facebook clothing page, the invitation to make Charly's dress still stood. Doubled with the fact that Blue Steak were booked to play at the forthcoming ball led to a dual invite from Charly for both Abigail and Nadine to join the Ashington's at Ascot's Saturday "Rock and Roll" themed race day. Robin Ashington had pulled some strings to book a box and had organised for the chauffeur to collect them from London to save them having to mix with 'commoners' on the train. It was overly generous yet again, thought Abigail guiltily, especially if Sam is upset. On the flip side, reasoned Abigail to herself, it is my birthday, and they wouldn't offer if they didn't want to extend the hospitality. If Sam wanted to be huffy and not come, or come and not talk to her, then that was his problem. Abigail told herself this over and over but couldn't convince herself.

"Yeah, Charly's great," Abigail replied. "Very confident and switched on. Robin's lovely too, as is Sam," she conceded. Nadine smiled inwardly. She knew her friend well enough to be able to tell when she was smitten.

"Did you get his birthday present sorted?" she asked. They had had a long conversation trying to decide what to get for his present. Abigail didn't want to spend a lot of money on a lavish gesture, despite the dress that he bought her costing a fortune. Especially now that he hadn't been in touch, she didn't regret going for the cheaper, but more thoughtful option. She'd tracked down an acquaintance from university that now had a silver jewellery business in Camden and commissioned a pair of cufflinks in the shape of horseshoes. Made in a fat chunky style there was room on the backs of the horseshoes to engrave today's date, his 25th birthday.

"They are gorgeous," gushed Nadine, as Abigail removed them from the tissue paper in their little small box. "I'm sure he'll love them. Let's hope he's there."

The Bentley crawled through the slow moving traffic on Ascot's bustling High Street and Abigail put the cufflinks back in their box and safely stowed into the gift bag. It had seemed easier than wrapping the box up. People were streaming up the High Street, most dressed for a wedding, many girls taking the rock and roll theme and wearing dresses with full skirts. Abigail was relieved that she wouldn't stand out in her dress that she'd made especially. Having performed a google search for 50s fashion and choosing one of the image results for inspiration, she'd made a dress from some cheap checked cheesecloth, matched up some heels and handbag from the depths of her wardrobe and pulled her hair into a high ponytail.

Nadine turned her nose up at the theme but wouldn't mind, nor barely notice, if she stood out. She was wearing a purple flaired trouser suit with a white blouse, platform boots and her hair covered in a thick grey headscarf dappled with purple beads. As always, Nadine looked interesting.

The Bentley dropped the girls on the road closest to the ticket office where they had been instructed to meet Charly. They thanked the driver, who had been pretty much wordless throughout their hour-long journey and Abigail clutched Nadine's arm to drag her to a pause before they approached the ticket office. She scanned the small crowd assembled by the entrance and spotted Charly straight away, her thick brown curls framing her smiling face. They hadn't been seen yet; Charly was gazing out into the crowded High Street in serene contentment. Then Abigail's heart plunged. Next to Charly was Kate. Nobody said anything about Kate coming, and if Kate was here, could it mean that Callum was here? Abigail suddenly felt a bit sick at the thought of Callum sharing the same space in the box as her. Surely Robin would be more sensitive than that.

"What's the matter?" whispered Nadine, reading the expression on Abigail's face.

Abigail shook her head and took a deep breath. "Nothing, I can see Charly." No Sam though, Abigail observed with a sinking heart.

Displaying a boldness she didn't feel inside, Abigail led Nadine up to Kate and Charly. Charly whooped in delight and hugged Abigail, before being introduced to Nadine and hugging her as well. Kate was smiling warily, but Abigail chose to act normally and greeted her with a huge smile and embraced her too. In relief, Kate held Abigail for a second longer than necessary.

"I'm so sorry about Callum," she whispered quickly in Abigail's ear. She knew then. There had been no communication between the two friends since Abigail left Sloth. The only person Abigail had made an effort to contact was a weekly phone call to Mrs. Angel, who had barely had chance to gather in the latest village gossip.

"He's not here, is he?" Abigail voiced her concern as she pulled away from Kate's arms.

"God, No," replied Kate emphatically, as if that was the most stupid suggestion. In the time it took the four of them to walk through the turnstiles and across the open expanse of the grand Ascot forecourt, Kate had filled Abigail in on how Callum had broken down in tears on the taxi ride home from the Ashington's party that night, and confessed everything that he'd done - or tried to do - to Abigail that night. They had stayed up all night talking, with Callum admitting to a raft of misdemeanors that he claimed he regretted. With a tone that wavered between hatred and devastation towards her husband, Kate revealed that Callum had also been sleeping with a groom in Lambourn, as well as an on and off relationship with a jockey based in Scotland and he'd had a one night stand in Aintree the night before the Grand National.

"He's gone back to Ireland to concentrate on racing there," Kate explained wistfully. "But he'll have to have access to Aidan, so we're keeping on civil terms." She smiled gratefully at Abigail. "I was worried you'd hate me."

"Of course not; you can't be responsible for Callum's behaviour."

They entered the building. It was a breathtaking space, like an airport terminal, spacious, glassy with escalators rising high up to the top floors, and smartly dressed race goers, buzzing with excitement and anticipation. Charly showed them how to flash their badge at the suited gentlemen guarding the base of the escalators.

They nodded politely in reply making Abigail feel like royalty.

"Mum and Dad are already here, Sam's joining us later as he's on his way down from somewhere up north. He was in York yesterday." Charly chattered on the escalator. Nadine nudged Abigail wordlessly in the small of her back at the mention of Sam. Charly pointed out the door to the Royal box as they ascended up higher and higher, although the door was closed shut, so there was nothing spectacular to note.

There was no need to flash their badge again at the door to the Ashington box as Charly was recognised by the lady guarding the corridor. The group were waved on through and Charly led them into a space the size of the penthouse in Cheltenham, complete with its own bar and floor to ceiling glass panels overlooking the final furlong of the course. There were sliding patio doors to one end of the glass leading out onto a stepped terrace. Towards the back of the box Abigail spied a long table laid out with preparations for a buffet; shiny crockery and cutlery, napkins and condiments. She was glad; it was already one o'clock and her tummy was on the verge of deep rumblings.

"Happy birthday," greeted Mr. Ashington, stepping forward to give Abigail a polite hug.

Abigail was surprised but pleased to see that Mrs Ashington was also in attendance, looking fresher and happier than their previous encounters. Even her outfit, a plain mint green shift dress, didn't look too clumsy with her brown eye shadow and chocolate coloured shoes.

"Free bar, what are you having?" asked Charly.

Relief flooded though Abigail, who wasn't feeling in an economic position to be paying posh racecourse prices for alcohol. She was acutely aware that Nadine was also in the same boat, clutching only a twenty-pound note to cover the day's expenses. Before the girls had chance to decide, Charly had already ordered a bottle of chardonnay, served in a large metal bucket of ice. No-one questioned her age.

She took control with a natural confidence and ease, pouring them each a glass of wine before leading them out onto the terrace and pointing out the finishing post, where the queen would be sitting during the Royal Ascot race meeting next month, and finally installing them into the row of fold down plastic chairs and distributing booklets to them all.

"Ah, a programme!" declared Abigail, taking her copy and flicking it open.

"Race card," corrected Kate with a fond smile. "The first race is in twenty minutes so we'd better decide who we're backing."

"I have no clue," muttered Nadine. "I think I'll just choose a cute name."

Abigail found the page with the listings for the first race and quickly scanned down the horse's names. Next to each listing was a small mugshot of the jockey. Halfway down the list she did a double take at the picture. There, smiling out from under his black silk cap, was the freckled face of Sam. The horse was Abigail's dream.

Everything suddenly slotted into place, like the twist of a murder mystery novel, and her mind reeled back to all the conversations they'd had. Doing jobs for his Dad, he'd said. Well yes, this was some job. He'd never openly said that he was a jockey, but then he'd never had the opportunity to deny it either. What had Kate said too, about jockeys being 'minted'. That would explain the Porsche and the budget for the flat, even the generous purchase of the dress from Betty Boo's Boutique.

Part of her was suddenly disappointed, remembering the scene in the kitchen between Kate and Callum, throwing dates around between them, scheduling in time to see each other. Hadn't she said to Sam the following evening that she could never date a jockey for that reason? She was getting ahead of herself, she realised. Who said anything about the possibility of them dating anyway? It would appear Sam didn't want any contact with her.

"Look Ab, a horse called Abigail's dream," Nadine pointed out.

"That's one that my Dad trains," Charly explained, for Nadine's benefit. "And Sam's riding her. We think she's got a great chance of stealing this, as long as Sam's fit. It's only his second ride back after his injury."

"Well, it's getting my twenty quid," nodded Kate, fishing in her handbag for her purse. Abigail sensed Nadine baulk at the thought of blowing her day's budget on the first race.

"Tell you what," she reasoned. "I'll stick a tenner on for both of us. If it wins, you can put the next bet on from your winnings." Abigail prayed it would win. She looked back at the race card and the photo of Sam. He looked so happy and carefree, and the black silk of his cap contrasted beautifully with the golden shine of his Moroccan Sunset hair.

"Where's everyone gone?" she asked, suddenly looking up and realising that the box had emptied out.

"Parade ring," replied Charly. "Dad and the owners - some syndicate from the banking world – need to go down and watch the horses circle, talk tactics to Sam. They'll stay down there and watch the race. So, shall I go and place the bets?" She had half an eye on her smartphone. "Abigail's dream is currently ten to one."

She gathered up the money and enlisted Kate to help her go

and find the best price at the bookies who were lined up on the tarmac alongside the track. Nadine and Abigail soaked up the May sunshine from the balcony, enjoying the rare opportunity to be sipping free booze.

"Oh look, horses," sang Abigail, spotting the graceful creatures emerge from several storeys below their feet and canter elegantly off down towards the starting stalls. She stood and leant over the railing, glass in one hand, race card in the other, open on the correct page.

"There's Sam," Mrs Ashington's voice said from behind them. She emerged from the patio door and joined them at the railing, as all three watched the dark horse with Sam on board follow the other runners down the course. It wouldn't have been easy to pick him out, the black silk cap covering any trace of his golden hair, and his oversized goggles masking his eyes. All the jockeys seemed to be carbon copies of each other; there was even a lady jockey amongst them somewhere according to the race card, but her body wasn't distinguishable from the others heading to post.

Abigail spotted with surprise that Mrs Ashington was clutching a glass of orange juice.

"Driving?" Abigail asked, nodding towards the glass.

"No, just cutting down," she confessed in reply. "I'll have some champagne when Sam wins." She paused, gazing thoughtfully down the track, looking as though she wanted to say something more.

"Have you gone back to work yet?" Abigail prompted. She was aware that she was coming across as being nosy, but Mrs Ashington didn't appear to mind the questions.

"Not yet, but I'm planning to when we come back from holiday. I'm not quite sure what's come over Robin, but he's taking a week off work and taking me away to some romantic spa retreat in Austria. It's the first time we've been away since... Well, probably our honeymoon."

"Good for him," laughed Abigail, bursting inside with pride that maybe she had instigated this change. She'd contributed to saving their marriage and Mrs Ashington's sanity. Well, she liked to think so.

The big screen on the side of the track was now showing images of the horses being loaded into their stalls, and the commentary was reverberating loud and clear through the speakers in the box. There was a large plasma screen on the wall inside the box, but somehow it seemed a waste to watch it inside. You could do that from home. Abigail was surprised to find her heart was starting to pound. She wasn't sure whether it was excitement or nerves for Sam, but she could feel the butterflies in her tummy and wondered whether Sam felt the same, or whether this was just another job for him. Kate and Charly burst back onto the balcony in the nick of time.

"And they're off and racing," came the authoritative voice of the commentator, as the doors of the stalls snapped open and ten horses sprang out like Jack-in-the-boxes and began their tenacious gallop for home. The horses were tiny blobs in the distance on the track, so Abigail kept her eyes on the screen alongside the track to match the action with the commentary. "and blazing the trail early on the far side is Henry the eighth in the red jacket, with Cool Aunt on the nearside with the white noseband. Also handy is Kazoom, followed on the nearside in the yellow jacket by My Mate Mark and behind these is McDonald…"

Abigail struggled to see Sam's colours within all the horses bunched up on the screen.

"Don't say he's right at the back," she groaned to Charly. "But then I suppose there's a long way to go yet. How many times do they go round?"

"Oh no, it's only a mile, which means they just come up the straight and cross the finish line."

"Oh." Abigail turned her attention back to the action, praying Sam would start nudging to the front soon.

"…chasing this leader Henry the eighth, who's joined by Butterfly moving up on the nearside. My Mate Mark, Cool Aunt and Prisoner on the far side. After these races McDonald and after those is Toffee and then Abigail's Dream on the far side."

"At last, he gets a mention!" exclaimed Nadine, but everyone was concentrating now, silently willing him on. Abigail looked down the track and could now see the gang of colour hurtling towards them, but was unable to make out who was who.

"As they stretch towards the final quarter mile, My Mate Mark is challenging Butterfly, over on the far side Toffee is running on under pressure, also coming in there is Kazoom and McDonald, but My Mate Mark is holding on. Abigail's Dream now starting to pick up, so too Mysterious…"

They could now see the black silk colours of Sam pushing through the middle of the pack, drawing up towards the front-runners. Abigail glanced from the finishing post to the pack of horses, there was still time, if they carried on advancing like that. The man in the commentary box was raising the pitch of his voice in excitement, and Abigail realized she was holding her breath.

"Abigail's Dream coming forward to wear down My Mate Mark, then Mysterious, now well inside the final furlong, but it's Abigail's

Dream under a well timed ride here from Sam Ashington clearing away to score. Abigail's Dream takes it from My Mate Mark, with Mysterious in third and Cool Aunt in fourth.."

It was amazing that the balcony didn't collapse under the weight of the five ladies jumping up and down in ecstasy, clutching their receipts from the bookies promising to pay them three figure sums. Abigail was partly euphoric at the winnings, but glowed inside with pride for Sam. Callum had described the need to win as an addiction, and Abigail suspected Sam was feeling ten times the adrenaline rush that any of them on the balcony were experiencing. She didn't take her eyes off the dark horse as they slowed to a canter and then down to a trot beyond the finish line and then began a steady walk back to the winner's enclosure. Sam was grinning from ear to ear but didn't look up to smile in their direction.

"Well, that certainly calls for more wine," demanded Charly, checking that the bottle in the bucket was empty, and carting it over to the bar for more.

"That was the easiest hundred quid we've ever made, eh Ab?" marvelled Nadine as she examined the bookies receipt in disbelief. Abigail felt no sympathy for the gentleman in a wax jacket who counted out a thick wad of ten pound notes into her hands a few moments later as the girls went to collect their winnings. There were plenty more people that had backed the favourite, Butterfly, that wouldn't be getting their cash back.

As promised, Abigail split the winnings with Nadine and let her have the pick of the next race. Although her friend was taking the task very seriously, studying names, looking in the race card to see what the verdict was on their form, and flirting with a random guy in a grey pinstripe suit to ask his opinion, Abigail knew deep down that the subsequent races wouldn't have the same excitement without Sam riding in them. She'd flicked ahead through the programme to see whether his face appeared again next to any of the mounts, but she was disappointed.

Having placed her ten pounds on a horse called 'Fabulous Frankie', Nadine accompanied Abigail back up to the box, which had now filled up with a lot more connections, gathered loosely around Robin like wasps round a coke can. Abigail presumed that they had all been downstairs earlier. The box was buzzing and there was no possibility of introductions.

Abigail went off to the ladies, a far cry from the toilet block at Wits End, with its polished marble surfaces, shiny tiled floors and posh hand soaps and moisturizers. She topped up her lipstick, re-squirted a dash of perfume behind her ears and stepped back into the charged atmosphere of the private box.

"Oh look, it's Sandra Dee," came a familiar voice. She turned to see Sam, now dressed in a smart dark suit with sky blue shirt and a chunky navy tie, which was slightly off centre and loosened rebelliously. His hair was freshly washed and ruffled untidily and Abigail found her heartbeat start to speed up uncontrollably. He wasn't smiling his usual friendly warm welcome as he hovered on the edge of his Dad's group and regarded her neutrally. "You came then."

Abigail opened her mouth to reply but no words came out. She took a deep breath and decided to use the same tactic as when she'd first seen Kate earlier. Act normal, you've done nothing wrong, a voice told her inside her head.

"Of course I came, Charly invited me. And I'm glad I did, to see you win like that, it was amazing, congratulations. Oh, and happy birthday too."

Sam smiled, but it looked like it was an effort and the smile didn't reach his eyes. "Yeah, you too." He looked down at his feet and shuffled awkwardly.

"Look Sam... are we OK?" she asked quietly, stepping closer to him.

He slowly raised his eyes from the floor to meet hers. He shrugged dismissively like a stroppy teenager. "You tell me."

Abigail sighed and wished she had her glass of wine in her hand. She could do with being able to take a large glug for courage right now. Out of the corner of her eye she saw Robin turn from the group he was commanding, and approach them, a glass of wine in each hand. Thank God. Her saviour once again.

"Right Sam, you take that," he instructed bossily, thrusting a glass of wine at his son. He handed the other to Abigail. "I think you two have some crossed wires and I suggest you go and sit somewhere quiet and uncross them. Agreed?"

Abigail looked from Sam to Robin and back to Sam and nodded compliantly. Sam shrugged again. "Come on then, we'll go out on the terrace."

He trudged across the box, briefly acknowledging a few of the connections that shouted out congratulations at him as he passed. Abigail followed, feeling Nadine's eyes watching her from where she was making small talk with Charly and Kate. The air was cooler outside and Abigail realized how stuffy the box had become with the additional people.

They sat on the plastic chairs furthest from the patio door and Sam gazed out over the racetrack momentarily before turning to her. She gulped at her wine.

"So..." he sighed.

"Why don't you start," Abigail suggested. "You tell me why you're pissed off with me. I don't really understand what I've done wrong."

There was a hesitation as Sam gathered his thoughts. "Well," he began. "I met a wonderful girl about a month ago. She took my breath away the first time I set eyes on her, and she was good company, and kind, we got on well and I thought she felt the same way about me too."

Abigail frowned and felt a tide of jealousy rising up in her. Why was he telling her about another girl, and what did any of this have to do with her pissing him off?

"She made such an impact on my life in a short space of time, she made me question who I was, what I was doing with my life and what I want to be doing with it. Anyway, I always knew she wasn't going to be around permanently but at the point when we were getting really close she just ups and leaves without saying goodbye, and then I find out she'd not really been truthful about who she was..."

Ah, he was talking about her. She suddenly felt foolish again. She opened her mouth to protest but thought better of it. He deserved the courtesy of being allowed to continue uninterrupted. Sam averted his eyes and stared out across the racecourse as he carried on his monologue.

"It seemed I did something to upset her, but she didn't say what. She just wrote all about it in a cryptic blog post, publically announcing something about a jockey letting her down, and that seemed to be a very clear message to me that I've overstepped some sort of mark and she no longer wants anything to do with me."

He had nothing more to say and turned his attention back to her. He raised his sandy eyebrows, inviting her response.

"Oh Sam," she sighed in despair. "You have got your wires crossed. I did lie about my name, I'm sorry, I'm Abigail by the way," she held out her hand for him to shake in an effort to lighten the mood but he wasn't ready to play. She put her hand back in her lap. "I thought I was in trouble, and just needed not to be Abigail for a while. It's a long story, which I won't go into here, but I'm sorry for not being honest about that. But everything else was true. And you weren't so honest with me. You never told me you were a jockey, did you?"

He furrowed his eyebrows for moment. "I presumed you knew. I just thought someone would have mentioned it."

"No, you said you did jobs for your Dad, so I thought you just shovelled horse shit into wheelbarrows and exercised them most days. So it wasn't you I was referring to in the blog." Abigail cast her mind back to try and recall the exact words she had written. She couldn't remember any sentences exactly but she knew the gist.

People that I thought were friends, people that I had learnt to trust over the week let me down badly, and one person in particular – a jockey that will remain nameless – betrayed me to the point where I couldn't stay any longer.

"Looking back, I can see how you may have interpreted that as being a dig at you, but I was actually referring to Callum." Abigail was both surprised and pleased that Robin had not breathed a word about the events of that night to anyone in the family. She had misjudged the propensity for gossip in the village it seemed. It could have avoided this big misunderstanding though if he'd told Sam a version of events. "He did something awful the night of the party," Abigail continued, not quite sure how much she wanted to reveal. A little voice in her subconscious urged her on; she had nothing to be ashamed of, and she shouldn't be keeping secrets from Sam after the misunderstanding that had just occurred. "He cornered me in the tack room and he was just so hideously drunk." The memory of the stench of his whisky-soaked breath and the clumsy wetness of his forceful kiss flooded back to her, and she felt a lump rising in her throat. "He's pretty strong, he completely overpowered me and if your Dad hadn't come along in the nick of time, he'd have ..." she couldn't say it. She looked up at Sam. "well, you know."

He flinched as though she'd slapped him, and instantly grabbed her free hand.

"Oh God, I'm so sorry," he gushed. "I feel pretty foolish now, and selfish, for thinking it was all about me. I'm sorry. Callum is *such* a bastard. Is that why Kate's thrown him out?"

"Well, that, and a few other recent misdemeanors that at least he had the decency to admit to." Abigail realized that Sam still had hold of her hand. His skin was surprisingly soft and warm.

"There were always rumours going around in the weighing room about Callum. I hoped for Kate's sake that there were no foundations in them, but I was obviously wrong. Poor girl."

"Oh, I've got something for you," Abigail remembered. She needed to free her hand from Sam's to delve into her handbag and pull out the gift bag containing his birthday present. He looked surprised that she had got him anything, but smiled gratefully and pulled the box out from the bag.

"They're amazing, thank you," he said, genuinely pleased with the cufflinks. She pointed out the engraving on the back and the fact that her friend had made them as a commission. He removed the pair he was currently wearing - the Playboy bunny logo – and replaced them with Abigail's gift. Holding out his arms, he admired them gratefully.

"Oh, and I've got something for you!" He began to reach into the inside pocket of his suit jacket.

"But you gave me the dress for my birthday, I don't expect anything…"

"Your winnings," Sam interrupted her, placing a fat envelope in her lap. "From the Grand National. Mum went to the bookies when we were in Cheltenham on the day after the party to pick them up, but you'd left by the time we got back to Sloth."

Abigail peered into the envelope and nearly fainted. The wad of matching twenty-pound notes was as overwhelming as the envelope Mrs. Angel had left in her handbag.

"It couldn't be this much, could it?" she argued with a frown. "Moroccan Sunset was fifty to one."

"He was eighty to one when Harriet placed the bet," Sam replied. "Eight hundred, plus your ten pound stake back. I'd say drinks were on you!"

Abigail stowed the envelope safely in her handbag. That was all going into her business, the same way Mrs. Angel's cash had been a lifeline for the start-up of April Smith's fashion empire. She'd never imagined that gambling would have been the investor she needed though.

The speakers crackled into action again and Abigail realized that the second race was about to start soon.

"Do you want to go down and stand by the finish line?" asked Sam. "The view's great up here, but there's something about feeling the thundering hooves as they cross the line in front of you."

Abigail nodded enthusiastically and followed Sam off the balcony and back through the box, where Nadine caught her eye with an enquiring look. Abigail smiled back enigmatically, giving very little away. They descended back through the building on the tall escalators and exited onto the trackside near the finishing post. A few people seemed to recognize Sam and gave him a pat on the shoulder for the win.

"So have you backed a horse this time?" Sam asked, taking a spot against the rail.

"Nadine's put a tenner on Fabulous Frankie for the both of us," she replied. Sam sucked air into his mouth disapprovingly.

"Not a hope," he replied adamantly. "He's been put up in trip and is carrying a bit of extra weight. I think Sly Fox has this one in the bag."

"What do you know?" teased Abigail. "You said that there

187

were thirty eight horses that had a better chance than Moroccan Sunset. My eight hundred and ten pounds suggests otherwise."

They fell silent as the horses jumped loose from the stalls on the big screen in front of them and hurtled up the track. The commentary boomed out, but Abigail was barely listening. She was distracted with her thoughts, thinking how brilliantly everything was working out. She was slowly starting to build up the fashion design business, with orders creeping in, and some funding to develop the website and advertising. She had reconciled differences with the people of Sloth that had brought about this change in her. She was changed. She had noticed a nursing home a few streets from her home that she had never bothered to acknowledge before. Having built up such a rapport with Mrs. Angel, and realizing how lonely and isolated she was, Abigail wandered into the nursing home and before she knew it, was part of a voluntary befriending service. She now spent her Wednesday afternoons playing chess with Mrs. Aker or cards with Madcap Mavis.

The commentator was getting more excitable, and Abigail leaned over the rail to peer in the direction of the race. Fifteen beasts topped with blazing colours thundered towards them, and in a matter of seconds sixty hooves had piled over the finishing line in an exhilarating climax. It seemed that Sly Fox had taken it by a nose. Fabulous Frankie barely got a look in.

"Have I really made an impact on your life?" Abigail asked suddenly, recalling his words from ten minutes ago.

"Definitely," he replied, turning to face her with his back against the rail. "I'd never met anyone that had never been on a horse before, and it was brilliant seeing you get on Grace like that. It got me thinking about people in cities that never get the chance to stroke animals or sit on a horse, and get close to things that we take for granted in the country. So I was thinking that – whilst I could never give up racing completely – maybe I should cut down the jockey activity and look to set up a riding school. I think there's a market for adult beginner lessons, maybe corporate days, team building, that sort of thing."

He paused and looked at her to get a reaction. She smiled back at him.

"You'd really be able to cut down on the buzz of wins like that one earlier just to help people learn to ride? There'd be very little money in running something like that."

"Yeah I know, but it's not about money though, is it? You've got to love what you're doing and whilst I love racing, there's a downside too. It's risky, my Mum hates it every time I race, and I think I'd get pleasure and satisfaction from working with horses in other ways. Spreading the joys of horses to others." He fiddled with his race card momentarily. "Of course, I'd need some help to get it off the ground. I'll have to find a place that's got land and accommodation in a suitable location, I'll need someone with skills in marketing and business to help guide me through the process, and I'll have to set up a website and so forth. Now, if only I knew a person with such skills..."

"Of course I'll help," promised Abigail. She could feel his enthusiasm already and knew he was being serious about his future.

"That would be great." He tucked his race card back into his jacket pocket and reached out to take her hands in his. He started shifting nervously again; his posture reminded Abigail of the time he'd presented her with the dress at the party so many weeks ago. She sensed he was about to ask her something.

"I know this might not seem like the most practical suggestion, given that we live so far apart, but I was wondering, er, whether you'd be my girlfriend?"

Abigail smiled back at him coyly and it occurred to her that nobody had ever officially asked her out before. In senior school, Martin Brompton had asked her if she wanted to go swimming on Saturday, and they'd had a hot chocolate afterwards, but most of Abigail's relationships had just 'happened'. Whether they'd started as a flirtation at a party, a slow dance in a nightclub, a snog at a wedding, but nobody had actually asked her permission before.

She leaned her body into his and slowly pressed her lips to his in reply. All around them, excitable punters, tipsy from wine and winnings, were laughing and chattering, but all Abigail could think about was how perfect everything was. Right at this minute. Right here. Perfect.

Her stomach gurgled. A deep, comical protest that curled up from the depths of her tummy; it was highly audible and impossible to ignore. She broke away from Sam and squeezed his hand.

"I think we need to eat. There's a buffet to demolish in the box," pointed out Sam, as they began to wander hand in hand back towards the stands.

"So what next? After the buffet I mean?"

"Well, I have no plans for the rest of the weekend, so I could run you home later and meet your parents? I can get a hotel or something and we can spend tomorrow together?"

"We have a spare room," Abigail offered. She wondered briefly whether her Mum would remember the lie about running off with the chap from work, and the connection to Sam. Ah well, she would cross that bridge if it came to it.

"Then next weekend Mum and Dad are going off on holiday,

and so I've got the place to myself. You'd be very welcome to come and join me and catch up with everyone in Sloth, get a proper swim in the pool…"

"Sounds brilliant," Abigail enthused. She'd never been happier as she rose up on the escalator, Sam pressed into her back with his warm hand still clinging onto hers. Her twenty-fourth birthday. It felt like the start of a new chapter in her life.

That bloke off the telly again

Ivan caught the barman's eye and with a flick of his head indicated that he was ready for another whisky and coke. It was his third, and it was only two o'clock in the afternoon, but fuck it, if the camera crew were going to keep him waiting, arseing around with getting endless footage that wouldn't be used, then that wasn't his problem.

The barman set his drink down with a polite nod and what looked like a smirk. It didn't help Ivan feel any less paranoid about his downfall. His relegation from being Mr "Saturday sport" to Mr "fluffy filler reports". Thanks to what he considered to be a sharp witty remark on Twitter, there had been sudden uproar, followed by a whirlwind of meetings involving senior executives and management, and out-of-proportion media speculation. Next thing he knew, suddenly he was on the sidelines "until it all died down". In his opinion, he felt things had very much died down, but the bosses seemed to disagree. Meanwhile, that young buck John Farthing was sitting in his hot seat, taking all the credit and all the glory. John, with his youthful good looks, and enthusiasm, not to mention slick comedy timing. The cock.

So that's why Ivan was here at Ascot, doing a silly pre-recorded "behind the scenes" report about the women's weighing room to be broadcast during Royal Ascot, instead of being involved in the thrilling buzz of live TV on the afternoon of the FA cup final. He'd spent five hours here already, he'd interviewed Jackie Simnel, one of the upcoming stars of flat racing and got her to show him around "backstage". He'd endured some demeaning "funny" shots of him peering around the sauna door asking if everyone was decent, and getting a vox pop with punters to see how many lady jockeys they could name. Riveting telly that. There wasn't even much decent totty to ogle at. Female jockeys all looked like his eleven year old daughter.

So he felt he deserved the whiskies. He paid the barman and took his glass to go and sit by the window overlooking the track. The 2.05 was about to start but he'd not had chance to place any bets today, he wasn't very knowledgeable about these low grade maidens anyway, and Jackie Simnel was certainly being very coy when it came to tips.

He scanned the scene below him. There was a hen party involving ten girls already high on bubbly and atmosphere, waving their matching fluffy boas around in the wind and giggling. The bookies were doing brisk business, taking the last bets before the start of the race, punters waving their sterling around and consulting the racecards.

He watched the horses gallop up the track with disinterest, and wondered whether there was anywhere in the grandstand that would be showing the FA Cup later. If the crew hurried up, they could get back to London and he could be in a pub watching it, surrounded by passionate fans and properly priced alcohol.

Swigging the whisky back in what he hoped was a stylish fashion, a blaze of ginger hair caught his eye. He was sure that was Sam Ashington standing next to the finishing post, his back to the track, leaning casually against the rail. And there was quite a hot blonde with him; really good tits being shown off in her Sandra Dee get up. He marveled momentarily at how a skinny, ginger lad like that could have a girlfriend that looked like she'd stepped off the pages of a lad's magazine. He on the other hand, worked hard to tone his abs, beef up his pecs, take care with his tan and haircut, and was in a totty dry zone.

The blonde leaned forward and kissed Sam gently before exchanging some fond words together and strolling hand in hand towards the building. Ivan stared, fascinated. There was something very familiar about the girl, the way she flicked her ponytail and had a natural waggle in her hips as she walked. He was sure he knew her from somewhere and he racked his brains to think whose daughter she might be.

They approached the window to the bar but were too distracted by each other to take any notice of the bloke off the telly perched at the window seat. And then it struck him, fell into his brain from nowhere, the recollection of the blind date at La Roulade a few months ago. Yes, she was that work colleague of his sister, the temp that didn't know who he was. She'd said she knew nothing about sport, yet here she was plonking her lips on Sam Ashington. Had she been playing with him all along?

He tried to picture how their date ended. He hadn't slept with her, he knew that much, but he slowly recalled her giving him her number. For confirmation, he tapped his phone with his thumb and brought up the contacts list. Abigail, yes, there it was at the top of the list. He briefly wondered why he'd never bothered to call her since, but it didn't seem to matter now.

He drained his whisky and with another swift tap, deleted the number.

ABOUT THE AUTHOR

Claire Fleming lives in Wiltshire, in the UK with her husband and cat. She works in social marketing and has a background in broadcast journalism.

She has loved reading and writing books since an early age, and has a passion for horses and horse racing.

Dark Horse is her first published novel.

Made in the USA
Charleston, SC
07 February 2016